In the California coastal town of South Cove, Jill Gardner, owner of Coffee, Books, and More, becomes more engaged in sleuthing than wedding preparations when there's a murder in a dress shop . . .

Jill couldn't love police chief Greg King more—so why does that engagement ring still feel funny on her finger? At least she'll have a chance to show it off this Saturday at their engagement party. Just in time for the event, a new dress shop has opened in town, Exquisite Gowns for You, specializing in designer wedding gowns and other custom-fit dresses.

But Jill's excitement turns to shock when she comes by to pick up her dress for the party and discovers a dead body in the shop. New owner Harper Sanchez is behaving strangely and becoming more mysterious than anyone expected. Despite Greg's warnings to leave the case to him, Jill can't help looking into the murder. Somebody in South Cove is dressed to kill—and if Jill's not careful, she may not live to wear her wedding gown . . .

Visit us at www.kensingtonbooks.com

By Lynn Cahoon

The Tourist Trap Mysteries
Wedding Bell Blues
Picture Perfect Frame
Murder in Waiting
Memories and Murder
Killer Party
Hospitality and Homicide
Tea Cups and Carnage
Murder on Wheels
Killer Run
Dressed to Kill
If the Shoe Kills
Mission to Murder
Guidebook to Murder
Novellas
A Very Mummy Holiday
Mother's Day Mayhem
Corned Beef and Casualties
Santa Puppy
A Deadly Brew
Rockets' Dead Glare

The Kitchen Witch Mysteries
One Poison Pie
Two Wicked Desserts
Novellas
Chili Cauldron Curse
Murder 101
Have a Holly, Haunted Christmas

The Cat Latimer Mysteries
A Story to Kill

Fatality by Firelight
Of Murder and Men
Slay in Character
Sconed to Death
A Field Guide to Murder

The Farm-to-Fork Mysteries
Who Moved My Goat Cheese?
One Potato, Two Potato, Dead
Killer Green Tomatoes
Penned In
Killer Comfort Food
Fatal Family Feast
Novellas
Have a Deadly New Year
Deep Fried Revenge
A Pumpkin Spice Killing

LYRICAL UNDERGROUND BOOKS are published by

Kensington Publishing Corp.
119 West 40th Street
New York, NY 10018

All Kensington titles, imprints, and distributed lines are available at special quantity discounts for bulk purchases for sales promotion, premiums, fund-raising, educational, or institutional use.

Special book excerpts or customized printings can also be created to fit specific needs. For details, write or phone the office of the Kensington Sales Manager: Kensington Publishing Corp., 119 West 40th Street, New York, NY 10018. Attn. Sales Department. Phone: 1-800-221-2647.

Lyrical Underground and Lyrical Underground logo Reg. US Pat. & TM Off.

First Electronic Edition: March 2022
eISBN-13: 978-1-5161-1107-7

First Print Edition: March 2022
ISBN-13: 978-1-5161-1108-4

Printed in the United States of America

WEDDING BELL BLUES

A Tourist Trap Mystery

By Lynn Cahoon

LYRICAL UNDERGROUND
Kensington Publishing Corp.
www.kensingtonbooks.com

To my Aunt Jackie. You will be missed.

Acknowledgments

I've always said it takes a village to write a book, and with South Cove in the mix, it's an upscale tourist town type of village. When I write these acknowledgments, I think of all the people who help me even when they don't realize how much. Like my sister, Roberta Gowin, who lives near the fictional South Cove and always sends me news pieces and interesting tidbits to make my mind wander from my Midwest writing cave to the California coast. She's the reason I visited the little town with the rundown house at the corner of Main Street and Highway 1 in the first place. A house that sparked Jill and her new life.

I'd be remiss if I didn't thank the Cowboy, my husband, Jim, for his ability to keep the house and world running while I go off in my bubble to write. A big thanks to my editor, Esi Sogah, who saw the possibilities in a story about an ex-lawyer turned bookstore owner who loved to read and solve mysteries. And thanks to Jill Marsal, my agent who helps me keeps the business part of the author job up front and center.

Chapter 1

Spring in South Cove, California, is beautiful. The days are warm, the nights cool enough for a firepit in your backyard or a bonfire on the beach. Now that we were out of the rainy season, which seemed to get shorter and shorter every year, I could count on clear days to take Emma, my golden retriever, running after I got off work. It was a great stress reliever and helped to offset my other stress activity, eating. Eating sweets, specifically.

Times like today I regretted putting in the treat bar at my bookstore/coffee shop, Coffee, Books, and More. It was the first Tuesday of the month, and my shop swarmed with local business owners, city council reps, and worse, Mayor Baylor and his wife, Tina. I hosted and ran the business-to-business meeting as one of my side gigs. A job I really didn't need to do anymore for the money. But I couldn't seem to walk away. As I sat listening today, I vowed that next year, when Amy sent me the annual contract, I'd send it back unsigned with a big "Thanks, but No Thanks" in red pen over the top.

Of course, I wouldn't. Amy Newman—no, now Amy Newman-Cross—was my best friend and sitting right next to me. I guess misery loves company.

Tina Baylor was at the podium introducing this month's speaker. Harper Sanchez was the owner/operator of our newest South Cove business, Exquisite Gowns for You—a special occasion and wedding gown designer. I loved her shop. Located down the street across from the Train Station, and on the other side of town from Vintage Duds, Exquisite Gowns was the only other clothing shop in South Cove. Vintage Duds sold gently used designer creations and was run by Sherry King and Pat Williams. Sherry was my fiancé's ex-wife. But Pat was the one who was usually at the store and in town where I could run into her. I wasn't sure what Sherry did as her part of the team, but as long as she wasn't around much, I didn't care.

Oh, the joys of living in a small town.

"And I'm sure you'll all be as fascinated as I am on today's topic, picking the perfect outfit for your shape, age, and event." Tina crooned into the microphone. "Harper? Come on up here and let's get this show on the road."

Harper followed Tina's instructions and set a pile of index cards on the stand. She cleared her throat and scanned the room. She hit the microphone as she straightened the cards a second time, and it squealed its discomfort. "Sorry, I'm a little rusty on this talking thing. I don't think I've done an hour talk since I was in college speech class. And I wasn't very good then."

"Great, put us in a receptive mood," Amy whispered in my ear. "I'm already tired enough to take a nap. Justin was up until one last night talking online to his history group. You would think just the topic would put me to sleep."

I shushed her. We were getting the glare from Tina. Man, that woman knew how to put the evil eye on someone. Deek Kerr came over and refilled our coffee mugs, leaving the carafe near us. At least we'd be caffeinated.

What felt like a lifetime later, Harper finally stopped talking. I knew more about her and her path to being a designer than I knew about my newest barista, Evie Marshall. And Evie had been in town for months.

Darla Jones, the town event planner, hurried up to the podium before Harper could start another story. "Well, wasn't that interesting. Thank you for being here, Harper, and welcome to South Cove. Now, we really have to talk about our Welcome Spring Saturday festival that will occur in two weeks. I've got a list of committee assignments that still need filled. In addition, I wanted you all to know that Jill and Coffee, Books, and More will be sponsoring a read-a-thon for the local schools' arts and cultural funding. We all know how strapped the schools are, and typically, the first to lose their extras are our band, choir, and art kids. So if you want to support the kids, be sure to pick up a pledge sheet. Jill's keeping the store open overnight to keep the excitement going."

I stood and pointed out Deek. "This was Deek's brainchild, so make sure you sign up on my sponsorship page since he's got two pages of sponsors already."

"Now, Jill, it's not nice to try to poach my sponsors." Deek stepped toward the table. He was California-surfer-boy cute with blond dreadlocks and a killer tan for March to complete the look. He struck a pose and put on a blinding smile. "I'm sure supporting the cause is much more important than supporting either one of us, even though I am taking selfies with my crew."

The table laughed, but I saw at least one of the women near me fan herself. Yep, I wasn't going to beat out Deek for pledges, but as he said, it was all for a good cause. I just didn't like to lose.

"Anyway, we'll see you all next month. If you have time, be sure to volunteer. Spring Saturday is only two weeks away." Darla held up the signup sheets, then spread them on the front table. "They'll be right here, on your way out. We're done here."

The entire group seemed to rise at once and race out of the café's front doors. I saw a few people stop and sign up, but Darla would have to do her famous face-to-face method of finishing the committees. She was strong willed, and not many people could tell her no to her face. Which was why so many people were trying to get out of the shop without making eye contact.

Loud voices from the bookstore section of the café drew my attention. Sherry King, my least favorite business owner, stood in front of Harper, shaking her finger at the poor woman. I hurried over to stand between them. "Sherry, what are you doing?"

"You just stay out of this. It's not your fight. I can't believe she even had the nerve to open a shop in my town. We already have a clothing shop, Vintage Duds. And we sell designer clothes. What am I supposed to do when people decide to buy new gowns instead of my used stuff? You're going to drive me out of business. You should have opened a store in the valley. They have a lot of celebrities who need dresses. Here, we have to deal with weddings and such." Sherry took a breath.

"Sherry, leave her alone. We'll be fine." Pat Williams hurried over and took Sherry by the arm. She glanced over at me, lowering her voice. "Sorry, she's been a little upset since she heard the news."

Sherry glared at me as they walked out, and I figured the news Pat was talking about had nothing to do with the new business moving into town. I glanced down at my hands, but the ring was at home, on the kitchen window. I'd forgotten to put it back on after rinsing out the coffeepot this morning.

Deek stood next to me, watching them leave. "That woman has a bad aura. Not completely black, but on its way."

I ignored his comment and turned toward Harper. "Are you all right? I'm so sorry about Sherry. She can get a little emotional about things."

"She tried to get into my shop yesterday morning. I thought I had a delivery, so I went out front when I heard the banging, but it was her, screaming about my shop driving hers out of business. Should I report her to the police? She's scaring me." Harper took the glass of water that Amy had poured for her and drank it down. "Thanks, I needed that."

"Who needs to report what to the police?" Greg King, South Cove's police chief in all but the name and my boyfriend—no, fiancé—stood behind me. I hadn't seen him come in through the crowd.

Deek and Amy looked at each other, then Deek stepped away. Amy took Harper by the arm. "Come sit down with me for a few minutes. Let's get you a brownie to calm your nerves. Nothing like a treat to get your sugar level back up."

I turned to Greg and led him back to the office behind the coffee bar. I sat on my desk and took a deep breath.

"Okay, you're scaring me. What's going on?" Greg took my hands, but then he dropped them. "Hold on a minute, I've got something for you."

"What?" I watched as he dug in his pants pocket and pulled out my ring. He slipped it on my hand, then kissed me. "You left this at home, again. That's the third time this week. Is there something you need to tell me?"

"No. I mean, yes, but not about the ring." Now he had me flustered.

He studied me. "So leaving it at home isn't a passive-aggressive way of telling me you don't want to marry me?"

"No. I don't think so." I sighed and ran my hand through my hair. "Look, I love you, and yes, I want to marry you. So stop asking. Anyway, we have bigger problems."

He sat in one of the other chairs. "Okay, tell me what's going on, then. Why did Amy and Deek take off like they were afraid I was going to throw everyone into my small two-man jail cell?"

"Well, before you came in, Sherry started yelling at that other woman. She's Harper Sanchez, and she opened that clothing design shop down near Harrold's Train Station. Sherry thinks she's trying to run Vintage Duds out of town." The words spilled out of my mouth, and I stood and went to the cooler to grab a bottle of water.

"Sherry's Sherry. I can talk to this Harper and see if she wants to press charges, but if Sherry was just upset, it's kind of a stretch." Greg grabbed my water bottle and took a drink before handing it back.

"That's not all. Harper said Sherry came over yesterday to her shop and tried to break in. Harper's scared. You need to talk to Sherry and tell her to knock it off before Harper does press charges."

He took my hand and squeezed it. "I will. But you do me a favor and keep that ring on. I didn't spend all that money to have to cut it out of your dog when Emma thinks it's a treat you left lying around."

"Greg, there's more." The ring, with its large marquise stone, felt heavy on my finger. I bit my lip before telling him what Pat had said. "I think

Sherry's upset about our engagement. Pat said she hasn't been herself since she found out."

He shook his head. "No. She can't lay that on me or you. We're divorced. That's what she wanted, so she got it. And now I'm happy, so she's feeling bad? Jill, it's typical Sherry. She only wants what she can't have."

"I know, but I figured you needed to hear it before you fell into one of her traps." I leaned down to kiss him.

"Sherry's traps don't work on me anymore. I've gotten attached to a new female who knows all new tricks to play on me." He stood and pulled me into a hug. "You let me worry about Sherry. You just keep that ring on your finger and get ready to have a huge engagement party this weekend. I even bought a new suit."

By the time we came back into the main dining room, Harper and Amy were gone. Deek had moved the tables back into their regular spot and was now serving up regular customers who'd been waiting for the meeting to finish.

Greg slapped him on the back and headed to the door to go back to work. He'd promised to go talk to Sherry and tell her to leave the new designer alone. I didn't think it would be that easy.

I checked the ticket Deek was working on, and after washing my hands and pulling on a clean apron, I dished up two of Pies on the Fly's new cheesecake brownies. I was kind of surprised we even had any left to sell since I'd been mainlining them since Sadie, Pies on the Fly's owner and local baker, had dropped them off on Friday with our weekly delivery. Since we were friends, she knew I was a stress eater.

The woman at the register beamed at me. "It's about time you two got hitched. You make such a lovely couple. Are babies on their way? Is that why you're getting married now?"

I about choked. "I'm sorry, what?"

Deek snickered next to me. "Mrs. Landstrom, I can assure you that Jill and Greg aren't expecting. I hear they're planning on at least a year-long engagement."

My face felt hot as I glanced around the room. Everyone was watching me now. I took off the apron I'd just put on. "Deek's right, no babies on the way. Maybe a second puppy soon. But I do need to leave. I just remembered I have a lunch date."

In the back room, I sank into my desk chair and laid my head on the desk. Seriously? Was that what everyone was thinking? That I was pregnant? I glanced over at a batch of double Dutch cookies that Deek had pulled out of the cooler to warm up before putting them in the sale case out front. They were better at room temperature, but I went and grabbed one anyway. It was cold to the touch, and I really wanted a cup of coffee to dunk it in. But I didn't want to go back out to the dining room in case I'd be asked more questions.

I wondered if Amy had been getting these same questions about her recent marriage? Or maybe it was just at the engagement stage that people liked messing with the newly engaged. I dialed city hall, hoping Amy was back from wherever she and Harper had taken off to.

She picked up on the first ring. "South Cove Mayoral Office. Amy Newman speaking. How may I help you today?"

"I thought you were taking Justin's last name?" Ouch, maybe everyone was too involved in this marriage convention, even me. "Never mind. I didn't mean that. Anyway, are you free for lunch? I need to clear my head."

"I saw Greg give your ring to you. Did you forget it at home again?" Amy's tone dropped from professional to that of a caring friend. Way different that the random woman at the counter.

Deek knew her name, I just knew her coffee order. Large regular coffee with two squirts of chocolate sauce to add some flavor, like a mocha without as many calories. I'd even suggested she try it when she'd been complaining about needing to give up the sweet coffee treat for her diet plan. Now that I thought about it, there were a lot of customers that I could rattle off their coffee and treat preferences and even the last book they'd bought, but I had no idea what their names were. Or their stories. I needed to get better about that.

"Jill, are you still there?" Amy broke into my mental wanderings.

"Sorry. Yes, I forgot the ring again. Greg thinks it's a red flag that I'm giving up on the marriage idea."

Amy was quiet for a minute; then she asked, "Are you sure it's not?"

"Amy, I love Greg. You know that."

"Look, I've got a couple of things to finish for Tina before I can leave, but I'll meet you at Diamond Lille's in about fifteen?" Amy's voice had changed back from her worried friend tone to professional.

"She's standing right there, isn't she? Don't answer that. I'll see you at Lille's." I hung up the phone and looked around for something I could do for a few minutes since I was still hiding from the customers.

I pulled out a piece of paper and listed out the things I knew about the woman who'd asked if I was pregnant. Then I wrote the name Deek had called her—Mrs. Landstrom. I tried to remember all of my commuters and put names to the ones I knew. It was about half. Tomorrow, I'd check their credit cards for names. Then I'd add them to my list. By the time the week was over, I should know most of my morning customers by name. The other shifts, well, they weren't on phase one of this new Jill plan.

I wasn't quite sure my brain had enough room for all these new names, but if I could remember how someone liked their coffee, I could remember their name. It was just a matter of focus.

Pleased with my new personal development goal, I put my notes into my tote. It wouldn't do for my aunt to find them and question the fact that I didn't already know my customers by name. Aunt Jackie had run a coffee shop with my uncle Ted before he'd died, and I was certain she knew each and every one of her regulars. But my aunt was like that. I'd rather chat with someone about a book they loved than about their three kids and the house they were remodeling.

Maybe I was a bad small-town business owner.

As I was tucking the pages into my tote, I saw a note in my aunt's handwriting. "Jill and Jackie at Exquisite Gowns at one p.m". I checked the date. Yes, this was the third. How could I have forgotten the appointment that my aunt had called me about three times last week? I checked my watch. I was meeting Amy at eleven thirty. And Harper's shop was right across the street from the diner. I'd be fine, but I set an alarm on my phone, just in case.

Aunt Jackie didn't like it when I was late. And I didn't like it when my aunt was angry at me. She was like that superhero who turned green and into a raving monster. Except Aunt Jackie got quiet and her face froze into a polite blank stare. For weeks.

It was awful. I wasn't going to make her mad just before my and Greg's engagement party. It would be horrible. I tucked the tote under my arm and left the store through the back door just to avoid the people out front.

Yeah, I worried too much about what others thought. But in my defense, I did live in a small town where the rumor mill was active and vicious.

Chapter 2

Amy walked into Diamond Lille's and saw me in our favorite booth. She hurried over and slipped into the bench across from me. I'd already ordered dessert to eat first. A slice of apple pie and a scoop of ice cream sat half-devoured in front of me. "I came as soon as I could get away. What's wrong? Well, besides Sherry's stunt at the coffeehouse. And Greg and the ring."

"Wow, I am a little predictable, aren't I? It's not about Sherry. Or Greg." I stopped talking when Carrie, our favorite waitress, paused by the table.

"What can I get for you?" Carrie asked Amy. She nodded toward me. "Jill's already ordered fish and chips to go along with her dessert. Do you want your usual? Cheeseburger with fries? Or are you going to do dessert first too?"

"I'll take the cheeseburger. No dessert, thanks." Amy pushed the menu away. "And an iced tea."

"Sounds normal. Not like your friend here." Carrie shot me a pained look, and I felt my face heat.

Amy leaned down after Carrie left. "Okay, now you're scaring everyone. What's going on?"

I would have stopped eating the pie, but Tiny, Diamond Lille's chef, made amazing apple pie. "I don't know. I just feel like everyone's expecting Greg and me to be this couple and pop out babies and, I don't know, just settle down? Did that happen when you got married?"

"He asked you to marry him, not give away all your brain cells and become a Stepford wife. And when did you start worrying about what other people thought?" Amy thanked Carrie for the iced tea and then waited for my answer.

My breathing slowed, and for a second I felt sick after eating that pie so fast. Tiny would be ticked if I got sick. I pushed the almost-gone pie away and then broke off a piece of crust and popped it in my mouth. So good. "Okay, so that was weird."

"It was probably a panic attack. You've been on the edge for weeks now, since Greg asked you to marry him. You've really got a keeper there." Amy saw my eyes widen and patted the air in front of me. "Calm down. You know that's true. Why are you freaking out about this marriage thing?"

"I'm not good married. I already ruined one relationship. Why should this one be any different? Maybe I should just break it off now. We'd both be better off." I wished I had a paper bag to breathe into. Maybe that would work. I started digging in my tote to see if I had anything. I found a bag with two brownies inside that I had taken home for dessert. I took the brownies out and set them on a napkin, then started breathing into the small Coffee, Books, and More bag.

Amy watched me and sipped her tea. She didn't say anything. She didn't have to. She was barely keeping from laughing at me to my face.

Finally, I sat the bag down. All my efforts had done was make me hungry for another brownie. The bag smelled like chocolate and, with every deep breath, reminded me of the brownies on the table. I stuffed them back in the bag along with the napkin, careful to not break them. Then I tucked the bag back into my tote.

"Do you feel better?"

I shook my head. "All I managed to do was make myself hungrier. I guess I could just wait to gain a ton of weight and have Greg cancel the wedding himself."

"Greg would love you no matter what size you are." Amy caught my gaze. "I didn't know you when you were married, but from what you've told me, neither you nor your ex-husband were willing to put the relationship above your careers. You and Greg aren't like that. You both accept each other the way you are."

Amy had a point. I didn't know why I was freaking out about a little thing like commitment and a ceremony. I already would do anything for Greg, and I knew he felt the same way. Marriage would just make that bond stronger. Now I just had to convince my head what my heart already knew. "Thanks for calming me down. So tell me how amazing married life is so I can start counting down the days."

Amy blew out a breath that moved her bangs. A signature move showing her frustration. Then she took a napkin and started shredding it. Crap, things were worse than I thought. "I can't say that. I guess I didn't know what to expect. Justin reads all the time. Or he's talking history stuff. I try to listen, but maybe we only had fun and surfing in common. Maybe we're not soulmates?"

"Amy, there's one thing I know, and that's you and Justin were made for each other. I'm sure it's just a matter of learning to live together." My friend and her husband had taken the traditional route and not moved in together before the ceremony. Now they were learning what it meant to share a home. "At least Greg and I got that adjustment done early. Good or bad, it's the way it is."

"You guys had problems at first?"

I laughed as a waitress delivered my fish and chips and Amy's cheeseburger. "Not just at first. He's still campaigning for a workout gym in Miss Emily's painting shed. I seriously think he'd kick Toby out if he didn't think it would affect him working as a deputy. He's a lot cleaner than I am. I feel bad that he's always cleaning something I think I should be doing and that I put off."

"Justin makes our bed every morning." Amy grabbed her hamburger. Before she took a bite, she admitted, "I only made it when I changed sheets. The rest of the time, it looked messy chic. At least to me."

We talked about the guys and what drove us crazy about them for the rest of the meal. I pushed away half my fries as we finished lunch. "I've got to meet Aunt Jackie at Harper's shop. She commissioned a dress for me for the engagement party as a surprise. Although, I think she ordered herself a new dress, and then Harrold guilted her into getting me one as well. I kind of love that guy."

"He's a great uncle." Amy grinned as she took out her credit card for the meal. "I'll get this since I needed some Jill wisdom today about relationships."

"I'm kind of thinking we should split it since I was on the edge of eating the place out of apple pie when you showed up." I stood and tucked my tote under my arm. "But I'll get you next week. Thanks for making time for lunch. I appreciate it."

"No problem, sis." She gave me a quick hug and took the check up to the counter.

I went past the hostess stand, where Lille stood, glaring at me. I knew the restaurant owner didn't like me, but I thought maybe her animosity would end after Harrold married my aunt, since Lille adored Harrold. In a grandfatherly way, that is. I would say something, but the woman had a mean streak, and I didn't want to get banned from her restaurant for life. I loved Tiny's food.

By the time I'd gotten across the street, Aunt Jackie was already at the front of the new shop. She glanced toward the diner and sighed. "I supposed I can't hope that you ate a salad when you were having lunch."

"Nope. Fried food and dessert. Why are you concerned about my eating habits now?" I put my arm in hers, and we walked into the shop.

"If you want to look good in your wedding dress, you probably need to lose at least ten pounds. Twenty would be better." She turned toward the counter, looking for Harper.

Before she could ring the bell to announce our arrival, loud voices floated out from the back. I stopped my aunt's hand from hitting the bell, holding on to her wrist in case we needed to make a fast exit. I figured I could drag my petite aunt out of the store before anyone even knew we were there.

"You need to leave," a woman said, not in a shout, but the determination in the tone made me turn toward the door.

My aunt held up a finger, slowing my planned escape.

"You're going to regret turning me down," a male voice shouted, and then a door slammed.

I waited, but no one said anything else. Now I wished I'd eaten the rest of those fries. "Do you think it's okay?"

She nodded and hit the bell. She shrugged out of my grip and whispered, "Keep your phone in your pants pocket. We may have to call Greg."

"Okay." Her words before the argument finally sank in. "Wait, what was that comment about me losing weight? You're not usually worried about my appearance. What's different now?"

She jerked her head back like I'd slapped her. "I didn't mean to criticize, dear. I guess I assumed you would want to look perfect for your wedding day. It's a special occasion."

I didn't get a chance to respond to my aunt's reasoning to question my appearance before we were interrupted.

"Oh, I'm sorry, I didn't hear you come in. Not to butt into your conversation, but I think Jill looks perfect just the way she is." Harper stepped out of the back with a tape measure over her shoulder. "Of course, in a gown I make, she'll look even more beautiful. Have you chosen a wedding dress or designer yet?"

"Not yet." Harper's words made me relax a little. At least someone was on my side. I glanced around the samples she had on mannequins around the room. "We haven't even set a date yet."

"Well, when you do, let me know. I'd love to be considered. And I'll give you the South Cove discount." Harper glanced at her calendar. "But you're not here to plan for the future, are you? I have both of your dresses ready for final fittings. Let's go get you changed into them so I can see what I need to do to get them finished."

"Will they be ready by Friday?" Aunt Jackie asked as we followed Harper into a second room set up for trying on dresses.

"I'll have them ready for you at noon tomorrow. I've got some things to do this weekend, so I need to get this off my plate." Harper pulled down two dresses and handed one to me and one to Aunt Jackie. "Let's see what a genius I am."

I took the dress she handed me. The color was a mix between silver and blue, and the touch of the fabric made me shiver. I'd bought designer dresses before on a sale rack, but I'd never had one made for me before. "It's so pretty."

"I thought the fabric would look amazing with your coloring." Harper smiled as she watched me hold the dress like it was made of glass.

"The changing rooms are back there." Aunt Jackie pointed the left of the room. "You try yours on first. Then I'll go. That way you can get back to your day. I'm sure you're busy."

There was no way I was going to leave my aunt alone with Harper until I found out who had been yelling at her when we came in. I paused before I went behind a curtain. "We heard voices when we came in. We didn't interrupt anything, did we?"

"No." Harper turned beet red. "I was watching television. You must have caught me listening to the soap operas. They're my guilty pleasure, especially during the day when I'm sewing."

I met Aunt Jackie's gaze. Nope, she didn't believe it either. But I let it go and went to change into this piece of heaven Harper had created.

Thirty minutes later, my final adjustments were done and Harper had promised the dress would to be available tomorrow. I sat reading a book and waiting for my aunt, who was still talking about the length of her dress. My phone was close by, but I'd had a minute when Harper had been focused on my aunt to find the back door and make sure it was locked. There wasn't anything or anyone suspicious in the alley, so I figured the guy must have left.

Had the man been an ex-boyfriend? Or maybe a rival designer? On the reality shows I watched on the fashion industry, people were always saying snarky and mean things to each other or behind their backs. Maybe it was just that. Although in South Cove, the only rival Harper had was Sherry and Pat's store, and that wasn't even a close race. Vintage Duds sold estate items, not custom, made-to-order dresses like the gown I'd just tried on. It was lovely, and I was going to wear it to every formal event I attended for the next ten years.

If I still fit into it. Aunt Jackie's words made me want a milkshake, just to be contrary. But maybe she was right. I hadn't been running with Emma in weeks due to the weather. Today, I'd change that. Food could be managed with just a little exercise. Look at Amy. The girl ate more than I even thought possible, and she was stick thin. Mostly because she surfed most weekends. Or biked. Or hiked. She had a lot of active hobbies.

I read books.

Okay, maybe a little exercise and a little less sugar and fat. I tried to focus on the story. Finally, Aunt Jackie was done and we stood together outside the shop. I nodded to a bench in front of the building that held Amy's apartment along with the bike rental shop. "Can we talk a minute?"

She checked her watch. "I've got a little time. Harrold probably has dinner ready. We like to eat early on days when I work so he can come with me. I swear, all his old cronies have been showing up for coffee while I work. It's just a little social hour for him."

I saw the smile on her face even though her words sounded harsh. My aunt didn't have a social filter when it came to monitoring what she said. She was who she was, and I loved her for it. "I'm glad he's going with you. I'd hate to think you were working the evening shift alone. Greg says we've been having some issues in town."

"I'm sure you didn't want to talk about South Cove's crime rate." Aunt Jackie glanced over toward the design shop. "I don't believe the story about watching television. Do you?"

I shook my head. "I've been trying to think of what the most likely issue is. I've got it narrowed down to ex-lover or rival designer."

My aunt patted my arm. "You always wanted to know the why on things. Why it happened. Why they would say that. But in this case, I think we should keep an eye out for Harper. I'm not sure she has any family in the area. She told me that her folks are out of Connecticut."

"Do you think I should ask Greg to check in on her?" I felt a knot in my stomach. Something bad was going on with our new business owner, Harper. I could feel it.

"Why are you sitting over there?" Harrold called from the doorway of the Train Station, which was right across the street.

"Girl talk. Never you mind," my aunt called and waved him back into his shop. "I swear, that man keeps close tabs on me. I'm feeling a little smothered."

"He loves you. He wants to know you're all right." I flushed as I said the words. It could have been Amy telling me the same thing about Greg. And I'd been whining about feeling unsure of our relationship. Some people never got this. Never got to find their soulmate either with a first marriage or a subsequent one. I was lucky. And so was my aunt. "You better go. I don't want Harrold to worry about you."

"Thank you for letting me do this for you. You're going to be lovely on Saturday." She leaned over and kissed my cheek. An action so unexpected it brought tears to my eyes. She rubbed them away with her thumb. "Now don't be going all sobby on me. We've got a while to go before the wedding where we'll both be complete messes."

"I'm sure I'll be a mess on Saturday too. I just hope I don't do anything stupid and drive Greg away."

My aunt laughed as she stood. "I'm not sure that's possible. That man is deeply in love with you. I've seen it in his eyes since you two started dating. I'll chat with you tomorrow about the weekly work schedule. And we need to talk about Deek. He wants a week off this summer to do some sort of writing retreat."

"Cat Latimer, that young adult author that Sasha set up to come talk a few years ago, lives in Colorado and runs a writer retreat. I'm pretty sure Deek's been talking to Cat about attending a session."

"You would think that boy would want to do something actually fun for his vacation. Not work on a book. Never mind, just make sure I know so we're not short-staffed that week. I'd hate to decide to book a cruise and leave you in a lurch so that you have to hire temp staff to cover." My aunt tucked her purse under her arm as she stood.

My aunt hated hiring temporary staff. She believed in bringing on people who would stay. I thought it was more that people were scared to tell my aunt they were leaving. She had a bad habit of talking employees who put in their notice into staying. I wished I had that kind of manipulation skills. I realized she was still talking to me.

"And don't forget, you need to pick up the dresses tomorrow by one. Harper's going out of town this weekend, and I don't want you wearing that old black dress you wear to everything."

"I like my black dress." I stood and crossed the road with her. "But I'll get the dresses picked up before one. I love my new dress. Thank you. It was thoughtful."

My aunt smiled. She smiled a lot now that she was married to Harrold. I kind of liked this new version of her. "Just remember to pick them up, dear. I'll leave you a reminder at the shop. That should help you."

"I'm not going to forget," I said again as I paused at the door to the Train Station. Aunt Jackie and Harrold were living in the apartment above the store. I waved at my new uncle, who was showing a customer a train engine car. He'd tried to get me interested in the model train world, but it wasn't my thing. He had bought me a train set for my Christmas tree this last Christmas, which I loved. But that was the extent of my interest. "I'll see you Saturday at the community center? The party starts at two."

"As long as you and Amy don't need me there early to help decorate or set up the food."

"I've hired caterers for the food. Sadie is bringing the desserts. Amy and Justin are doing the decorations, so I think we're fine." I kissed her on the cheek. "Thanks again. The dress is lovely."

"So are you, my dear." She disappeared into the store and paused at the counter to give Harrold a kiss. Then she slowly moved up the stairs.

I loved my aunt. Warts and all.

Chapter 3

On my way to the beach to run with Emma, my neighbor and South Cove's resident fortune-teller, Esmeralda, waved me down and crossed the street to chat. Esmeralda also worked for Greg as a police dispatcher, so the topic of conversation could be the state of the road that separated us, rumors from South Cove's city hall, or maybe just a friendly chat. Sometimes she even shared her visions with me. A practice that always freaked me out just a little.

Everyone has their own beliefs, but hearing voices from the beyond was pushing it just a bit for my tastes. I clicked my fingers, and Emma sat next to me, wiggling in excitement to see one of her favorite people.

Esmeralda gave my dog a rub on the top of her head, then focused on me. "Jill, I was just wondering if everything is all right. Your aura feels a little off these days. Please don't tell me you're reconsidering Greg's offer?"

"No, I love Greg. There's really nothing going on with me. I'm just a little distracted, that's all." Why was everyone focused on my feelings right now?

Emma whined and stared at me with those deep chocolate eyes. Even my dog knew I was lying. But maybe they'd all leave it be.

"If you say so." Esmeralda studied the connection between Emma and me. "Just remember, if you need a tune-up, sometimes, it's good to have a friend you can talk to about anything."

"Seriously, I'm good." I tried to change the subject. "So when is that guy of yours coming back to visit? He was very nice looking."

"Nic is handsome, isn't he? I'm actually heading to New Orleans next week after your engagement party. I thought it was a good time for a little vacation. I don't take as many vacations as I should." Esmeralda looked out over the ocean as it sparkled in the mid-afternoon sky. "I guess when you live in a place as beautiful as it is here, you get your vacations in every day."

"We are lucky to be able to live here, that's for sure." I scanned the coastline. Surfers were starting to show up for the evening waves.

She touched my arm, and my gaze met her own. "Just remember, I'm here this week. If you need to talk, about anything."

"Unless you know of any fast diets where I can lose twenty pounds by Saturday, I'm fine."

Esmeralda studied me. "I can brew a potion, but I don't think it will solve your problems. It would only mask the pain."

I wasn't sure what pain she was talking about, but Emma saved me by pulling on her leash. "Don't worry about it, I was kidding. I guess that's my cue. Emma's been dying to get out on the beach for a few days, but with the rain, we've been staying home and she watches me on the treadmill."

"Be careful, Jill. You're not completely protected during this season. I see some grayness in your future." She checked the road for cars, then crossed over, leaving Emma and me on the sidewalk.

I glanced down at my dog, who was watching Esmeralda leave. She looked as confused as I felt. "Yeah, I know, girl. Let's go run."

Greg was home when we returned, and he pointed to the dish on the table. I'd put my engagement ring in the bowl so I wouldn't lose it when I was running. Or worse, get robbed because of the ring. And then Emma might get hurt. It was easier all around for me to just take precautions. "Do we have to have the talk again?"

"You can talk all you want, but there's no way I'm wearing jewelry while I'm running. Especially a ring that you probably paid way too much for and has way too much meaning for me to lose." I kissed him on the cheek. "Let me get showered, and I'll help with dinner."

"Point taken, and you win that argument. Are we doing those salmon steaks in the fridge?" He leaned down and greeted Emma. "How's my girl? Did you do your duty and protect the house today while we were gone?"

"She slept on the couch with her monkey and the blanket. But she didn't eat the sofa pillows I left out, so I'd call that a win." I paused at the stairwell. "I've got a recipe for an Asian cabbage salad I want to make to go with the fish. You can have whatever carb you want, but I'm off carbs until the party on Saturday."

"You can't lose weight in four days." He took out a potato and some aluminum foil. "Besides, you look great to me. Are you sure you don't want one?"

"My aunt wants me to lose twenty so I'll be ready for the wedding gown. We haven't even set the date." I rolled my shoulders. "I'm not freaking out about it, but this dress she's having Harper make for me is freaking gorgeous. I want to do it justice."

"You'd look amazing in a potato sack." He held up his hand. "But I'm not going to stand in your way, unless you go all crazy on me and stop eating sweets."

"Oh no." I ran over and pulled out the bag from my tote. "I brought home brownies for you. I hope they aren't squished."

He took the bag from me and opened it. "They look fine. Looks like there are two of them. Are you having one?"

"No. I actually ate two at work." I leaned in to smell the chocolate. "Don't judge, you know the business-to-business meeting drives me bananas."

"Why don't you let someone else run the meetings? You've done it for a while, and we don't need the extra money." He took a brownie out and took a bite. "Oh, these are amazing. Maybe I should marry Sadie instead."

"I think you'd have to get in line. Pastor Bill seems on the edge of a proposal. At least I'm hoping so. She deserves a good guy." I turned and ran upstairs and away from the second brownie just sitting in the bag. I thought about his statement about running the meeting for the chamber. It was true. We didn't need the money like I had when I'd taken on the role. But I had let Sherry King be in charge once, and attending that meeting had driven me crazy. She'd turned it into a circus. Literally.

Maybe I had a bit of a control issue around the meetings, but if I was going to have to attend as a South Cove business owner, I wanted to be in charge of the agenda. And, I'd learned how to keep our constant complainer, Josh Thomas, in line. Even without my aunt's support after she'd dumped Josh for Harrold.

When I got back downstairs, the salmon steaks were out and seasoned. And he'd found the recipe I printed last Sunday on my kitchen desk and had started chopping the vegetables. Greg had his faults, like watching way too much football on television, but he was handy to have around in the kitchen. And he grilled like a master chef.

I stood beside him and started making the salad. "So what's up at city hall? I hear Tina's redecorating Marvin's office again. Doesn't he have to run for reelection again this fall?"

"He does. And he reminds me of that fact constantly. Sometimes I think he wants me to run against him so he could fire me for not doing my job and campaigning on work hours." Greg dumped the shredded cabbage into the largest bowl we had. "As far as rumors, there's none going around. Except Amy's been grumpy lately. Is there trouble in paradise?"

I didn't want to answer that question. If I told him, I was a bad friend. If I didn't, I was a bad fiancée. It was a catch-22. "Why would you ask me?"

"You had lunch with her. I expected she would have told you if she and Justin were having troubles." He glanced over at me. I was mixing the dressing for the salad and not meeting his gaze. "I hit it on the head, didn't I? That's what's going on with her. You don't have to answer, I know you probably swore to never tell."

"It's kind of an implied promise, not a case-by-case promise." I crushed the dried ramen, and Greg dropped in the slivered almonds.

He held up the green onions. "Before or after the dressing?"

"After." I poured the dressing over, tossed it a few times, then nodded to the green onions. "Put them on top. I'll toss it one more time, then let it sit in the fridge. How long on your potato?"

"At least another twenty. Let's go outside and sit on the deck for a few while the grill heats up. I want to talk about Sherry."

"Oh, I'm not going to like this conversation, am I?" I poured two glasses of iced tea, then handed him one.

"Probably not." He nodded to the door. "Let's go sit."

I followed him out the door and sat on the wooden swing. He started the grill, then set his iced tea down and sat next to me. "Tear off the Band-Aid."

"Horrible expression." He shook his head. "Anyway, Pat came to see me this afternoon. She's worried about Sherry. She thinks our engagement is, well, making her crazy."

"So you want to call off the engagement since it upsets your ex-wife?" If I'd ever had any questions about our relationship, it was paling in comparison to the conversation we were having right now. "Don't tell me you're still in love with her."

"I'm in love with you. And no, we're not calling off the engagement. We have a party in four days. Besides, we are supposed to be together. I know it." He took my hand. "I'm going to go over to her place and talk to her tomorrow. Let her know that she and I are fully and completely done, and she needs to accept it. I just didn't want to go over there without telling you first. You know how rumors fly in this town."

"Like Amy's wedded bliss."

"Exactly. If there's dirt to be had on anyone, there's a rumor floating around South Cove. I'm not risking our relationship on me just not telling you what I'm doing." He squeezed my hand. "So what do you think?"

"I hate to be the one who can't forgive and forget, and it's your ex-wife problem. Thanks for telling me though. You're the best." I was going to take the high road here, no matter how Sherry reacted. "I'm sorry that Pat dragged you into this though. If Sherry's having problems dealing with your breakup, isn't it a little late?"

"I think so, but I'd be in the wrong if I didn't at least try to make the woman understand that she didn't have a shot at a second chance, even if she'd tried." He squeezed my hand. "I'm not sure I'd be so understanding if your ex-husband was upset about our new status. I'd probably tell him to go pound sand."

Laughing at his honesty, I sipped my tea. "Well, I guess I'm acting like the better person here. I'm not going to show my true hand here because I want you to think I'm an angel."

"That I do." He glanced at his watch. "I'll go get the salmon and get it started. Maybe we can watch a movie after dinner?"

"Sounds good." I watched Emma in the yard, hunting rabbits. She'd never caught one, but she was certain that they visited her yard during the day when she was locked up in the house. And I'd seen the rabbits out in the yard in the morning while I was drinking coffee and standing at the kitchen window.

My thoughts turned to Greg's upcoming visit to Sherry. I didn't like the idea, but when you lived in a small town, taking care of others was part of the deal. Even when the others were people you didn't like. I didn't only dislike Sherry because of the way she'd treated Greg during their marriage. I didn't like her because of her attitude and the way she treated everyone, including me. I had no idea why Pat stayed friends with the woman. But I guess someone had to. And it wasn't my issue.

Not my circus, not my monkeys. One of my aunt's favorite sayings. Sherry was one of Greg's monkeys. Aunt Jackie was one of mine.

* * * *

The next morning after I opened the store, I had an early morning visitor. Deek Kerr was my barista and soon to be a local author. Or he would if he got the right break and kept going. The guy was amazing and one of the best booksellers I'd ever known, including myself.

"You're not on the schedule today. It's Toby's day, or did you switch?" I was on the couch, engrossed in a new time travel advanced reader copy. My commuter traffic had come and gone, and this was my quiet time before I had to get everything ready for the next shift. I stood and went to refill my coffee cup.

He waited for me to get coffee, then filled his own. Following me back to the couch, he set his cup on the table and sat in the wingback chair facing me. "Jill, I need to talk to you."

"Do not tell me you're quitting. You have the summer reading program all set up and a ton of authors coming in. You know no one's as good with the kids, especially the teenagers, as you are." My heart started racing. If I had to replace him now, it would be months before I found the right fit. And I just got Evie comfortable in her job.

"Relax, I'm not quitting. But it's good to know you need me so much. Maybe we should talk about a raise." He held his hand up and laughed. "I'm just kidding. You should see your face."

"I'm trying to figure out how I can carve out a raise for you." I sipped my coffee. "Okay, now that you gave me a heart attack, what did you want to talk about?"

"You gave yourself the heart attack." He squirmed uncomfortably on the chair. "I really trust your judgment, so that's why I'm asking you."

"Asking me what?"

"I want you to read my manuscript. I need someone's opinion that I trust. My professor, well, I've already told you that he thought it was garbage, but the other book I turned in, the one I hated, he loved. Said it was a clear, new voice in the literary world. Then he told me I needed to get my PhD and teach." He took a sip of his coffee. "Jill, I love working with the book clubs here, but if I had to do that all day? I'd hate it. I'm not a teacher."

"It's important to know what your strengths are. Look, Deek, I know you won't work here forever. You're too ambitious to be a coffee shop/bookstore seller forever. But I'm hoping the experiences you get here will help you decide what you want to do with your life." I was going to talk my barista into quitting, I knew it.

"I know what I want to do with my life. And working here is part of it. You give me the social outlet I need so I can go back into my writing cave and focus my time there." He took a pile of papers out of his backpack. "Okay, so there's this guy who's telling me if I sign with him, I'll probably make a million dollars the first year on the book. My issue is he hasn't even read the full thing. Maybe only the first three chapters are good?"

"Who is this guy?" I held out my hands for the packet. The book was heavy, probably five hundred pages from what I could tell. I understood his fear.

"Brandon runs a publishing company out of Colorado. One of my friends from my writing group gave me his website. I got five rejections from agents last week, but this guy loves what I sent him." Deek paused and looked away. "I think it's a good book."

"I think it probably is a good book. But you're not telling me something about this offer. What's bothering you besides the fact he hasn't read the full book?" I didn't read auras like Deek and his fortune-telling mother, but I could tell something was wrong.

He scooted up to the front of the chair and tapped the table. "It's just that…"

The bell on the door rang, and several people walked into the shop.

"Oh, I know this group, they just need coffee. Let me help them, and you can look at the book and see if you want to read it or not." Deek jumped up before I could even think about standing up and heading to the coffee bar.

There was something he was holding back, and I was going to find out what it was, but right now wasn't the time. And before I could even start reading, another group came in. I recognized a bus driver. We had a tourist group visiting South Cove. I picked up the book and tucked it under my arm, then took my cup and went to join Deek. "Thanks for the help. It looks like we're going to be busy for a while."

He flashed me a smile. "I've got time. And you know I'm always up for extra hours."

By the time the tour bus customers had been served and bought books and left, my shift was over and Toby was working with Deek.

I tucked the book draft into my tote bag. "I've got to go pick up the dresses for the party on Saturday. Deek? You're working tomorrow, right?"

He nodded. "We can talk more then."

Toby glanced between us. "I'm picking up on something. What's going on?"

Deek shook his head. "It's good, man. Jill is just helping me out with something. Nothing to worry about."

"If you say so." Toby glanced around the shop. Every table was dirty. "Do you mind staying for a bit before you take off? Or at least until Evie shows up? I need to get this place cleaned up."

"I can do that." Deek grabbed a tub and headed out to the coffee shop area.

Toby leaned closer to me. "He's not leaving, right?"

I laughed. "That was my first reaction. No, it's just something with his writing."

Toby fake-wiped sweat off his brow. "Whew. That's good to know. He's always great about switching out with me if Greg needs more hours from me."

"We're fine. Don't worry." I nodded to the group that just walked in the door. "The beauty school students are here. I'll let you flirt."

He threw a towel over his shoulder. "I have to admit, Deek's just as popular with these women as I am. It took a while for me to accept it, but I can share the love."

I checked my watch. I needed to go and meet Harper. "Gotta go. Thanks for all you do."

"Easy to work for good people," he called after me as I made my way to the front door.

As I passed by Deek, I patted my tote. "Looking forward to digging into this tonight."

He blushed. "Thank you again."

As I left the building, the sunshine wiped away my fears about Deek's future with Coffee, Books, and More. And I felt blessed that he trusted me enough to read his book. I just really hoped it was as good as I wanted it to be.

Chapter 4

I was making my to-do list in my head as I headed to the dress shop to pick up the dresses for Aunt Jackie and me. I had a key to their apartment over the Train Station, so I'd drop hers off before heading home. Then a quick run with Emma and I'd make some lunch. Finally, I'd be able to start reading Deek's book. I knew it was a mash-up of fantasy and time travel, so I was really excited to dig in. I wasn't sure about this publisher who was pushing him for a commitment and I hoped Deek hadn't signed anything. I paused outside the dress shop and texted him a note to caution him about signing any contracts until we talked. Maybe I could ask one of the authors who visited the shop to talk to Deek about publishing. I knew a few authors pretty well. I bet I could call in some favors.

I waited for an answer and wasn't disappointed when Deek responded with an "I know, I know" and a smiley face emoji. Apparently, he'd been given the warning about signing before checking out a publisher before.

Relief filled me, and I tucked my phone back into my jeans and opened the shop door. Like yesterday, the lobby entry was quiet. Harper had been expecting me to show up, so I knew she had to be there. The room just felt so empty.

I walked over to the counter and rang the bell. I heard a box fall in the back. Harper must be finishing things up so she could take off for her trip. I called out, thinking if she'd heard the bell, she probably would appreciate a warning that I was the one in the front. She really should consider hiring a receptionist or only opening by appointment and keeping the front door locked. "Harper, it's Jill. I'm here for the dresses."

As I waited, I picked up the silver heart frame and looked at the two little girls smiling up at the camera. The picture was older, and the frame said "Sisters," so using my top-notch detective skills, I deduced that this must be Harper and her sister. The girls were the same size and wearing matching dresses. Was Harper a twin? If not, they were very close in age. That was one piece of history she hadn't mentioned during her business-to-business talk.

Still no Harper. I set down the frame and glanced at my watch. Greg would probably be home about five. Unless something kept him. And we were going out to dinner tonight, so I wanted to shower and change into something date-night worthy. The party on Saturday might be considered a date night, but we both knew it wouldn't be relaxing. So we'd kept our Wednesday night tradition.

"Hello? Harper? Are you back there?"

The sound of a door shutting made me jump. Laughing at myself, I decided to check out the dressing room. Maybe she'd left the dresses there and hadn't heard me come inside. She could be out packing her car.

I moved into the dressing room, and someone was on the stand in front of the mirrors. But she wasn't standing up, she was lying down, and it looked like she was reaching under the mirrors for something. "Harper, did you lose something?"

But Harper didn't look up. Or respond. I started to get a bad feeling as I stepped closer. "Harper?"

When I got to the stand, I saw pruning shears sticking out of her chest and a pool of blood on the floor. I hurried out of the room, pulling out my phone as I moved to the front entrance. When the call went through, I pulled open the door and, after it closed, turned to watch inside the windows. I didn't see anyone following me. And, bonus, I couldn't see the body anymore. Although I wasn't sure I'd get that out of my head anytime soon.

"Jill? Did you butt-dial me again?" Greg's voice was comforting as he chuckled.

Hearing his voice, I started shaking. "Greg? I need help."

"Where are you?" His voice turned all cop in two point two seconds.

"Outside the dress shop. The new one? Greg, I think she's dead."

"Oh, Jill," Greg said. I heard noise from the other end of the line. "We'll be there in a few minutes. Stay out of the shop. And don't touch anything."

"Okay." I hung up the phone and sank onto the bench outside the shop. My tote was still on my shoulder, and I let it drop to the ground as I kept my gaze on the front door. I jumped when my phone rang. Not recognizing the number, I answered the call. "Hello?"

"Jill, it's Esmeralda. Greg asked me to call you and keep you on the line. Are you hurt?"

Relief filled my body as I listened to a friendly voice. "No. But I think…"

"Stop, don't talk about it yet. I just want you to feel the sunshine on your arms. Can you feel the warmth?" Esmeralda asked, her voice calming. "Take a deep breath in and blow it out. One, two, three, and four."

"I feel the sun." My gaze didn't leave the door. "I heard a box fall, so I went to the back."

"Jill, stay with me. What do you hear? I bet you hear birds. Can you hear the ocean waves on the beach?"

I was surprised that I could hear the birds. They were singing a short song, over and over. I never was good at picking out what type of birds they were. "I hear the birds."

"Good, what about the waves?"

I shook my head, then realized I was talking to someone a few buildings away who couldn't see me. "Sorry, no waves, but there are a lot of cars on the highway."

"True. What do you smell?"

I thought for a moment. Then I turned away from the dress shop and toward Diamond Lille's across the street. "Tiny's chili. It's Wednesday, he always makes chili."

As I sat there, I watched a woman walk across the street, a bag in hand. She was drinking a milkshake. I froze as I watched her approach the dress shop. I was seeing a dead girl walking. "Harper?"

She hurried over to me. "Sorry, Jill. I ran to get some lunch so I didn't have to stop when I was driving north. It's hard to find anything but fast food when you take the freeway."

"You're alive?"

Harper had just taken a sip of her milkshake as my words hit her. She startled slightly. "Of course I'm alive. What are you talking about?"

Greg pulled up at the side of the road with a patrol car that Tim, his other deputy, was driving. He looked at Harper and then at me. "Jill? What's going on?"

I hung up the phone and tucked it into my jeans. "I think I'm going crazy. I swear, I saw Harper lying on the floor in the dressing room."

Harper turned white and dropped her shake and the bag. She ran to the door, but Greg was faster and grabbed her arm.

"Stay out here with Jill. I'll check it out." He led Harper over to the bench and sat her next to me. Then he nodded to Tim, who pulled his weapon, and the two of them went inside.

Neither Harper nor I said much of anything until Greg came back outside. I watched her milkshake spill out into the flower bed where it had dropped. It appeared to be chocolate. I reached over and picked up her bag and handed it to her. Being polite, I added, "You dropped this."

"Thanks." She took the bag and set it on the bench next to her.

Greg came out but Tim wasn't with him. He walked over to the bench and we both stood up.

"Well?" I expected him to put me into his truck and drive me off to some private facility where I'd be treated for stress. I wondered if they'd still let me read Deek's book.

"There is someone inside." He turned to Harper. "And she looks a lot like you. Do you know who might be inside your shop?"

Harper burst into tears and hid her face in her hands.

There was more going on with this story, but at least I wasn't going crazy and seeing things. I put my hand on her back. "Are you okay? Do you know who it might be?"

"It's impossible. I need to see for myself." Harper started to stand, but Greg put a hand on her shoulder.

"I'm sorry, I can't let you into the crime scene. If you want to stay until the coroner gets here, we can escort you inside then. But for now, we need access to the shop." He turned to me. "Do you need to be somewhere? Can you stay with Harper?"

"I can stay here for a while. I'll need to let Emma out sometime this afternoon." My only appointment was with Emma for a run and date night with Greg, but it looked like that appointment just got canceled.

Harper shook her head. "My boyfriend will be here at one. We were planning on spending some time in Mexico at a retreat. I guess that's off."

"It would be better if you stayed around for a while, at least until we found out who was killed in your dressing room." Greg had pulled out his notebook. "Was there anyone in the shop when you went to get food?"

Harper shook her head. "No one. I was expecting Jill to come and get the dresses, and then like I said, Colton was coming to pick me up."

Her gaze darted to the shop, and for a second, I felt like she was lying. That she knew who was in lying dead in her shop. I turned toward her and met her gaze. "Why did you say it was impossible?"

This time I saw her face change as she lied. "Would you think there could ever be a dead body in your shop? I just remodeled this building. I studied the crime rate for South Cove, and my Realtor swore to me it was a safe town. Now, I'm here less than six months and someone is killed in my shop? I shouldn't have left the door unlocked when I left."

"Typically, we're a pretty safe community," Greg responded, but then a large blue pickup truck pulled up and parked across the street. A tall man wearing a blazer and dress shirt over a pair of new jeans got out and hurried across the road. He looked like he was dressed for a date.

This must be Colton, I thought, and then my suspicions were confirmed when he took Harper into his arms, squeezing her tight.

"What on earth is going on? When I pulled up, I thought maybe something had happened to you before I saw you sitting here. Was the store robbed?" He put his arm around her and turned toward Greg. "Colton Canyon. I'm seeing Ms. Sanchez. Full disclosure, I'm also an attorney, so if she's in any trouble, I guess I'm serving in that capacity too until we get different representation."

"Ms. Sanchez isn't in trouble. Someone was killed in her shop. So unless she's the killer, she's fine." Greg's look took the guy in, and from where I sat, Mr. Canyon had come out lacking. "Right now, we've just started collecting evidence, so I will need to interview Ms. Sanchez as soon as we secure the scene." He turned his focus toward me. "And I'll need to interview you as well. I suppose I can let you go home until I'm ready."

I knew it wasn't a question. Greg wanted me as far away from the crime scene as possible. Especially since I had a habit of getting involved in his murder investigations. This time it wasn't my fault. I was just picking up the dresses. "Oh no. The dresses. Do you think we'll be able to get them before Saturday? Aunt Jackie will be…"

I didn't finish the statement, but Greg knew my aunt. His tone softened. "I'm sure we can make arrangements for you to finish your transaction with Ms. Sanchez. But for now, go home."

I glanced at Harper, but she and Colton had sat on the bench and were holding each other. She was in good hands, even if the guy was a lawyer.

"I'll see you at home, then." I picked up my tote from next to the bench and turned to leave.

Greg stepped away with me. "Do you need Tim to walk you home?"

"Why? Do you think I'm not safe?" I shook my head but kept my voice low. "Look, I found the body, that's all. I didn't see anyone else in that shop."

"You know that, but maybe this killer doesn't." He studied the path toward the house. "It looks fine. Just keep your eyes open."

"And don't take candy from strangers in a white panel van. I get it." I leaned up and kissed him. "I'll make some soup so if you come home late, there will be food on the stove."

"Sorry about date night." He rubbed my arm.

I shrugged. "It happens. The joy of being engaged to a cop, I guess. You're always out there protecting the good citizens of South Cove."

He laughed quietly. "And sometimes the bad ones. I'm glad to hear you say *engaged* though."

"I love you, Greg King. Don't let my moody behavior get in the way of that one thing." I squeezed his hand and started walking down the street to my house. It really wasn't that far away, and traffic was light for a Wednesday. On Saturday, when the weather was nice, there would be cars inching their way up to the town parking lots or people walking up the road from the beach parking area. Today was a ghost town.

Especially for that poor woman in Harper's shop.

On the way home, I called my aunt. When I got her voicemail, I explained the situation at Harper's shop and Greg's promise that we should be able to get the dresses before Saturday. I hoped my fiancé kept his word on that, or my aunt was going to be so mad at him.

When I arrived home, Esmeralda called me.

"I'm supposed to verify that you went straight home," she said as soon as I said hello.

I laughed. "Nope. I stopped in every shop on the way back and still made it here in ten minutes. Of course I went straight home. But he's also going to tell me not to take Emma running today, isn't he?"

"Sorry, that was the second part of the message I was supposed to deliver. Look, I can go running with you after my shift. I don't have any clients tonight."

"Okay, that would be awesome. We'll be ready. Just stop by when you are. But you don't have to do that." I appreciated my neighbor's offer, but I didn't want to take advantage of our casual friendship.

"No problem. I've been meaning to get in a few workouts. Nic wants me to come down to New Orleans this fall for a marathon. He runs every day, kind of like you. Me? I'm more of a couch potato."

"You also work more hours than anyone I know in South Cove," I reminded her. "Sometimes, that makes it hard to fit in self-care."

"Well, not today. And maybe I'll keep running with you if you don't mind. I know you like to clear your head during your runs."

"You're welcome anytime." I did like my solo running time, but I had a feeling Esmeralda wouldn't be a Chatty Cathy during the run since she rarely played the social small talk game anyway.

"I'll see you at ten after four," Esmeralda said, then she hung up.

I wondered if she just wanted off the phone or if another call was coming in. Emma was watching me and the running leash. "Sorry, girl, we'll go in a little while. I need to get a few things done first."

Emma went over to her bed and flopped down. Message received but not appreciated.

I pulled out the laptop and decided to do some research on our newest business owner. I had been certain the body was hers, and Greg even said it looked like her. I thought back to the picture of the sisters in the shop lobby. Could that have been Harper's sister? A twin?

I could tell that Harper had been holding something back, especially when her boyfriend slash lawyer showed up. It was almost like they'd played this game before. I wrote down his name, too, hoping something I found would explain away the bad feeling I was getting. Greg didn't hate it when I found out things via the internet. Not as much as when I went chatting with people. That really got under his skin. I get it. I wasn't a trained investigator, but some things just fall into your lap.

I keyed in Harper's name and "designer." A lot of the hits matched the history she gave us at the business-to-business meeting. But there were things she'd left out. Like how she was born in a small Idaho town. I was pretty sure she said she went to a California university right near her house. Had she meant to ignore her childhood in Idaho? I made a list of questions that omission brought up. If anything, Greg would have a great interview guide for his chat with Harper.

She didn't have a Facebook page, which I found totally suspicious. Of course, she would have found me friending her today probably just as suspicious. Especially with my history of investigating crimes in South Cove. Twitter had an account for the business, so I went back to Facebook to see if there was a business page. And, yes, there was. I went through all the posts for the last year. She'd announced the opening of her first shop as soon as she'd signed the lease, if not sooner. There were a lot of South Cove pictures, including a recent one of Coffee, Books, and More, with a caption from Harper that read: "My favorite coffee shop, ever."

I hearted the post. She'd know I had been here, but really, social media was part of my job. I saw Darla had done the same thing after the meeting and invited her down to the winery for a glass.

A message from Darla popped up. "Did you hear about the murder?"

I thought about ignoring it, but I knew that would just get me a phone call from our weekly newspaper's roving reporter. Darla was in the know about everything. So I thought I'd see what I could find out.

I leaned back and typed in a question. "Did you hear who was killed?"

"They haven't released a name yet. Lille said it was at Harper's shop right across the street from the diner."

"Really?" I urged her on.

"Yeah, and she said she saw you talking to Harper when the police went inside the shop. So what are you hiding?"

Chapter 5

When Esmeralda got to the house, I was ready. I'd hurried off the internet so Darla couldn't see me ignoring her question. I'd turned my phone to silent so I wouldn't hear the calls that came as soon as the computer went off. And now, I was just waiting for Darla to show up at my doorstep. So when the clock hit four and no one had shown up, I figured the winery must be hopping and Darla couldn't get away.

And if she left the winery now, she'd miss me since I'd be out running.

I'd have to talk to her sometime, but I didn't want to add any fuel to the flames of what was probably a sensitive investigation for Greg.

Esmeralda had stopped at her house and changed so she was ready to go. I led Emma out to the porch and locked my door, glancing up the road to see if I could spot Darla's car. No traffic yet. "Let's go."

"Who are you watching for?" Esmeralda asked as we made our way down the stairs and out of the gate that pretended to keep Emma in the yard. She could jump it, but it had been there since she was a baby, so she didn't even question it now.

"Darla. She's on the story. I don't want to tell her anything that would upset Greg's investigation." I hurried down the driveway to the sidewalk to meet Esmeralda. I needed to change the subject. "So how was your day?"

"Better before there was a murder in town. Look, I know you talked to Harper. Did she tell you anything? She's stonewalling Greg at the station. Her lawyer just keeps interrupting." Esmeralda reached down and rubbed Emma's head. "Greg's getting a little grumpy."

"Thanks for the warning." I started jogging toward the beach parking lot entrance. Hopefully traffic wouldn't be crazy and we could get across Highway 1 without risking our lives. Last Fourth of July, Greg had to have an officer directing traffic all weekend to make sure people got across the road safely. "I'm making some soup tonight for dinner and maybe some bread. That way maybe he'll eat something when he comes home late."

"He does take his job seriously." Esmeralda stopped at the road and looked both ways. "It looks clear. Don't kill the messenger but I'm supposed to tell you that he'll need Toby this week."

"I figured. I called Deek and asked him if he could work with Evie to pick up Toby's shifts. I think we'll be fine." We crossed the road, and the small talk stopped. At least for the run.

We paused at the stairwell afterward, and Esmeralda took out two bottles of water and a small bowl from her backpack. "Let's sit for a minute and take in the ocean."

"Sounds good to me." I poured water into the bowl and offered it to Emma. She drank it all, then sat next to the stairs and watched the seagulls. I sipped my water and turned to Esmeralda. "So what aren't you telling me?"

"I was just waiting for you to ask. I pulled Harper's business license application while Greg was talking to her, just to verify some things, and I found something interesting." She pulled out a copy of the application and pointed to a column. "Harper has a partner. Did you know that?"

"No, and she didn't mention a partner at the meeting. I take it he or she is a silent partner?" I scanned the name. "Alicia Sanchez. Mother or some other relative?"

"Maybe. I didn't find anything on my search. Did she mention where she grew up?" Esmeralda sipped water while watching me.

"She said California at the meeting, but the information online says Idaho. I was going to point that out to Greg when he got home." I held up the copy. "Can I have this? Or are you breaking some kind of law?"

"It's perfectly natural for the person who runs the business-to-business meeting to do some information gathering on a new resident. Otherwise, how could you help them?"

"Smart." I tucked the paper into my jacket pocket. "It feels weird though, looking into Harper. She's kind of the victim here since the murder happened in her shop."

"We're not investigating her, we're proving her innocent so she doesn't get in over her head. Her lawyer seems like he's more worried about how things would look than protecting her rights." Esmeralda stood and threw the empty bottle into the recycler near the beach entrance. "I've got to go get some housework done. I should just bite the bullet and hire someone, but I hate to have someone in my house while I'm gone. I've got too many sensitive things there."

"I'm sure they're bonded. Besides, I don't think someone would steal from a police dispatcher." I handed her the pet bowl she'd brought for Emma. "Thanks for the water."

"No problem." She took the bowl and put it away. "But I wasn't talking about things being stolen. I don't want anyone touching anything in my reading room. It throws off the spirits."

"If you say so." I snapped my fingers, and Emma followed me up the stairs. "Thanks for running with me. I appreciate getting out of the house without Greg worrying."

"You need your space as well." She pointed to the fruit stand. "I'm stopping to get some kale for dinner. Do you need anything for your soup?"

I shook my head. "I've got everything. I'll see you tomorrow, or at least Saturday? You are coming to the party, right?"

"Of course. I wouldn't miss it for the world. And don't you dare push it off because of this. Greg can take one night off during an investigation. Besides, it might help him think if he's not focused on finding a murderer twenty-four seven." Esmeralda crossed the highway with us, then turned to cross Main Street to the fruit stand.

"You tell him that. I'm not poking the bear," I called after her. Emma whined and looked across the street. "Your friend will be fine. We, on the other hand, will be in double dutch trouble if we don't get home before Greg."

We hurried up the hill, and as I unlocked the front door, Emma stood watch. I grabbed the mail out of the box, and we went inside. Emma went right to her water dish and drank again. Then I let her outside, just in case. She wasn't a puppy, so we didn't have a lot of accidents, but she needed her time outside, even when she'd just got home from a run.

I set the mail on the kitchen table and went through it quickly. I needed to get the soup started, but I had a minute. Bill, bill, bill, junk, junk, and a catalogue on wedding dresses. The marketing lists had found me. I might not be ready to say yes to the dress, yet, but the wheels of sales had already started. I'd tried to decide what type of figure I had to see what I should look at and what I should stay away from, but mostly, for me, it was certain colors. And since I was determined to be a pretty bride, I focused on the classics. I knew I'd have to try on some dresses before I could even see myself in an all-white gown with a train and a veil without seeing a white cupcake or marshmallow. Maybe Aunt Jackie was right, maybe a few pounds off would make me feel better about the dress part of the upcoming event.

Of course, we hadn't set a date yet, so after this engagement party, I didn't really have to worry about it for a while.

The soup simmered on the stove and a loaf of bread baked in the oven when my phone rang. "Hey, Amy, what's going on?"

"Are you kidding me? I was in a meeting with Marvin all afternoon, and I get home and Justin asks me how you're doing since you were at the crime scene? Did you even think about calling me?" Amy was talking a mile a minute.

"I didn't call you because I wasn't hurt or even involved. All I did was find a body. I don't even know who it was." I opened my laptop and keyed in "Alicia Sanchez" to see how many hits Google would give me. Way too many.

"You found a body. That's enough. Do you need me to come over? Justin has supper ready, but I could have him hold it for a while."

"Amy, I'm fine. No bumps or bruises. Esmeralda came over, and we went running. I'm calm and relaxed. Eat your dinner. Don't worry about me. Come by the shop tomorrow, and we can have coffee together." I paused, not wanting to rat out Esmeralda, but maybe Amy knew more about Harper's partner. "Hey, what do you know about Harper having a partner in her shop?"

"How did you find that out? She wanted it to be a secret. I told her it had to be part of the business license, but no one would see the original paperwork."

"Don't be mad."

Amy sighed loud enough that I could hear it over the phone. "I'm not mad. I should know better than to think anything is a secret in this town. Anyway, it's a relative. She didn't tell me how close, but she did say they wanted to support her in this business."

"I just don't understand, one, who would have been in Harper's shop, and two, who would kill someone in Harper's shop. It feels like someone must have been trying to kill Harper, don't you think?" My mind was wandering.

"I have no idea. I'm just glad you're okay. I'll come by for my break tomorrow. Marvin's heading into the city for a meeting. I think they're taking a long weekend, but you didn't hear that from me." She laughed and added, "And that's why no one can keep a secret here. I'm just as bad as the rest of you. Have a good night and stay safe. I take it you're alone?"

"I'm not alone. I have Emma." My dog thumped her tail on the floor when she heard her name. "Go eat. We'll talk tomorrow."

I texted Greg, letting him know that soup and bread would be ready at seven. The response I got made me smile and sad at the same time. He loved me, but he'd be late. Keep the soup warm.

I closed my laptop and went to the living room to find a movie I could eat my dinner with. I wouldn't be alone. I had my dog and a new rom-com

I wanted to see. I missed Greg, but he'd hate this movie. So watching it tonight was perfect.

* * * *

The next morning, my alarm woke me to find Greg had been home and his side of the bed had been slept in, but my betrothed was already out of the house from the sounds of it. Emma was watching me from a spot on the floor near the door.

"Did Greg leave?" I asked her and got a bark in return. "Did he feed you?"

No answer. I knew he had, but Emma would never admit it in the hopes of getting a second breakfast. "Give me a few minutes, and I'll let you out."

She laid her head down, so I knew she wasn't in a hurry to go outside. Another clue that she'd spent some time with Greg this morning. I got ready for work and slipped on some tinted sunscreen and some ChapStick to count as makeup.

Downstairs, I found the soup pot washed and put away and a note from Greg. "Soup was great. Maybe I'll be home tonight. I'm working it out so I can be off on Saturday. Don't worry."

Me? Worry about missing a party? I guess I should be, since it was our party, and if Greg couldn't come, that meant I'd have to do it alone. I poured my coffee and let Emma out for a few minutes.

I turned on the television, but the local news was out of the city and a murder in South Cove rarely rated a spot in the reporting. Instead, I heard about all the robberies that were going on in the city. One had been in the apartment building where I used to live. My neighbor, Kara Bailey, was on the television talking about how she didn't feel safe at home anymore.

I made a note to call her after work when I got back home later. I hadn't talked to her for months. I hadn't told her about my upcoming marriage. She'd been there for me during and after my divorce, but once I'd moved to South Cove, we didn't seem to get together much anymore. She didn't like driving out to see me, and I wasn't ever in town. Especially after I opened the store.

I hated that I'd lost touch with Kara. I was going to fix that tonight. I filled my travel mug, gave my dog a kiss and a chew bone, and went to hide my sofa pillows. Emma had been good for a long time, but she did love tearing up sofa pillows. Especially when she was left alone for a while.

Walking up the street to town, I enjoyed the birdsong and the echo of the ocean waves. I loved walking to work because I got to relish the quiet. And the sounds of nature. I waved at an artist who was working on a painting outside her studio. We smiled at each other but didn't talk. She was in the groove, and I knew it. Besides, my commuters were on their way, and I needed to have coffee ready for them so they could get to their jobs.

I was an essential part of the community and of commerce everywhere. I provided coffee, the elixir of working and creative people everywhere.

Okay, maybe I was a little over the top today.

By the time the commuter traffic slowed down, I was ready for a break. I still hadn't started reading Deek's book. I took a handful of pages and put a clip on them and the rubber band back around the other part. Then I took it and the coffee to my favorite part of the sofa where I could watch the front door, just in case.

When Amy came in at ten, that section was read and my coffee was cold. She met me at the coffee bar. "What are you reading?"

"Deek's book. It's really good. Engaging. I didn't want to stop." I dumped out my cold coffee and refilled it with fresh. "What can I get you?"

"A copy of that book, for one." She sighed when I shook my head. "Okay, just plain coffee with room for sugar and cream. Esmeralda's watching the phones, so don't let me forget to take her back a large black coffee."

"Sounds good." I came around the bar after pouring the coffee and sat on a stool next to Amy. "I'm so glad you stopped in today. I'm a little less calm about this whole thing than I was yesterday. What if it's just some random killer who's targeting businesses in South Cove? Maybe I should have two people on each shift just in case."

"Might not be a bad idea, but usually these things settle out that someone was killed for a specific reason. Sherry would be the only one who'd want you dead, and she's been saying that for years." Amy sipped her coffee. "But you're really okay? You weren't hurt, were you?"

"No, I walked in, called out for Harper, then went to the back where she was the day before." I paused, trying to think. Something had been weird the day before too. Loud voices. Loud male voices. Or at least one male voice. "She'd been arguing with someone on Tuesday when Aunt Jackie and I were in the shop. I wonder if I told Greg that. Yesterday was a little crazy."

"He's in Bakerstown today with Doc Ames. I guess you'll have to tell him tonight when he gets home." Amy patted my arm. "Let's talk about Saturday. What time are you showing up at the community center? Justin's already committed to helping me with decorations, so we should be good there. I just don't want everyone to be there before you are."

"Greg and I were going to pick up Aunt Jackie and Harrold at one since the party starts at two. Which will give Aunt Jackie an hour to change around everything before people start showing up. I hope he'll still be able to get away from this case for a few hours on Saturday."

Amy sipped her coffee, but I saw the same worry in her eyes. We both knew how Greg got during an investigation. He took his job seriously. But if I had to be at this party to celebrate our engagement, he had to be there too.

I took a deep breath and smiled. "Why am I even thinking about that? Of course he'll be there."

From the look she gave me, I didn't think Amy believed me.

Chapter 6

Deek came in at eleven, and Evie was scheduled to join him at noon. I was handling the start of the lunchtime coffee rush and the South Cove Rumor Society at the same time. Okay, so the Rumor Society wasn't a real club, but for the number of people who came in to find out more about the murder at Harper's shop, it might as well have been. I handed an iced coffee with two pumps to my latest customer, who wanted something sweet and vanilla in her coffee. I wished I had some murder mysteries up on the counter. I could have sold them a book when they asked me about what I'd seen. "Nothing, Mrs. Parks. Just a dead body, but have you read *The Murder on South Cove Hill?* It's a page turner."

Deek glanced over at me. He was stocking the treat shelves. "What did you say?"

I felt my eyes widening as Mrs. Parks walked out of the shop. I excused myself and turned my back on the next customer. "Did I say that aloud?"

"Just the part about some book." He took in the line at the counter. "Why don't you go in the back and cut another cheesecake. I'll handle this."

What he didn't say was "before you scream at someone," but it was implied. I took off my apron and threw it in the dirty clothes. I was tired and wanted to go home to my dog and that pint of ice cream in the freezer. Vanilla rocky road.

Maybe I should have eaten something before I came to work. Footsteps sounded on the stairs, and I watched as Evie came down from her apartment. She didn't have Homer, her dog, with her and she was dressed for work. I glanced at my watch, but she was an hour early. "What are you doing here?"

"Deek just called and said I needed to come early to replace you before you attack our customers." She studied me. "What's wrong with you?"

"Nothing's wrong with me. I'm just tired of answering questions about the murder."

Evie frowned. "Wait, there was a murder? Where? Did they catch the guy?"

"Did you not just hear me saying I was tired of questions." I glanced up at her. The easy confidence she always portrayed was gone. In its place was fear. "Sorry, like I said, grumpy. Anyway, I can't believe you didn't hear about this from anyone."

"I only talk to you guys and Sasha. Oh, and Homer, but he rarely adds anything to the conversation." She smiled to put me more at ease. The woman was filled to the brim with sweet.

"Sorry, you're right." I glanced out the doorway. There was still a line, but not quite as long. Deek was dealing fine. "A woman was killed at the designer dress shop. I went to pick up my and Aunt Jackie's dresses, and I found the body. That's all."

"Man, you're a cool one. I would be totally freaking out. I've never even seen a dead body before." She shivered. "I can't believe you're upright. I would still be lying in bed with chattering teeth."

"I'm fine, but Deek's right. Having you come in early isn't a bad idea. Thanks for bailing me out."

"Oh, Jill, there are so many things I need to thank you for, so don't worry about me working an extra hour. Besides, if I'm going to buy you anything for your engagement party, I need some overtime to pay for it."

"Aren't you saving up for a house? You don't need to be getting me an expensive gift." I tucked everything back into my tote, and for the second time this week, I got ready to sneak out the back door. "I'll see you tomorrow."

"If you need someone to take your shifts, I can do it. It would give me a great excuse. My sister's kids are on spring break. She keeps asking me to come over and hang at their pool, but I don't want to be around those kids. Blood kin or not. It's not worth it."

I paused at the door. "I didn't know your sister lived here too. I thought it was just you and Sasha once your grandmother passed on."

"Her grandmother, not mine. I'm related from Sasha's dad's line. Still a cousin, but we were raised with more money and fewer kids around us. My sister is trying to single-handedly fix that oversight from our parents. She already has four kids. I told her I'd help with her college costs, but she just laughed at me, saying that wasn't her future. Just mine." Evie picked up the cheesecake I'd cut before she'd gotten downstairs. "And if you want me to help you investigate this murder, just let me know. I had fun the last time."

I went back to my desk and wrote down "Harper and Alicia Sanchez" on a piece of paper. "Nothing but internet searches, but if you could find something interesting. I came up blank. Maybe you have a better feel for this since Harper is more your age."

She took the paper and tucked it into her jeans. "As soon as I'm off work, I'll check it out. Homer and I aren't doing anything tonight."

I thanked her and went out the back door, locking it after me. Then, instead of taking the pathway to the road, I walked down the alley that would take me toward my house. I would have to go onto the road just past Harper's shop, but at least I'd miss all the people who wanted the dirt on the latest murder. I was surprised Darla hadn't shown up at the coffee shop this morning. The girl was always looking for a scoop for her articles at the *Gazette*.

When I went past Harper's building, there weren't any cars in the back parking lot. Apparently, she was still out dealing with this murder at the shop. I'd stop by tomorrow and see if I could get the dresses. Looking up at the apartment above the shop, I saw a woman looking down at me. I waved, thinking it was Harper, but instead of waving back, she moved away from the window. Maybe she hadn't seen me.

I considered knocking on the door, but thought I'd give her another day. I'd be upset if someone died at the coffee shop, so I could understand if she didn't want to talk to anyone. I rounded the corner and ran straight into Toby Killian. He was my barista, Greg's deputy, and our renter. And he didn't look happy with me right now. "Hey, Toby, what's up?"

"Greg sent me to walk you home, but Deek tells me you're in the back. Then Evie comes out and says you just left. I assumed you'd walk through the pathway between your building and the antique store, but no, you decide to walk the empty alleyway. Are you crazy?" He was out of breath, and I didn't think it was from running after me.

"If the alleyway was empty, isn't that a better place for me to walk rather than the crowded sidewalk? I was safer here, at least." I stepped around him and started walking to Main Street.

"No, Jill. You weren't safer. What if this killer had been following you? You could be dead, and then Greg would kill me for not watching out for you." He hurried to catch up. "My truck's back at the shop. I was going to drive you home."

"Then go get it, and I'll beat you back to the house." I turned onto Main Street. Traffic wasn't bad yet, but it would be tomorrow. Thursdays were always good tourist days since people came in early for a longer than normal weekend.

"No, I'll walk with you to the house, then walk back up to move my truck back to the station. Man, I wish the council had approved those side-by-sides. I wouldn't have to drive my truck for little errands like this." He nodded to a woman sunning herself in front of the bike shop.

"You didn't need to drive me home. I suspect this means Greg's going to tell me I can't walk to or from work now? What did he find out that has him worried?"

Toby didn't answer.

I stopped and waited for him to turn around.

"Jill, you know he hates it when I spill case facts to you. Don't ask me. You're putting me in a bad position." He tucked his hands in his jeans and didn't meet my gaze.

"As your boss or as your landlord?" I saw the pain in his look when he met my gaze. "Oh, never mind. You know I wouldn't fire you or kick you out. But there must be some reason Greg's getting a little protective around this murder."

He didn't say anything else until we were at the house. When I moved to go into the gate, he grabbed my arm. "Look, Jill, I can say this. We can't find a connection between the dead woman and Harper, which means this might be a random killer. There's a string of break-ins in the city that have escalated from just stealing things to killing people who happen to be there. He's worried the guy moved from the city to here. So yeah, you're going to get some extra attention."

"Aunt Jackie works nights. Maybe we should close the store." Fear stabbed me in the stomach as I thought of Jackie and Harrold in danger.

"Either Deek or I will be working that shift with her. Besides, Harrold brings all his friends in for a few games of bridge. I think she'll be fine. It's the early shift where you're alone that we're more concerned about. We're telling all the business owners to be on high alert." Toby pulled me into a hug. "Stop worrying so much. Nothing's going to happen."

But that was the problem, I thought as I opened the door and greeted Emma. Something bad had already happened at our newest business owner's shop. And unless we found out that the murder was something personal, South Cove would always be in fear until this guy was caught.

My mail was in the box already, so I pulled it as I came through the front door. Emma was waiting, doing the happy dance since she'd heard Toby's voice, but my babysitter had taken off as soon as I'd opened the door. He'd heard Emma's happy barks, too, and knew there was no chance for anyone to be actually inside my house with my dog. She didn't like strangers, especially not in her house. I'd heard about her reaction before when someone had tried to break in. She wouldn't let anyone she didn't know get over the threshold.

"Sorry, girl, your buddy had to go back to work." I pointed to the kitchen as I shut and locked the front door. "Ready to go outside?"

Her short bark and mad dash to the kitchen door was all I needed from her as a yes. As I waited for her to want to come back inside, I flipped through the mail. Bill, junk, bill, junk, and a letter from Vintage Duds. I'd signed up for their newsletter to try to find some good designer jewelry for my aunt for gifts, like her birthday or Christmas. Aunt Jackie liked high-end items. My wallet liked gifts I didn't have to spend a week's worth of wages from the bookstore on. Greg had started talking to me about what I was putting away for retirement. He had a pension and another retirement account. I needed to check and see what we did a few years ago when my aunt had brought up the subject. I knew she'd set up the program for the bookstore, but most of my employees weren't looking at retiring. They were trying to live in our high-cost-of-living area and still eat real meals. Or in Toby's case, save for a house. It was always something.

I opened the Vintage Duds envelope expecting to find a sale flyer. Instead, I had a personal note from Pat, Vintage Duds' co-owner and Sherry's friend. I read the note twice, the content surprising me.

Pat had sent me a "congratulations on the upcoming wedding" note. She wished me and Greg a happy married life. One line stuck out, and I read it a third time. She knew Greg deserved to be happy, and she thought I was the woman to do that.

I tucked the letter away in the spice cabinet. I didn't know if I was going to show it to Greg or not. On one hand, the note was about our upcoming wedding, but on the other hand, it was addressed to me. I decided I'd show it to him as soon as this murder investigation was over. He had enough on his mind other than what his ex-wife's best friend thought about our upcoming nuptials.

I brewed a cup of coffee and sat down at the table, going over the last few loose threads for the party on Saturday. We still needed to pick up the dresses and check in with Sadie about the food. Amy was in charge of the decorations, so I wouldn't need to deal with that. Darla was in charge of the music, which meant Matt was probably DJing the event. I wrote down to pack some slippers from my closet into my tote so when we started dancing, I'd be able to kick off my shoes without going barefoot. I had some cute ballet-type slippers that would be perfect with the dress. If I'd ever get the dress.

My phone rang as I was writing up a new list to keep on the table so I could cross things off when they got done. It was Greg. "Hey, sweetheart. Are you coming home tonight?"

"I was home last night." He chuckled.

"Okay, I'll rephrase. Are you coming home at a time I'll actually be awake?"

"I think so. We're waiting for DNA and fingerprint results on the victim. Your new designer isn't being very cooperative with the investigation."

I sighed. "I heard that from Esmeralda, but I thought maybe she'd warm up and actually answer a question or two. She can't still be in shock. I mean, I would be upset if someone was killed in the shop, but at least I'd be trying to help you find the killer."

"I'm stopping by Vintage Duds this afternoon for my chat with Sherry, then I'll be home. So six at the latest."

"She's working today?"

He grunted. "I talked to Pat yesterday. She gave me Sherry's schedule. Apparently, there's a rumor that someone from the city paper is going to be there, so she wants to be the face of Vintage Duds, rather than Pat. But at least it gets her in the shop. Pat said she hasn't been working more than twice a week, if you're generous with the word *work*."

"Ouch. That's rough." I decided not to wait. "She wrote me a letter congratulating us on our engagement."

"Sherry?"

I probably should have waited to tell him, but I wasn't good at keeping secrets. At least not with Greg. "Pat. I've got it in the spice cabinet. You can read it when you get home."

"Did she threaten to kill you or me?"

I felt confused by the question. "No?"

"Then we're at a good place. Pat has wanted to shoot me since I divorced Sherry." He groaned. "Sorry, I've got another call coming in. See you around six."

"I'll take some chicken out to grill." And then I realized he'd already hung up the phone. Either way, we needed to eat, so I took out the chicken to thaw. I set an alarm on the stove for five p.m. Hopefully they'd be thawed by then, and I could soak them in barbecue sauce. I got out the makings for a pasta salad and put water on to boil in two pans. One for boiling eggs, one for the pasta. Then I started dicing and slicing veggies. I'd make enough pasta that I could make me a lunch out of it as well. I was starving.

By the time Greg arrived, the chicken was marinating and the pasta salad was chilling. All we had to do was warm up a vegetable and we'd be set for dinner.

He locked his gun in the gun safe in the den, then took off his shoes. "You should be proud of me. I didn't even think about killing Sherry."

"Not once?" I thought he was probably trying to look like the good guy.

He grabbed his work boots. "Okay, maybe once, but I resisted. I'm running up to shower and change. Did you set up anything to grill?"

"Chicken that's been marinating in sauce for about an hour. I didn't know if you'd need to go back in." I poured him a glass of iced tea and handed it to him.

"I'm planning on not going back. Unless something breaks tonight. Toby's on watch and Tim's on call, so I'm home and doing my usual 'not thinking about a solution' method of investigating. Do we need to go over Saturday's schedule?" He took the tea and drank down about half of it before setting it down on the table.

"Timing probably. And I need to get those dresses from Harper. Will she be able to open tomorrow?"

He frowned and paused at the stairwell. "She said she was calling you today about the dresses. I'll follow up and pick them up tomorrow morning. It will give me an excuse to ask her a few questions without her lawyer boyfriend butting in."

"Unless he's sleeping over."

He shook his head as he headed up the stairs. "You always know how to ruin a good plan."

Chapter 7

Greg was still home when I came down on Friday morning after getting ready for work. He nodded to the plate on the table. "Just eggs and bacon, but there's still fruit salad in the fridge. Coffee or OJ?"

"Both, but I can't stay long. I've got commuters showing up in an hour, and it takes me fifteen minutes to walk to work." I sat and picked up a slice of bacon. As I devoured it, I noticed my dog watching me with a bit of drool on her chin. "Emma, you have food in your dish."

"Oh, but human food is so much better," Greg said as he set the coffee and juice in front of me. "And you just got ten more minutes to eat since I'm driving you to work today. And you're off tomorrow and Sunday, so we'll see where we are on Monday."

"You don't have to drive me to work. I'm sure the killer isn't targeting random South Cove businesses." I took a long drink from my orange juice, then realized Greg hadn't responded to my statement. "Unless you think he is?"

"Look, I don't want to get into the investigation. I just want a nice breakfast with my fiancée." He sat and started eating his eggs. "Anything I need to know about today?"

"Like what?" I knew what he wanted me to say, but he could just ask.

"Are you working until noon, then coming home? Or do you have other plans?" He didn't even look up to meet my gaze.

"Yep, that's the plan. Although I need to fit in some time to read Deek's book. He's going to think I don't like it, when really, I just haven't had time to finish reading it." I should be able to finish today, then I'd call him and tell him what I thought. Or send him an email if it was too extensive to just talk about. I really, really wanted to just love the book.

"Tim will come by and drive you home, then. Please wait for him and don't go down the alley to avoid him." He stood and refilled his coffee. He sat back down and took a sip.

"I didn't try to avoid Toby, I didn't know he was even waiting for me. I was trying to avoid everyone asking me if I was expecting."

Greg inhaled the sip of coffee he'd just taken and started coughing. I handed him a napkin. When he finally came up for air, I nodded. "That was kind of my reaction too."

"Who on earth was asking you that?"

I tried to remember what Deek had called the woman, but I couldn't. So much for my "get to know South Cove residents" campaign. "One of the customers. Deek knows her name, I just know her coffee order. Is that horrible? Am I a horrible person you don't want to marry now?"

"Because you can't remember names?" He shook his head. "That's not why I'm marrying you. I don't want a social butterfly this time. I want someone who wants to be with me. I'm thinking you fit that bill."

Smiling, I kept eating.

Finally, he leaned back in his chair. "People are really thinking you're pregnant and that's why we're getting married?"

"According to Deek, that's been the gossip at the shop. He's done his best to say no, but it keeps coming up." I finished my breakfast and went to rinse my plate. "Thanks for cooking. I need to go change my shirt now. I spilled ketchup on the front."

As I hurried upstairs to change, I thought about the look on Greg's face. Shock? I knew he wanted kids, but just not now. The problem was, if we waited too much longer, we wouldn't have the chance. But again, this was a discussion for another day. Like when we settled on a date for the wedding. Baby #1 needed to arrive at least a year after that happened. No matter what.

Small towns had long memories.

* * * *

I might not have had a second person working with me, but after the commuters came and left, I had someone from city hall coming in every half hour for coffee. I figured probably each and every one of them had been sent to check in on me. By the time Amy arrived, I had the visits timed to within five minutes. "Hey, Amy, coffee? Or do you just want to let Greg know I'm still alive?"

"So you figured it out? I told Greg it was a bad idea, but your man can be a little determined." Amy sat on the stool. "Since I'm on city hall time, I'm doing a mocha with two cookies so we can have time to talk too."

I glanced at Deek's manuscript on the back counter. Every time I'd sat down to read, someone else had come into the shop. But Amy was my best friend. Telling her to leave would be rude, and I didn't want to hurt her feelings. Deek, on the other hand, was going to be freaked out. He knew how fast I could read when I fell in love with a book. "So how are you and Justin getting along? Things a little better in happy honeymoon land?"

"We had a talk last night. I told him I thought we needed to spend some more time together. Surprisingly he agreed. So Sunday, after your party, we're heading out to find some waves. The water might be cold, but it will be fun to spend some time, just the two of us." Amy bit into a cookie. "This married life sure has its potholes."

"As soon as you get used to living together, you'll be fine. Before, you just saw each other during the fun times. Now you get the boring times too. I bet Justin's just acting like he normally acts when class is in session. You just weren't around then to see it." I sipped my coffee and tried to act casual. "Have you heard anything else about the woman in Harper's shop? Do they know who she is?"

"I'm sure you and Greg already had this conversation, but no. I heard him and Bill Sullivan talking. Greg was supposed to be reporting on the case to Marvin, but he's out of town. Again. Anyway, Bill says the council's very concerned about this recent murder and wants Greg's assurance that this isn't random. Like he could tell them anything so early in the investigation. We all know how this goes. It takes time to find the killer." Amy finished her cookie. "Bill and the council want this solved like it's an hour-long drama on television. Greg told him as much, so I'm thinking Greg's not on the council's good side right now."

"Well, I know something." Evie came out of the back room with Homer in her arms. The little Pomeranian wiggled his pleasure in seeing us. Homer and Emma were getting to be fast friends. "You are talking about the murder, right?"

"Grab some coffee and sit with us." I pulled another stool closer. "And a couple more cookies if you want."

"I'll pass on the cookies. Having Homer back here is probably violating more of the health codes than I'd like. Or I should say, than your aunt would like." Evie poured a cup and came over to sit. Homer curled up on her lap. The dog was well trained and precious. "Anyway, I ran the names. Harper isn't from California. She moved here when she went to the fashion school in LA. Then she worked for a local designer, and early this year, her sister, Alicia, joined their inheritance to open the shop here in South Cove."

"That was her sister who signed the business application?" Amy sipped her coffee. "How did you find that out?"

"I made some calls. I'm friends with someone who went to the same school as Harper. She was surprised to hear that Harper opened her own shop. I guess she was on scholarship at the school and really strapped for cash. She worked weekends at the fabric store near the school." Evie set her cup on the counter. "So when I asked about family, Tasha, that's my friend, said she remembered a sister and her husband coming to one of the school shows. She said the sister was fun, but the husband, he was on his phone the entire time and stood outside on the sidewalk waiting for her to come out so they could leave. The sister, Alicia, said they were flying back to Boise the next day."

"I thought I found evidence she was from Idaho." I wasn't feeling quite as bad about my Google investigation techniques than I'd been yesterday. "Did she remember anything else?"

"No, we talked about people we knew after that. I'm running downstate to meet up with her in a few weeks. I've put it on the vacation board in the back." She glanced at her watch and stood. "I've got to take Homer out now. We're on a strict schedule."

After Evie had left the café, Amy was staring at me. "What?"

"Now you have Evie involved in your whole Nancy Drew crew. You know Greg's going to flip if he hears that you're investigating."

A real customer came in the front door, and I slipped off the stool and took my cup back to the sink. "Kind of like I flipped when I realized he was having all of you check on me?"

"Okay, you have a point there." Amy's phone rang. "I've got to get back to the office. I told Esmeralda to call if things got too busy. See you Saturday at the party." Amy grabbed the rest of her cookie and hurried out the door.

"Do you have any books for teenagers? My niece is coming to stay with me for a month, and I need some reading material at the house. My personal library is filled with thrillers and nonfiction about the Supreme Court." The customer walked over to the counter while she scanned the bookshelves for the right section.

"Of course. How old is she?" I grabbed the cups and wiped the counter before drying my hands and hurrying out toward the bookshelves. This was the part of the job I loved. Introducing people to my book friends.

* * * *

Tim stood outside the café by his personal car when I left the shop. It was an older sedan whose paint was beginning to crack. Tim was saving for a wedding and a house, so a new car wasn't high on his list. Deek and Evie had come just before noon and took over the shop from me. I had Deek's manuscript in my bag, and as soon as I was dropped off by my babysitter, I was making time to read. No interruptions. "Hi, Tim. Thank you for taking me home."

"You're welcome." He opened the door for me and then shut it after I got inside. When he settled into the driver's seat, he grinned. "Greg made this sound like you were going to be a problem. Like I'd probably have to chase you down to give you a ride."

"I'm not unreasonable. And I figured you'd just find me anyway. Why make today any harder on you than is necessary." I fastened my seat belt. "Are you and Winn coming tomorrow?"

"We'll be there. Greg hired Bakerstown officers to cover until five when I'm back on duty. Winn is so excited we get to come celebrate with you both." He started the car and, after checking his side and rearview mirrors, pulled out into traffic. "And I have a surprise for you."

"You really don't have to bring a gift," I protested. I knew Tim was hoarding away every extra dime. I'd feel bad if they'd bought us some appliance that we'd just have to take back for store credit.

"Winn took care of that. No, this is something from Greg." He pulled the car over and parked in front of Exquisite Gowns for You. "Greg says your aunt is already there to get her dress. I'll come in with you, if you don't mind."

"If *you* don't mind." I climbed out of the car and hurried over to the door. I looked through the window before opening the door. Aunt Jackie was inside talking to Harper, and the dresses were hung on a rack near the counter. I opened the door and hurried over to greet them. "I can't believe we get the dresses even with all that's gone on."

"If I had to make you new ones on my machine upstairs in my apartment, you were going to have a dress this morning for your party. Your fiancé called this morning and said the shop was clear and I could reopen. Since I was planning on being closed anyway this week, you're my only appointment. Then I'm vegging in my apartment until Monday. Not quite what I had planned, but he says I'm stuck here until we find out more about what happened." Harper handed me the silver-blue dress in a clear plastic hanging bag. "Here you go."

"I'm so excited to wear this. You should come to the party. Especially since your plans got changed." I held the dress out, then pulled it close to hug it. "I'm going to look like Cinderella at the ball."

"You'll be beautiful," Aunt Jackie said, then pulled a tissue out of her purse. I stared at her, dumbfounded. "Are you crying?"

"No. I just have allergies." My aunt turned and headed to the door. "Don't forget to pick Harrold and me up tomorrow on your way to the hall."

"We won't." I turned to Harper. "Thank you again. This is really something special."

"That's what I'm here for. To make your special days even more special." She paused at the counter. "I might stop by tomorrow, if you really want me to."

"We'd be honored to have you. Besides, you're part of South Cove now. You might as well meet all of the family." I told her where and when the party was being held, just in case the rumor mill hadn't gotten to her.

"Jill, I've got to get back to work," Tim said.

"I can walk from here." I laughed when I saw his face. "Don't worry, I'm coming. Thanks again, Harper, and I hope I see you tomorrow."

When I got home, I carried the dress upstairs and took off the plastic cover. Holding it up against myself, I looked at my reflection in the full-length mirror in my room. It was lovely. I hadn't been this in love with a piece of clothing since my first prom dress. Or maybe one of my suits that had been cut just for me. It was amazing how a well-made piece of clothing made the moment just a little more right.

I hung the dress in my closet and closed the door. "Emma, you stay away from my dress, okay?"

Emma whined, and I realized I hadn't let her outside yet.

"Sorry, girl. Let's go outside and we can play ball for a few minutes." *Sorry, Deek*, I thought as I headed downstairs. *Five minutes and I'd be completely focused on the manuscript.*

As soon as I'd gotten back inside, the doorbell rang. Setting the papers down on the coffee table, I hurried over to glance outside. A delivery guy stood there with a floral arrangement.

I opened the door. Emma sat next to me, watching.

"Jill Gardner?" He handed me his clipboard and a pen when I nodded. "Sign there."

I signed and then traded the clipboard for the flowers. "Thank you."

"Just doing my job." He hurried down the stairs and out of the gate into a Bakerstown Floral van.

I closed the door and set the flowers on the entry table, looking for a card. There wasn't one. I opened the door to see if he'd dropped it, but there wasn't a card on my porch either. I grabbed my cell phone and, after finding the phone number, called the florist.

"Bakerstown Floral, may I help you?" a cheerful woman answered.

"Yes, this is Jill Gardner. I just got a delivery, but there wasn't a card. Do you know who they are from?"

"Where were they delivered?" Now the woman didn't sound so cheerful. I gave her my address.

"South Cove? Are you sure? I didn't think we had any deliveries out there anymore." She paused, and I heard the phone ringing. "Look, give me your number, and I'll ask Sheila. She's out for lunch right now, and things are crazy here."

"Okay." I gave her my phone number and then my name and address again. "So you'll call me later?"

"Sure." The line went dead.

I took one more look around the flowers to see if I could find a card, but nothing. So I'd leave the mystery to later. I needed to read Deek's manuscript now. Tomorrow was going to be a zoo, and Greg and I were supposed to be heading to the city for some couple time, but I wondered if that was off the table now with the open murder investigation. I was probably lucky the party hadn't been canceled too.

Chapter 8

I stood in front of the mirror, glancing at the full effect of the outfit. I'd pulled my hair up into an updo with a few tendrils of curls hanging down around my face. I'd chosen a silver necklace Greg had given me our first Christmas. It hit the perfect spot on my neck. The shoes had a small heel and wouldn't kill me after a few hours. I was ready, but for some reason, nerves threatened to overtake me. I kept reminding myself it was just a party.

"You're beautiful." Greg came into the room dressed in his black suit. He wrapped his arms around me. "I love that dress."

"I know. Harper did a great job on this. Aunt Jackie wants me to talk to her about doing my wedding dress. But it feels like that's too soon." I met his gaze in the mirror. "I mean, we still haven't set a date."

"We will. As soon as this investigation closes up, you and I will take a drive up the coast and spend a week at one of those bed-and-breakfasts you like so much." He leaned down and kissed my neck. "Or maybe we could rent a place so Miss Emma could come along. She's part of the family, so maybe she should be there for the discussion."

"I like renting a full house. It gives us more privacy." I glanced at my watch. "We need to get going. Aunt Jackie's going to have Harrold standing outside on the curb in his suit waiting for us."

"She's a stickler for time. I get why you're the opposite. It must be hard to live with that." He let me go and grabbed his suit jacket from the closet.

"She's always been on a schedule. I think running the café made her that way. I don't remember my mom much. But Aunt Jackie I can tell you a ton about."

He stood by me now, a steady hand on my arm. "Do you want to talk about your parents?"

I shook my head, swallowing away the tears that threatened to fall and ruin what appeared to be perfect makeup application. Of course, Amy would probably pull me into the bathroom when we arrived and fix something. "Not today. I miss them and wish they'd met you. They would have loved you."

He shrugged. "What's not to love? I have to say I'm glad Mom decided to not come this weekend. I'd hate to dump handling her on you since I'm going right back to work after the party. Besides, Jim will fill her in on all the bright spots. He's taking pictures during the party and will send her a copy as well as us."

Greg's brother Jim didn't like me. He had actually told me that Greg and Sherry were still married when Greg had started coming around to chat with me. But we continued our relationship, much to Jim's disapproval. He felt marriage was forever, and since Sherry was still alive, he held out hope that his brother would return to her unloving arms.

I didn't mind Jim's disapproval, mostly because I couldn't do anything about it anyway. And I knew Greg deserved to have his family and friends at the party too. It was just going to be uncomfortable.

Speaking of Sherry, I followed Greg downstairs. "Hey, do you have any updates on the murder investigation?"

"No."

"No what?" I checked Emma's water and food. Then I let her outside for a quick run around the yard.

"No, we are not talking about this. I have four hours of not being the city detective, and I'm taking advantage of it." He grabbed the water from the fridge and filled a glass. He held it out as a question, but I shook my head.

"So you have to go back to work after the party?"

He nodded. "Sorry. No champagne for me. I'll be the designated driver. I've got some witnesses I want to talk to before they leave town Sunday."

"Witnessess? Someone saw something?" I leaned on the counter, watching Emma run around the yard. I wondered if my house arrest was still in effect. "So I can go running?"

"Good try, but no. I don't want you alone until we catch this guy. I finally got you to say yes, I'm not losing you now." He went to the door and called Emma inside. "Time to go."

Nerves hit me as I followed him out of the house. I didn't want to throw up, so I said, "It's just a party. It's just a party."

He opened the truck door, and I slid inside. He brushed a curl out of my eyes. "What kind of mess are you going to be for the wedding?"

I laughed, but it came out a little tinny. "Probably a total wreck."

As I'd predicted, Aunt Jackie and my new uncle Harrold were waiting out on the bench in front of his shop. At least there was shade still on that side of the street.

Greg parked, then got out to help them into the back seat. I really needed to get a real car so when I had to take my aunt places, she didn't have to climb into Greg's truck. Or we could have taken her sedan, but it was in the shop getting something replaced.

"You look lovely, Aunt Jackie." I turned to see her scoot over so Harrold could sit beside her.

"I look hot and sweaty. I thought you were picking us up at one?" She threw the evil eye my way. Which I thought was totally unfair since it was my engagement party.

I pointed to the clock on Greg's dash. "It's one minute after, so we were exactly on time."

She sighed. "I'm sure I told you several times if you're not ten minutes early, you're late."

Harrold patted her leg. "I tried to tell her we should stay in the house in the air conditioning for a few minutes. That you'd call us if you were here and we weren't downstairs, but you know your aunt."

"Harrold, don't stand up for them. Jill knows she's late." My aunt glanced at me, taking in the outfit and my hair. "I suppose Amy's doing your makeup when you get there?"

I pulled down the visor and opened the mirror. "What's wrong with my makeup?"

"Oh, I didn't realize you had any on." My aunt turned and watched out the window.

Sometimes she could be a pill. But she was my aunt and the only blood family I'd have at this event. I needed to be nice. And the look that Greg shot me told me he thought I needed to be nice too.

I took a deep breath. "So how have you been, Harrold? I don't think we've talked since you guys got back from Napa."

"You two need to come to dinner next week. I'll open one of the bottles we brought back, and I can show you the pictures we took. I love wine country." He beamed at me, and I knew I'd asked the right question. My new uncle was easy to please. Not like my aunt. Not at all.

"We'll call as soon as Greg's finished with this murder case. Until then, I can't count on him even coming home to sleep, let alone dinner." I squeezed Greg's hand. The comment was true, but I didn't want to hurt him either.

"Bad deal, that murder. I hear the woman's sister came down to see Harper and was just in the wrong place." Harrold shook his head. "I'm glad we have doubled up on Jackie's shifts until you catch this guy. Me and the guys are there, but I'm not sure we are as imposing of a deterrent. Not like Deek or Toby."

My aunt patted his leg. "You are all I need to keep me safe. No one would come in to do me harm even if it was just you and me."

I loved their banter, but then I realized Greg was gripping the steering wheel tightly. I reviewed what Harrold had said. "Wait, I didn't hear that the victim was Harper's sister. It wasn't Alicia, was it?"

Greg glanced back at Harrold. "Where did you hear that? The information wasn't released to the public."

"Lille told me this morning when I went down to the café for breakfast. She was very concerned that I make sure I'm not alone in the Train Station. The girl has a good heart."

I swallowed a laugh, which turned into a choking noise.

"Now, Jill, just because you and Lille don't get along doesn't mean she's not nice." My aunt chided me.

"Look, we're here, and the party's announced on the marquee out front." I pointed to the sign and tried to change the subject. This had been the most uncomfortable five-minute drive of my life. Even Greg was feeling the strain. But why was he upset? "Greg, can you help me with something before we go inside?"

My aunt made a noise as he parked the car. "You can wait for a kissing session until you get home. People are here to see you. Don't make them wait."

"We're an hour early. The only people in there are Sadie, Amy, and Justin." I watched as they got out of the truck.

Before the door closed, my aunt said, "Don't be too long."

I waited for them to go inside the community center before I turned toward him. "It was Alicia, wasn't it?"

"That's what the grieving husband said when we matched her description to the missing person's report he filed on Monday. He said she'd been gone since Friday when he got home from work." He rubbed his face. "Clearly our new business owner should have been able to recognize her sister, don't you think? Yet her lawyer said she didn't know the deceased. It's creepy. I know she didn't kill her sister, because she was at the diner having lunch when Doc says the murder happened. Besides, she's not tall enough to have done it unless her sister knelt down before her. Which could happen, but that's a stretch, right? I hate it when it's family. I want to think that people are actually good and can be counted on to take care of one another."

I was torn. On one hand, I wanted to comfort Greg and tell him that some families do take care of each other. On the other hand, he'd let out a lot about the murder that he probably didn't mean to tell me. If I interrupted, I might not find out anything else. I decided to go with my better side. "Sometimes people don't think about others before they act. Why would Harper lie about the body in her shop being her sister?"

"That is a great question. The better one is who is leaking information about my case to Lille? I figure she only told Harrold to keep him safe. She loves him like a father." Greg reached up to run his hand through his hair, then stopped halfway. "We've got a party to put on, and I was the one who said no murder talk. I guess I need to hold up my end of the bargain."

"You know I'm always here for you to throw some thoughts around about your cases. And I'm kind of good at this investigation thing." I squeezed his hand.

"Good try, but that was my slipup. Harrold knowing all that made me react instead of just keeping it inside until I got back to the station. I'm trying to keep you safe and out of these investigations. Telling you my problems only drags you in deeper." He leaned down and kissed me. "But thanks for listening. Now forget everything I told you."

"Okay, but you need to know I invited Harper to the party. I don't know if she'll come, but I don't want you to be surprised if she does." I glanced in the mirror to make sure my makeup was fine. Then I realized that Amy was going to fix me anyway. "Ready to go celebrate our engagement?"

"Yes, but we need a united front on the wedding date. Party line is we're taking some time at the end of the month to set a date and make a plan. Does that work for you?" He studied the outside of the community center like it was a war zone that he needed to get through.

"Works for me." I moved to open the door, but Greg stilled my hand.

"Thank you for being you." He nodded to the door. "And wait a minute while I open that for you. It's supposed to be a romance kind of day. Maybe we don't have all day to enjoy, but we should make the most of the next few hours."

As we made our way into the community hall, I realized that was what I loved about Greg. He wasn't into the big grand gestures. Instead, he tried to make all of our moments together special. Every day. I guess being in law enforcement had given him the "live in the now" perspective since tomorrow wasn't guaranteed for any of us.

Amy hurried over to my side. "Thank God you're here. Your aunt is going off on Sadie about the food. Can you go rein her in?"

I saw Aunt Jackie pointing to the food table, but I couldn't hear what she was saying. If Sadie's face was any indication though, it wasn't good.

Harrold was over chatting with Justin and hadn't seen the problem. "I'll handle it."

When I got to the table, my aunt was explaining why having the mini eclairs next to the chocolate brownie bites was an issue. Sadie's eyes looked like saucers. I stepped between the two of them. "What's going on?"

"Your aunt doesn't like the food setup." Sadie waved at the table. "She's right. I can't believe I didn't think of some of her ideas before."

"Well, we'll let Sadie fix the setup. I need your help with Amy and my makeup. I think she's going overboard. I just want something simple."

"Jill, you know on special occasions like this, it's all about the presentation." Aunt Jackie glanced at the table. "Sadie, I'm sure you can fix this. Thank you so much for all you've done already."

As she walked toward Amy, Sadie gave me a grateful smile. My aunt liked things a certain way. And if they weren't that way, she'd let you know. I mouthed, "Sorry" to Sadie as I hurried after Aunt Jackie.

Once the party started, things settled down. Darla and Matt had brought in an actual band, not a DJ like I'd expected. Kathi Corbin, the owner of Tea Hee, a local tea accessory shop, was dating an up-and-coming country music star. Her boyfriend, Blake, had brought his band to South Cove for my party. I chatted with Kathi for a while about his schedule. "I can't believe they were available to play this event."

"Blake and the band are heading into the city after this and doing a concert tonight. Your party was a favor for me. He's gone so much anymore since the band started to take off, I had some chips to cash in. And bonus, I get him home for the weekend after the concert tonight. He'll have to leave again on Tuesday to get to Cleveland, but it's nice that you gave me a reason to have him home."

"They're really good." I hugged Kathi. She'd become a close friend after moving into South Cove. Even with her southern belle drawl and gorgeous looks, I'd come to respect her business savvy and sharp wit. We had a lot more in common than I'd expected when she'd moved into town a few years ago.

Amy pointed to the gift table. "You're racking up the stuff."

"Not my plan." Inwardly I groaned at the large number of items I didn't have a need for.

"Don't worry about it. I'm a pro at this now. We'll sort through, get your thank-you notes written, and then get them returned and buy something fun for your deck." She nodded to a very large box near the floor. "I spent a lot of the mayor's money on that one, and I made sure it was returnable. Tina wanted to make sure their present was the biggest one on the table since they care about the two of you so much."

"And it looks good to the rest of the town?" I added. This party was filled with people who like looking good to others, but mostly, people were here to have a good time and wish us well.

"It's about time you made an honest woman of her." Bill Sullivan slapped Greg on the back. "And now you can join the ball-and-chain club. We meet monthly at the community hall to express our gratitude for the women who put up with our idiosyncrasies. Harrold and Justin are our newest members, and when the time comes, they'll bring you into the meeting."

"Sound fun." Greg hugged me a little tighter.

After Bill and Mary had left to visit with Aunt Jackie and Harrold, Greg turned to me. "I couldn't tell. Was he joking? Or is there really a club for husbands?"

"Not a clue. In South Cove, you never know. I guess you'll find out when we get back from our honeymoon. Do you have something beachy and warm planned?" I pulled him out to the dance floor when the band started a slow ballad.

"Are we supposed to go somewhere different than our normal life? I was thinking if we do a winter wedding, we could go to Colorado and ski." He nuzzled my neck. "Get a chalet all to ourselves and hang out there for a week."

"I'm not much of a skier." I laughed as he twirled me.

The voices in the room died down, and after the song was over, the band took a break. I looked over to where the door had just opened, and Harper had just walked inside with a gift in her hand.

No one said anything, they just watched her. So Harrold's information hadn't been limited to Lille, it seemed like the entire town knew Harper's sister had been the one murdered in her shop. I hurried over to greet her, hoping it would break the tension in the room.

"Hey, I'm glad you came. The band just took a break, but there's plenty of food and drink left. I should introduce you to a few people."

She shook her head. "I really can't stay. I just wanted to drop this off. You and your aunt were one of my first customers here and I wanted to see you in the dress. You look lovely."

"Don't be silly. Come over and meet Amy. She's my best friend, and you need more customers. There are a lot of women here who are asking where I got my dress. I feel like I'm a walking business card for you." I took her arm and walked her into the room.

The voices started back up, and the tension in the room eased. Whatever they'd been thinking must have been calmed by my acceptance of Harper into our group. Now to find out why she didn't identify her sister, and my doubts would be eased too.

Chapter 9

By the time the party ended, Harper had chatted with several of the women I knew and had spent a lot of time with Kathi. Still, she was getting some looks from others in the group. I figured she'd get at least one dress ordered from the visit. I was eating the last lemon drop bite when Amy came over to my side.

"So how was it?" She glanced around the slowly emptying hall. "Did you have fun?"

Greg had already left, with a truck full of gifts in the back, to take Aunt Jackie and Harrold home. I was waiting for him to come back and pick me up with the few stragglers.

"I'm beat. It was fun, but it's hard being on display. I can't remember ever talking to this many people in four hours before. All I want is dinner and to get into my jammies and watch television." I nodded to Deek, who was leaving the party with a girl he'd brought. He'd told me he was bringing a date earlier in the week. A date, he'd clarified, not a girlfriend, so I wasn't supposed to make a big deal of it. "Since we're not heading into the city tomorrow, I'm going to sit down with Deek's book and read all day."

"Did he tell you he has a publisher who wants to buy it?" Amy kicked off her shoes and rubbed her feet. "He's so excited."

"He did mention it. What else did he say?"

"Just that this guy found him online. I guess they've been talking, but Deek's not sure about the investment he'd have to make."

"What? They're asking him for money?" I grabbed my phone and looked for Deek's number. When no one answered, I left a message. "Absolutely don't sign anything until we talk."

"What was that about?" Amy looked confused.

"Deek shouldn't be paying anyone to publish. From what I've read of it, this is an amazing book, and he'll be able to get an agent and or sell it to a publisher that pays *him*." I groaned. "I don't know much about the author part of books, but even I know that. I'm going to reach out to Cat Latimer. She's an author that I know out of Colorado. She should be able to at least tell Deek if this guy is on the level."

"You are really worried about him, aren't you?" Amy studied my face.

I finished my last glass of champagne before I answered. "Deek's a smart kid. The book is starting out to be pretty amazing. I could see him making a career of this author thing. If he makes the right moves now. Sometimes it's the little things that make a difference."

"Well, I'm glad I'm not starting out again. Although Justin has been talking about what happens if he doesn't get tenure this year. I guess it's a sign that he needs to change universities and start over. I don't know all the details, but if he gets a job in Iowa, I'm going to kill him. Then I'll be a widow and I can still live here." She watched as her new husband strolled over to where they were sitting. "Were your ears burning?"

"You're talking about not moving, aren't you?" He sat next to her and handed her a full glass. "I told you not to worry. I'll get tenure here. I've got a good feeling about it, and I've had great reviews. As soon as this book gets done, I'll have one more item off my list."

"You're writing a book? How come I didn't know that?" I studied Amy's handsome professor husband. They were so alike in some ways and so different in others. Justin was the calm to Amy's storms. He had dark hair to her blond, but they were both in surfer shape. "Who is your publisher? Or do you have an agent?"

"I'll be published by the university press. Not sure if many of your customers would be interested in California history. Unless they like pirate stories that are real. I'm trying to make it feel like a novel and less like a college term paper, but everything has to be cited and footnoted, so no fiction there." He sipped his drink. "And your eyes have already glazed over."

"Actually, I'm just thinking. Deek's ready to start looking for an agent on this book he's written, so if you know anyone who's currently writing fiction, maybe you could set up a meeting? He needs to know how the book world works." I scanned the almost empty hall. "If you guys have plans, I can wait here for Greg."

"We don't have plans, and I told Greg I would be here until he got back, so you're stuck with us." Justin leaned closer. "Since it's just us, maybe you know something we don't. Everyone's talking about that designer and how she didn't identify her sister's body. How weird is that?"

"Something's definitely going on with that family." I glanced at Amy. "Did you meet the sister? Did they seem like they were close?"

"Actually, the sister never came into the office. Everything was just sent in the mail. It is weird, though, isn't it? Maybe she didn't get a good look? If someone showed me a dead body, I'd probably have my eyes closed so I couldn't see it." Amy leaned onto Justin's shoulder. "I don't even like watching zombie movies."

"That's the truth." Justin laughed. "I should have asked before we got married, but I just assumed you'd love watching zombies as much as I do. It's a guy thing I guess."

Darla sat at the other side of the table. "I love a good zombie flick. Matt isn't a fan though."

"Where *is* your better half?" I glanced around the room and saw that everyone else, including the band, had left.

"He took off to play roadie for Blake's band tonight. Since they're playing just down the road, he wanted to help out." Darla adjusted the jacket on her dress. "I can't blame him for going. The winery has been dead for the last two weekends. Maybe it will pick up tonight. I'm so looking forward to summer and some good crowds. Anyway, tell me everything you know about this Harper chick and her sister."

"Funny, we were just talking about that." I touched the sleeve of my dress. "I sure hope she's not a killer, because she's an amazing designer."

"If she is, the value of your dress just went up tons. There are websites where you can sell almost anything. Especially if they're made by a serial killer." Darla pulled a notebook out of her purse. "So far, no one is saying they've even met her before tonight. And I know some of them were at the business-to-business meeting where she spoke. I guess having her labeled as a murderer has affected their memory."

"Tina's going to freak out. I think she's ordered a full summer wardrobe to be made, and Harper doesn't do refunds. Full cost up front, and if you don't like it, too bad. She's very good about showing you what she wants to do, but yeah, she has a strict no-refund policy. Tina was griping about it last week," Amy said when everyone at the table turned to stare.

"Tina told you that?" I prodded my friend for more information.

Amy's face turned pink. "Okay, so the door to Marvin's office was open when *he* griped about what she'd spent on her credit card last month. Sometimes my job is very boring, so I eavesdrop."

"You're amazing." Darla wrote something down. "You need to become my new best friend."

"Anything I say is off the record, or Marvin will fire me. Sorry, I'm in the no-comment crew." Amy tried to see what Darla had in her notebook.

"Don't worry. I'll put you as deep undercover. Marvin will think that Tina was talking at the salon again. She does, a lot. I have sources there, too, who call after she comes in for a touch-up. Anyway, her spending money on clothes really isn't news." Darla turned to me. "I did hear that you had to pull Sherry off her at the meeting. Maybe Sherry thought she was killing Harper? You know the girl has a temper."

"Stop fishing in this pond." Greg stood beside Darla. "I'm going to have to revoke your license."

"You can't blame a girl when the police chief doesn't give me a quote for my column." She held her pen out. "Or are you doing that now?"

"Now, I am off the clock and taking my girl out for a quick dinner at Lille's before I have to go back to work and find out who killed that poor woman in South Cove." He held out his hand to me. "Ready for some real food?"

"I didn't think we were getting dinner time too." I slipped my shoes back on and hurried toward him. "Thank you all for such a lovely engagement party. I had a blast."

"It's about time we got to celebrate the two of you." Justin stood and shook Greg's hand. "Have a great dinner, and if you need anything, we're still in Amy's apartment until we find a new house between here and campus."

"I might take you up on some babysitting. But it looks less like a random South Cove killing and more like a specific motive. Which is a relief." Greg put his arm around me as they talked.

"I *knew* you were looking at a South Cove killer angle. Too bad it wasn't one. That would have really sold the papers and brought in the tourists." Darla bubbled. When no one said anything, she shrugged. "Well, it would have."

I decided this was a good time to escape before Darla decided she had questions for Greg. "Thank you all again. It was amazing. I appreciate all of you."

"You are welcome. You deserve some appreciation." Amy waved us off. "Go on. I need to turn the key in to the caretaker by nine. They're having basketball camp for the middle school kids tomorrow morning."

I smiled as we walked out of the sparkling ballroom slash gym. They'd done a great job with the decorations for the party. It hadn't felt like a gym. But that was the special thing about South Cove. It was always changing and becoming something else depending on the season or the businesses. I wondered if Darla had ever thought of doing a history day for the tourists. I was playing with those ideas as Greg pulled the car out into the street.

"What's going through your mind? Did you have fun?" Greg asked as he drove the couple of blocks down to Diamond Lille's.

"Actually, I was thinking about South Cove and its history. We should do a South Cove History Day. I bet there's a lot of historic things around." I thought about the gold coins we'd found in the shed when I'd taken over the house. They were in a safety deposit box and would stay there. "I bet there's a lot of pirate stuff around. I could order pirate books for the kids."

"Sounds like a fun weekend." He parked and hurried around the truck to open my door. "Emma was sniffing at the gifts, so I locked them in the study. I think there must be something stuffed in one of the boxes."

"You know we probably don't need half of that stuff." I took his arm as we walked into the restaurant. "And we'll get more at the wedding. Who made up this tradition?"

"Someone who needed to set up a new household with the bride and groom?" He squeezed me. "Don't worry about it. Justin says Amy's a genius at these things. I'm sure we'll be able to trade it all in for a new grill or maybe a weight bench."

"Or a hutch for the kitchen area." I smiled at Lille, who was at the hostess stand. "Good evening, Lille. Harrold said you couldn't make it to our party this afternoon. I'm sorry you missed it."

"Two for that booth over there?" She ignored me and pointed to our favorite booth. Which in Lille-speak told me that she was happy for us and hoped we had many happy years together. At least, that's what I thought she meant by slapping down the menus and walking away. "She's in a good mood."

Greg laughed and opened the menu. "Sorry about the trip to the city. I know you were looking forward to trying that new seafood place on the harbor."

"It will still be there in a month when you feel guilty about working all the time and decide to take me out." I decided this was a fish-and-chips night with a slice of ice cream cake to go with it. I set down my menu and glanced around the room while we waited for Carrie to come take our orders. The woman worked all the time. At least, all the time I was in the restaurant. But on the other hand, she was the best waitress Lille had. And, after a rocky start last year, she was now dating our local funeral home director slash coroner, Doc Ames. The guy had a heart of gold, and they deserved each other.

Greg set his menu down. "I'm going to have the pot roast. Tiny's roast is always so…"

He trailed as he watched someone come into the restaurant. I knew immediately who'd he'd seen. Sherry—and she had his brother, Jim, in tow. "If you want to invite them to share a table, I don't mind."

"Yes, you do. And this is our time. I've got to be back at the station by eight. I'll ignore them now and call Jim in the morning." He smiled over at me. "So did I tell you how beautiful you are in that dress? Can we special order a week's worth?"

"Sorry, I don't think we can afford a full week of outfits. Besides, she loves to do party gowns. I think this being above the knee is considered out of her comfort zone. But Aunt Jackie can be determined."

Greg barked out a laugh. "That's one way to describe her."

"Hey now, be nice. She's trying." Although I had to admit, sometimes she was a little hard to figure out.

"Seriously, Greg, can't you afford to take Jill to a real restaurant at least for your engagement? I think for ours we went to that Italian place downtown with the chef who came out to our table? What was it called?" Sherry stood at our table, looking at my man as if he were on the menu.

"Sorry, can't remember." Greg squeezed my hand. "Jill and I are just grabbing a quick bite. The personal celebration will come in a few weeks when this case is solved."

Sherry laughed. "It's always after some investigation, isn't it? I'm surprised Jill puts up with it as well as she does. I couldn't stand your job."

"Which is why we're divorced." He waved toward Jim. "Tell my brother I'll call him later."

"It's not what it looks like," Sherry protested.

Greg shook his head. "Doesn't matter if it is or it isn't. He's his own man. Good night, Sherry."

He stared at her until she turned around in a huff and stomped back to her table. Greg's brother, Jim, raised a hand in greeting, then turned back to his menu.

Carrie paused by the table. "Is this a bad time?"

"Are you kidding? If you came a couple of minutes sooner, I could have ignored Sherry completely." Greg pushed the menu toward Carrie. "Pot roast for me, and I'm guessing Jill's having fish and chips."

"You're right, but I haven't been here this week." I paused, thinking about my week. "Scratch that, I came with Amy on Tuesday. Still, fish and chips. What can I say? I'm addicted."

"Sorry I couldn't make your shindig earlier. I've been working doubles since Lille fired Gretchen. Or was her name Allison? I can't keep up with them anymore. All I know is she better get someone in here who can waitress before my feet give out on me." Carrie glanced at the table. "Iced tea for the both of you? I'm suspecting you're going back to the station tonight."

"Guilty as charged." He nodded at Jill. "Tea's good for me. What about you?"

"Same." I put my menu on top of his. "Thanks, Carrie."

"Don't mention it." She glanced over at Sherry and Jim's table. "I'm glad they aren't in my section."

When she disappeared, Greg took my hands in his. "Sorry about that. She's going to realize some day that she doesn't affect me like she thinks she does."

"Did you talk to her about the engagement yet?" I knew the answer. He'd been too busy with the investigation.

"No, but because everyone is calling in to the hotline with reports of her fight with Harper, I probably need to go and make sure she wasn't in town on Wednesday. Pat called and told me she was in LA that day, but I've got to confirm." He rubbed my palm. "I don't think she killed Alicia. Do you?"

"No, but it would make things so much easier around here." When he laughed, I knew he was relaxing at least a little. "I guess fitting in an engagement party around your job was always going to be hard. I'm just sorry you're dealing with this on top of the other things on your plate."

"I'll be fine. I take it Darla was pumping you for information?" He changed the subject away from Sherry's visit.

"She says you're not helpful." I smiled as Carrie dropped off our drinks with a plate of nachos. "Hey, wrong table. We didn't order these."

"I'm not senile yet." Carrie dropped napkins on the table in front of us along with small plates. "Those are from me. Congratulations on your engagement. You two are the perfect couple."

She walked away, and I grabbed a chip. "She always knows just how to cheer me up."

"Food. That's how people make you happy. They feed you." He took a bite. "And when it's as good as this, food makes me happy too."

When Greg dropped me off at the house with the rest of the presents, I pulled out the thank-you notes and put them with the pile in the office. Then I shut the door. Greg needed to be here for this part of the fun. Or at least I felt like he did. If this case pushed off for another week, I'd start working on the gifts and thank-you notes myself, but I was optimistic. Besides, his handwriting was much better than mine.

Emma stared at her leash, and I was tempted, but Greg had specifically asked me not to run alone. I didn't think he'd accept my definition of being with Emma as not being alone. Esmeralda had cars at her place, so I knew she was working. Besides, I didn't need any more excuses not to read Deek's book. I filled a large glass with ice, put a handful of raspberries inside, and then filled it with tea. Then we went outside to the porch swing.

Emma was almost as happy hunting rabbits as she would have been with a run, so I didn't feel horrible guilt. Especially after starting to read and falling deeply in love with the story. By the time I was done, the light had dimmed and our porch light had come on. Emma lay near my feet, sleeping. I set the book aside and thought about the story.

Before I lost my train of thought, I grabbed a pen out of the kitchen and started writing down areas that either I'd gotten lost or things that could be shored up. Not big things, but just tweaks that would make the story easier to follow.

I heard a truck pull up in the driveway and stood to walk to the edge of the porch to let Greg know I was out back. Instead of Greg's truck, it was Toby's, and he was running to my front door. My heart raced as I called out to him. "I'm back here. What's wrong?"

"Oh, Jill. Thank goodness." Toby jogged over to the fence, where Emma met him. As he scanned the empty deck, he used the fence pole to vault himself over the top of the fence and ran up to me.

Chapter 10

"What's wrong? I'm just on my back porch. This babysitting is getting a little crazy, don't you think?" My mind went back to Deek's story and a chapter where the main character had been missing for a day.

"Greg's been trying to call you for hours. Why didn't you pick up the phone?" Toby jogged over and looked behind his shed and out of earshot.

I waited for him to return to the front of the backyard before I answered him. While I waited, I pulled my cell out of my jeans pocket. It was dead. "Why is Greg trying to call me? Is everything okay?"

"Everything's fine. He just had a break, so he called. No answer, then called again. And so when he couldn't reach you after multiple tries, he sent me to check on you. He would have come himself, but he's interviewing Harper and her lawyer. Now that he knows it's her sister, he's expecting some answers from the woman." Toby groaned as he walked up to the porch. "Maybe you could just forget I mentioned that last part."

"The part about him reinterviewing her? Or the dead sister part? I already knew Alicia was the one I found in the dressing room. Harrold already beat you to the punch for letting out that info." I went back to the table and grabbed the papers. "Let's go in. Do you want something to drink before you go back to work?"

"A soda would be great." Toby held the door open and followed Emma inside. "Wait, you said Harrold already knew who the victim was? Greg just found out. He was trying to keep it under wraps."

"Yeah, I saw that in his face when Harrold spilled the beans. Which one of you deputies has been talking in your sleep? Because it sure wasn't Greg. That man is tight lipped on these things, especially around me." I pulled out two sodas and set one in front of Toby. Then I got out my stash of cookies from Pies on the Fly. Sadie was a sugar goddess. That was all there was to that.

"It's not me. I've been sleeping alone for a while now." He took a cookie. "Besides, I'm too busy to have a girlfriend or a real life. I've got two jobs, and I'm shooting pool on league for four more weeks."

"Well, someone told Lille, and Greg's not happy." I plugged my phone into the wall socket and texted him. Then I set it down. "I've reported in, so he should see that even if he's interviewing. How are things going with you? Besides being too busy."

"Good. I keep thinking I'm close to having my down payment, then prices go up. One day I'm just going to have to bite the bullet and buy something." He took in the kitchen. "You could sell this to me, and you and Greg buy something bigger."

"No way. I love my little house. Besides, I don't want the property to fall into the hands of an investor. At least not while I'm alive." I munched on the cookie.

"I'd never sell it." He held up his hand like he was swearing on the Bible.

"And if you get married, then wind up missing or dead, and your new wife decides she's a city girl, she'd sell to the highest bidder." I'd thought the whole scenario out. Mostly, though, with me dead and Greg inheriting and then dying. We probably needed to talk about wills sooner rather than later. Not a subject I wanted to bring up, but I'd hate to have any surprises if I was left Greg-less.

"Wow, you've really thought this through." He shivered. "Why am I the one who winds up dead in your daydreams?"

"You're not. At least you're not the only one." I smiled. "So speaking of your widow, are you dating?"

"No. And I wouldn't tell you if I was. I'm thinking it's time for me to get back to the station. I'm sure there's a DUI or jaywalker I need to deal with." He drained his soda and put the can in the recycling bin under the sink.

"Tell Greg I'm sleeping with the mailman and running with scissors, but staying home." I followed him to the front door.

"I don't think he'd believe any of those things. Including the staying home part." He pointed to the flowers. "Those are nice. What did Greg do?"

"Actually, they aren't from Greg. I don't know who they are from. The florist never got back to me. Maybe someone who couldn't make the party. I hate not knowing. How am I supposed to thank someone if I don't know who they're from?"

He frowned and looked for a card.

"I already did that, but thanks for thinking I'm an idiot."

He blushed. "That's not why I did that. I was just checking. Your boyfriend says to never assume anything."

"Okay, Sherlock, who do you think sent the flowers?"

He shook his head. "I have no clue."

After Toby left, I wrote out my thoughts about the book to Deek and emailed it to him. I also included a few authors' names that I thought might be able to help with the publishing process. Once that was done, I considered starting to clean out the gift piles, but I decided to put it off on the hope Greg would be home tomorrow.

Instead, Emma and I curled on the couch with a bowl of popcorn and a movie I'd been wanting to see.

* * * *

Sunday morning, I got up too late to see Greg before he left for the station. I knew he'd come home, because Emma was lying in her bed downstairs with a bone. And there was a note on the fridge for me. During investigations, our lives were like this. Typically, I'd have to take dinner down to the station if I wanted us to eat a meal together, but I knew the beginning of the investigation was the hardest, so I'd give him some room. Besides, this was my first three-day weekend in a while, so I had a plan. A few of the items would have to be put off until I could run into Bakerstown without Greg freaking out, like adding to the flowers in front of the house. There was one project I'd already bought the supplies for. I needed to clear out and paint the third bedroom upstairs. The one I'd started to call the junk room.

It was cleared of furniture, except for the bookcases I'd bought at several yard sales that I'd planned on painting. This room was going to be my library. Greg had taken over the office downstairs, even though he said we shared it. He worked in there a lot more. When I was home, my work was more about finding a good place to read. This would give me a place to store my keeper books as well as a place for a reading chair and a table.

Greg still wanted to turn the room into a home gym, but I'd promised him the shed when Toby finally moved out. It would give us a lot more room for machines and such. Besides, this was my room. But right now, it was boxes and shelves and junk. The boxes would go into the attic. The boxes of books would eventually go on the shelves. And the junk would go outside to be trashed or given to the community yard sale pile.

I figured I could get the boxes sorted, moved, and maybe the walls painted before I had to go back to work on Monday. Then I'd finish it off after work and during any weekend time I had. By June, this room was going to be a library.

Maybe August.

I grabbed my radio and my fully charged phone along with a travel mug full of coffee and went upstairs to work.

I'd been at it for a couple of hours and had one more pile of boxes to go through. My legs and arms were killing me from moving boxes either to the second bedroom (the boxes that held my books), the attic, or downstairs for the giveaway/junk pile. I pulled a box close and opened it up to find pictures and papers.

None of this looked familiar, so I glanced through some of the papers. Utility bills, rent receipts, and tax forms for Greg. This was one of his boxes he'd moved over from his apartment. Most of his stuff was either in the rooms or we'd decided not to keep it since my kitchen stuff was better than his. I started to put it away, thinking I'd let him clean it out or store it in the attic, when I found several pictures of his wedding. He and Sherry staring into each other's eyes. Putting on the rings. Cutting the cake. He'd loved her once. These pictures were proof of that.

Did that love affect his love for me? Did my love of past boyfriends and the short-lived husband change the way I felt about Greg? Was this marriage going to be the forever kind? Or just something where pictures would be stashed in a box to be found by the next fiancée?

I put the pictures and the papers back in the box and took it to the second bedroom. I'd let Greg figure out what to do with it. I didn't need to make that decision.

After the boxes were done, I went downstairs to grab something to eat. I was tired, achy, and hungry, but there was only one of those things I could deal with right now. I scanned through the fridge to see what I could warm up and found nothing. Then I opened the freezer and found a serving of spicy chicken rice I'd stashed after we'd made too much the other night. Score.

I tucked the bowl into the microwave and grabbed a glass of tea. Then I went to check on the mail. The living room was filled with boxes, so I moved them to the side so we could get around the room until we put them in Greg's truck and took them to the donation-site.

A knock sounded at the door, and when I went to answer it, Evie and Homer were on my porch. An excited Homer greeted Emma with a yip, and Emma sat at attention. Her body vibrated with her glee of seeing her doggy friend. "Evie, what are you doing here on a Sunday? I thought you would be relaxing."

"I heard about Alicia. I wanted to see if you had any more news." Evie glanced at the flowers. "Those are pretty."

"Come on in. I've been clearing out a room upstairs, so forgive the mess. Come in the kitchen. I was about to eat something. Are you hungry?"

She shook her head. "I ate before I came down this way. I didn't want to be tempted to stop at Diamond Lille's. I'm trying to spend less money on food so I can save some. It's hard around here. Everything's so expensive."

"Are you okay? I mean, do you need a raise? I could talk to Aunt Jackie about it." I opened the fridge. "What about a soda or some iced tea?"

"Iced tea would be great. And I'm fine, I'm just trying to figure out how to live here. I didn't have to budget when I was married, so this is different for me." She let Homer down on the floor, and he ran up to greet Emma. "Be good, little man. We're visiting."

"He's fine. I love having you and him over." I set the glass in front of her, then sat down. "I don't know much more than what you just said. Or what you told me earlier. I'm not sure why Harper wouldn't have recognized her sister, unless she was in shock."

"So, funny thing, I saw a missing person's post on Alicia that her husband had filed a few weeks ago. He went to the police, and when they didn't help him, he went to the media. He said she'd been abducted." Evie pulled out some papers and handed them to me. "As someone who has left a bad relationship, it felt off. I would have bet money that he'd killed her weeks ago and this was a cover-up. But she must have really left and headed down here to be with her sister."

I scanned the papers. He'd been insistent with the media that his wife loved him, that they'd had a happy marriage. "I wonder what the papers are saying now about what happened?"

"That's the thing. Greg might not have been able to keep this a secret here in South Cove, but the news media hasn't seemed to figure out who was killed. Or at least tie her missing status to her death. At least until Darla files her story." Evie pointed to the pictures. "If Greg's looking for a suspect, I think he needs to talk to this guy and see where he was this week. He even looks like he could kill."

Evie had that right. The man in the pictures looked more like a model for a weightlifting gym than a grieving husband. "I'll give these to him when he gets home. Or you could stop by the station yourself."

Evie blushed. "Actually, that was my first stop. I didn't want to get you involved if it wasn't anything real. Especially since you two just had your engagement party. I didn't want to cause an issue. Besides, he was in a meeting so I came here."

"There's not going to be an issue, believe me." I pushed the papers aside. "So tell me what else is going on with you."

After Evie left, I took out my laptop and scanned the papers for Alicia's husband's name. Then I started my Google investigation.

Later, Greg came home with a bag of Diamond Lille's chicken with the fixings. "I hope you haven't eaten dinner. I should have called first, but time got away from me and I just ordered on my way back from seeing Doc Ames."

"Actually, I didn't even have lunch." I'd gotten lost in the internet search and had left my reheated leftovers sitting in the microwave too long. I'd just thrown it out and had been thinking about what else I could eat when I'd heard Greg's truck. "So how's Doc?"

"Good. Did you know Carrie's moving in next week? I guess they're getting pretty serious." He set out the food on the table while I grabbed plates and silverware.

"I didn't know that. I guess they're keeping it kind of quiet." I was overwhelmed by the smell of the chicken. Sunday afternoon memories flooded through my mind. Recent and those from when I was a sullen teenager living with my aunt and uncle. "You said food makes me happy yesterday. I think it's the memories I hold around it. Like Sunday chicken."

"I know. My mom didn't do Sunday dinner, not like your aunt, but I've grown to appreciate the tradition since we've been together." He leaned over and kissed me before sitting down. "I don't even look at the menu. Not on Sunday."

"And I appreciate it. Was Carrie working when you picked up the food?" I found my favorite two pieces, a breast and a wing, and put those on my plate before going for the mashed potatoes.

"Yes. And boy was she grumpy. I guess Lille had promised her the day off, but when Doc told her he was working today on this case, she went in anyway." He laughed as he grabbed a leg off the plate. "You would have thought I killed Alicia from the look she gave me."

"It's hard to be with someone who doesn't have standard nine-to-five hours. Being at the beck and call of the safety of the community makes me feel guilty when I feel upset because we have to change an outing." I thought about Carrie and her new relationship with Doc. "Maybe I should take some time and talk to her."

"That would be nice." He set the leg down without taking a bite. "You're okay with my job, right? I mean, I know it screws up our plans at times, but I've always been in law enforcement since we started dating."

"Yeah, I know. But knowing it and living it are two different beasts. Intellectually, I know that when you have to break plans it's not because you just didn't want to do it. But in my heart, sometimes I miss you. Especially during cases like this one. You're gone a lot. And I've gotten used to having you around." I squeezed his arm. "It's not a big thing. I'm just telling you how I feel sometimes. It's not a breakup-able issue."

"It was for Sherry."

The words hung in the air for a second. I knew when his first marriage had gone down in flames it had wounded him. But just like I couldn't worry about how my workaholic past killed my first marriage, this wasn't our issue.

"I'm not Sherry." I leaned back in the chair. "Speaking of your first marriage, when I was cleaning out the library, I found a box you need to go through. It has old tax returns, receipts from your rental, and your wedding pictures. I put it in the second bedroom with the book boxes. You have two choices, trash or attic. There's lots of room up there, but I didn't want to sort through your stuff."

"You could have." He studied my face.

I felt like there was more here. A fight I didn't understand the rules to. Or even the reason it was brewing. Something was bothering him that was more than just a box I'd moved from one room to another.

I decided to leave it for another day. With the case going on, if it was a fight, we might not be able to get through it before I didn't see him again for days. And I hated it when we weren't on speaking terms. Even though I knew we'd get past it. Eventually.

"Honestly, I saw the pictures and stopped. I don't need doubt running through my head right now. We're too busy to deal with it." I picked up my fork and took a bite of the mashed potatoes. So good. I turned to him. "Please tell me you brought home apple pie for dessert."

Chapter 11

Monday morning, I was surprised to find Greg still at the kitchen table when I woke up. I didn't set my alarm for my days off, but I still got up early. Just not as early as when I needed to serve coffee to my commuters. "Hey, I expected you to be off and running already."

He handed me the cup of coffee he'd just poured for me. "I wanted to spend some time with you before I went into the office. Yesterday felt a little off."

"We're both going through some emotions regarding our change of status. It's funny how you can be exactly the same person in the same relationship, but slap a label on what we have together, and it feels different." I took the cup and curled into one of the kitchen chairs. I loved having Mondays off, but they seemed to fly by. I tried to slow them down when possible. Like now.

"Bad different?" He sat next to me and continued to peel an orange while we talked.

"Different, different. I feel it. I know you feel it. And having this case is probably making it more pronounced. Did you see the papers on the counter about your victim's husband?"

"Yes. I know you didn't print them, because the office is still filled with gifts we need to deal with." He separated the orange sections and ate one.

The smell of the orange was overwhelming. I grabbed a section and popped it into my mouth before answering. "Don't get mad at her, but it was Evie. She started researching Alicia since she was listed on the business license as being a part owner."

"Well, I have him on my list to interview this afternoon. He drove down from Idaho a few days ago and is staying at the Castle until Doc releases the body. Then he'll go back and make funeral arrangements." Greg ate another slice, then stood to throw away the peels. He washed his hands at the kitchen sink before sitting back down. "And yes, after talking to him on the phone yesterday, I let my emotions cloud my thoughts about us. I don't know what I'd do if I lost you. And that scared me. A lot."

"Are you saying you want the ring back?" I held out my hand where it sat. I still didn't sleep with it on, but I did have a start on a routine at bedtime and after my shower of putting in on and taking it off to store it where it would be safe. Wearing it was beginning to feel routine.

"No. I'm saying I'm happy we made the jump. I have to say that I see your side of the ring issue. It feels different now. We feel different now. In a good way, but more important." He shook his head. "I'm not explaining it well."

"Actually, you're explaining it better than I was able to. I think we both thought it wasn't a next step. That it was just a thing. But becoming engaged is important. And different. We needed to acknowledge it formally, like we did yesterday with the community. I make fun of the 'ceremonies' around these things, but I think they're important for our emotional state." I stood and kissed him. "I'm so happy to be marrying you, Greg King. I know we'll have our ups and our downs. Our fights and our makeups. I can't see a future without you now."

"I feel exactly the same way." He squeezed me. "Okay, so now that we're done with the touchy-feely side, what's your take on Alicia's husband? Grieving widower or possible cold-blooded killer?"

"I don't know. But Evie had a strong reaction. I don't know her whole story, but I know she left a bad relationship to come here. And she feels like Alicia might have been escaping the marriage, not kidnapped." I shook my head, trying to let the conflicting emotions fall into neat little piles. The way I liked my emotions to be contained. It wasn't working. "I can't give you more than my reaction to Evie's reaction, but I think she's seeing something we aren't."

"I got that. He had a desperation to his call. Like I needed to understand how happy they were. That she wouldn't just leave him." He checked his phone. "I've got to go. We're having a strategy meeting at the station. Can I have the printouts?"

"As long as you don't rat out my source, yes." I pushed the papers toward him. "Will I see you for dinner?"

"Maybe. It depends on if anything breaks today. You know the drill." He paused. "And I'll go through the box and put what I'm keeping up in the attic. If I keep some of the wedding pictures, is that going to bother you?"

"No. I knew you were married before. I just need to know you love me more. Just so I can rub Sherry's face in it the next time we meet on the street." I laughed as I followed him to the door. "Do you think I could take her one-on-one?"

"Just letting you know, she fights dirty." He kissed me, laughing. "Just stay out of trouble. You can go running if you're careful."

"Thank you. I'll text you when I leave and when I get back." I felt giddy at the idea of running on the beach. "So you think this is personal, Alicia's killing?"

"Yeah, I've kind of ruled out a South Cove business owner serial killer scenario. There's too much going on in this family for it to not be something surrounding them. But be careful anyway, okay? Just in case?"

"No taking candy from men in white panel vans who seem to have a maniacal grin. Got it." I rubbed Emma's head. "Besides, I have my own protection squad."

"She's not going to stop a bullet. But she does make me feel a little better about you being out here alone. Besides, we need to get back to normal life. Before I go crazy with unfounded worry."

"Just wait until we have kids." I pushed him toward the door, laughing as his face fell.

He grabbed me around the waist. "You're evil, Jill Gardner."

"And you love it."

Once Greg had left, I grabbed my planner and looked over my to-do list. The thank-you notes were still there, and I moved the item to next weekend. Greg was so going to help with this. I needed to do a grocery run that I'd been planning on doing later this week, but maybe it would be better to get it over with today. And I could drop off some cookies to Doc Ames and check in on him and Carrie.

Which really meant see what gossip he'd tell me about Alicia's death, if anything. Doc was hot and cold on information. Sometimes he was super chatty. Other times he was a locked vault. Cookies should open him up. And besides, I felt bad since he didn't get to come to the party yesterday because of work.

And maybe Deek would call me back and we could talk about his book.

With my plans for the day set, I grabbed laundry from the hamper, set up a washer load, then returned to the kitchen. Laundry was always on my list. I poured a second cup of coffee and grabbed a book that I'd tucked in my tote Friday morning. A few chapters, and then I'd start on my list.

It was almost noon by the time I'd finished the run and two more loads of laundry. And I was halfway done with the New Zealand–set women's fiction I'd picked up. This would be my staff pick of the month, and I'd need to write a review for Deek's newsletter, but this would be easy. Good books made for good reviews. As I got ready to head to town, I thought about the review and how I'd start it. Since Deek had begun this staff review column, I'd grown to love sharing my favorite books with my customers even more. And I reached more people than when I just did it by word of mouth.

I stopped at Coffee, Books, and More, going in the back door since we weren't open on Mondays for a couple more weeks. I boxed up the cookies and, on the way out, grabbed another book off the Advance Reader Copies shelf in the office. I might need another book to read before the end of the day, especially if Greg didn't come home for dinner. I figured if he did, we'd spend an hour a day on the thank-you notes until the gifts were all opened and cards sent.

This was our elephant, and we were going to eat it one bite at a time. At least that was my plan.

I drove straight to Doc Ames's funeral home. I pulled in the crowded parking lot and realized that he must be having a funeral at the chapel. So much for my investigative skills. I probably should have looked at his website to make sure he was free.

Instead of parking and dropping off the cookies, which seemed a little inappropriate, especially since I was dressed in a tank, shorts, and flip-flops, my usual off-work attire, I pulled out of the lot and headed to the grocery store to do the shopping.

If I was lucky, I might run into Harper or maybe her lawyer boyfriend. Or maybe a South Cove business owner who had some gossip. Everyone always thought I knew everything about the investigations that Greg handled in South Cove, but really, most people around here knew more than I did since neither Greg nor Toby told me anything unless it was by accident. Or to throw me off the scent. Which rarely worked since I'd stumble into something and not realize I was actually in danger.

Amy was out, since she worked Mondays at city hall. So I just did my shopping.

My phone rang as I was checking out. It was my aunt, probably checking on my progress with the thank-you notes. Aunt Jackie was queen of the local manners club.

"Good morning, Aunt Jackie. How's your day off going?" I used my shoulder to hold on to the phone as I pulled out my wallet and swiped my debit card.

"I'm busy getting the plans set up for Saturday's spring festival. Have you bought the prizes for the readathon?" My aunt had me on speaker phone, and I could hear Harrold talking in the background.

"Crap. No. I forgot all about the supplies." We were doing book coupons to everyone who finished the twenty-four hours. They had to check in with us every hour they wanted credit for. Some of the kids would start early and go home to sleep, others were treating it like a sleepover. No matter how they set it up, everyone needed a bag of candy that they'd get when they signed up. I had to have full-leaded and sugar-free stuff and at least two hundred bags. I was hoping we'd bring in a lot of kids for the readathon. Twenty-four hours of reading started Friday morning at six when the bookstore opened. Then we'd be open from Friday to Saturday at noon. We had Lille's delivering a late-night snack run for all the kids who were sleeping over. And it was all hands on deck until they started leaving on Saturday after hitting their twenty-fourth hour of reading. "I didn't get snacks at the store. I'll go back in and do a second run. Anything else you can think of?"

She listed off a ton of things like sodas and juices and individual chip bags and mini pizza treats we could warm up in the microwave. This event was going to cost a fortune in food supplies alone. But it was worth it. Kids could bring their own books or buy them at the store. And everyone who finished won a book coupon. And all the parents would be there, looking at books too. We suspected we might have our biggest sale day ever. At least that was the plan.

I made a quick stop at the party place before leaving town. I bought paints, crayons, white paper, bags, and after a groan, glitter and glue. Evie was hosting a craft table, with one of the projects painting a rock. The store would be cleaning up glitter for weeks, if not months.

I dropped all the supplies off at the shop and was walking out to the Jeep when Evie called out from the apartment balcony. "Hold up. We'll be right down."

I grabbed my soda from the stop I'd made at the drive-through on the way out of town and leaned on the side of the car. She and Homer made their way down the stairs, then Evie hooked him to a lead and came over without him. He barked a greeting, then went over to the side of the building where the grass grew and lay down.

"I didn't expect to see you today. I thought you and your man were in the city." Evie handed me a sheet of paper.

"That trip was canceled due to murder." I shrugged as I took the paper. "It happens. What's this?"

"I found it when I went back to Alicia's husband's Facebook page. I took a chance and friended Scott Draper. Weird thing was he accepted. A lot of condolences on the loss of his wife. I guess he's enjoying the attention. I'd be too wiped to be posting on Facebook if something happened to someone I loved." She pointed to the paper. "That woman chats him up a lot. And they've been going to dinner a lot. One of the other people on the page commented that it must be nice to have people to take care of you. Then this woman stopped posting. That was yesterday. Like they thought it looked odd?"

"Maybe. Or maybe she's a late sleeper and hasn't been on. Or she's at work." I wasn't seeing what Evie was seeing in the comments, but I only had her report of the issue, I hadn't read the comments myself. I was beginning to worry that I was getting Evie down a rabbit hole and she was seeing unicorns instead of horses. "Maybe you should back off on this. You seem invested."

She sighed and looked over at Homer, who was watching us. "Maybe. I just wish I'd seen the signs in my own relationship. Maybe that's why I'm seeing them here. My eyes are open now, and all I can see are warnings. Even when they aren't there."

"Greg thinks something's off with the husband, too, so your instincts were good there. I just worry you're getting too invested in him being the killer."

Evie nodded and went back to gather up Homer, who was barking now. "I get what you're saying. And I'll cool it. But you know, it's always the husband."

"So the book says." I laughed and waved as she went back upstairs to her apartment. All of us who worked at the bookstore had read a thriller by that name and had a fun time discussing the book and its themes.

That was the good thing about working with people you liked. You had a lot to talk about. I went back down the alley and onto the road. By the weekend, I'd have to walk into town it would be so busy.

When I got home, my aunt called. I thought she must have seen my Jeep in town, because she always knew exactly when to call. "Everything's bought and at the shop. I'll start putting together snack bags tomorrow after my commuters leave."

"Good, I was just going to tell you to put that on the daily to-do list for all shifts. Harrold can work on them during my shifts this week too. We should be done by Thursday night."

I thought we'd be done with the prep work earlier than Thursday, but my aunt never shortchanged a plan. "I wanted to talk to you about staffing for the Friday sleepover. If this investigation is still going on, I don't think we can count on Toby being there. Greg's going to need him as deputy."

"Especially with the festival going on. Even if there wasn't this unfortunate murder thing." She sighed. "I thought I was being smart by hiring a police officer as a part-time barista, but he's giving us a lot of staffing issues."

"Toby is not. He takes care of his shifts and then switches with Deek when he can. We should be supportive of local law enforcement." I didn't like the way she was talking about him.

"Says the woman who's engaged to the head detective." She chuckled. "Never mind, I was just questioning my own decision-making, not yours. So if Toby can't be there, I guess I'll plan on being there through the night. I'll send Harrold home about ten. The man needs his eight hours or he's a wreck. And he has to open his shop on Saturday anyway."

"Actually, if you both go home at ten and then you come back around seven the next morning, I think we'll be good. I'm going to stay the full night, and I'll have Deek do the same. We'll send Evie up for a power nap from midnight to eight. And then I'll send Deek home as soon as breakfast is over." I grabbed a notebook and started mapping it out. "I don't feel comfortable with just one of us there overnight, but Deek and I should be able to handle seven hours with just the two of us. As long as these kids actually sleep. I suspect a few parents might hang around for a while as well."

"Are you sure? We could call in a temporary or two. I'd have to get them trained, but mostly it would be kid wrangling, not handling the store." My aunt never suggested hiring temps for the local events, which meant she was really worried about staffing for this one.

"Hold off on that idea. I have a better one." I just wondered what I could offer to make it work.

"Are you going to tell me?" my aunt asked.

"Only if it pans out. Hold on. Let me call you right back. Then, if I strike out, you can hire two temps for the week."

"Jill..."

I did hear my aunt call my name, but I could pretend I didn't. And if my plan worked, she'd be happy anyway and maybe forget that I'd hung up on her.

At least that was my hope.

Chapter 12

I dialed the number I knew by heart. When Sadie answered, I quickly asked, "I didn't wake you, did I?"

Pies on the Fly was basically a wholesale bakery that had a home base in Sadie's garage. A very clean and remodeled garage that looked like a baker's dream kitchen. She had been a stay-at-home mom when her husband died years ago, so she'd taken the life insurance money he'd left her and started her own business. One where she could be home with her son, get him off to school, and be available at three when he got home. The only problem was she worked nights. Now that Nick was living in London and working in finance, she didn't need to be awake when he got home. So she slept during the day so she could have a little time for herself at night. And the Methodist pastor she'd been dating for a few months.

"Nope, I'm awake and waiting for Bill to pick me up for dinner out. We haven't been out in months it seems. Usually, we're doing something at the church." She giggled. "I feel like a teenager, getting dressed for a date."

I smiled, happy that her new love life was working out. Sadie had tried dating once before, only to have it end when the man in question went back to his ex-wife. "So how busy is next weekend?"

"Nothing really. The church decided to suspend normal activities so we could support the town. Why?"

"Will you be baking on Friday night?" I knew she typically took Friday and Saturday nights off from baking, but with the additional orders for the festival, she might have to work.

"No, unless there's an emergency with my Friday deliveries, I don't plan on baking again until Sunday night. Why the twenty questions?" I could hear the question in her tone as she followed up, "What's going on, Jill?"

"How would you and Pastor Bill like to earn a donation to the kids' program at the church? Or I could pay you for your time? Either way."

"Doing what?"

"I need a couple of adult bodies to stay overnight with me and about fifty kids that have signed up for a readathon at the store on Friday night. We need you from about nine to eight the next morning." I held my breath, hoping Sadie would say yes.

"I don't see why that would be a problem. And no, you don't have to pay us. But the youth group is looking for a sponsor for summer camp fees this July. Maybe you could reach out for that. Let me confirm with Bill to make sure he doesn't have plans, but I'll be there after dinner on Friday. Can I bring my own books? I have a few of Nick's old favorites I'd love to read aloud again if we have kids that age."

"Of course." I should have known Sadie would say yes, as long as it didn't interfere with her own business. She just had a big heart. "Thanks for doing this."

"No problem. I'll call you tomorrow with Bill's answer, but I've got to go. He's ringing the bell."

After I hung up, I thought about how fun it had been when Greg and I were first dating. Maybe that was the chemistry everyone talks about. When you're finding out how much you have in common. Of course, it might just be the red car theory where you focus on the things that bring you together rather than the differences. Which was probably why most of my relationships hadn't lasted. I only looked for the good things.

Greg had his bad points, mostly his dedication to his job and his tendency to be a workaholic. But since I was the same way, I guess I saw it as a positive, not a negative.

I texted my aunt the news that Sadie and maybe Pastor Bill would be joining us. I'd let her know about the donation after Sadie and I finished our conversation. Now, staffing for the weekend was marked off my list, and I could settle into reading.

When Greg got home later that night, I was curled up on the couch with a cooking show on the television and the new advance reader copy in my hand. I'd already written my review for the first book and sent it to Deek's email. I assumed I'd get a shocked response back, since I was actually a day early on my deadline, not a week late, but by the time I'd shut down my laptop, I hadn't heard a thing.

I had already eaten a sandwich for dinner along with two of the cookies I'd planned on taking to Doc Ames. Maybe I could head that way tomorrow. I'd checked his website, and he didn't have a funeral scheduled. I decided

I'd call in the morning to make sure he was available and grab a fresh box of cookies from the shop for the trip.

I set my book down. "Do you want dinner?"

"I sent out for Lille's about seven. How about you? Did you eat?" He fell down on the couch next to me, watching the television host make a Cuban sandwich. Of course, the chef had roasted an entire pork shoulder beforehand. "That looks amazing."

"It's in Ohio. Do you want to take a foodie road trip sometime? We could start writing down all the places we want to stop, and by the time we got home, we would have gained ten pounds."

"I don't gain weight. That's your fear." He squeezed my hand. "My metabolism takes care of me."

"You work out at the city rec hall gym three mornings a week before you go into work." I turned down the volume on the television. "That's what takes care of you."

"True. So what have you been doing today?"

"Nothing much. I went shopping. Did some work on next weekend's festival, and then read." I studied him. "What about your day? Did you find a killer?"

He shook his head. "No, but there's a suspect. At least one that the DA thinks is pretty viable. Known to have a temper. Was seen in an altercation a few days before with someone. And had a pretty good motive, if not that it was Harper's sister that was killed."

"No. They aren't thinking that Sherry killed Alicia. That's crazy."

He leaned his head back and shut his eyes. "I feel the same way. She just doesn't have it in her. She's all bluster and no bite. But the DA's pretty sold on Sherry being the killer. So I'm building a case against her."

"If she didn't kill Alicia, there's no case to be built, right?"

He stood and started toward the kitchen. "Darling, if you look hard enough at any of us, we could convince a jury that you were a killer, even if you never picked up a gun or a knife. I'm looking for a good alibi, but she doesn't make it easy. She says she was walking and window shopping in Los Angeles during that time. That she didn't see anyone. And then she decided not to spend the night, so she drove back and slept in her own bed."

"Maybe someone saw her," I said.

"That's the hope."

* * * *

With Sherry being suspect number one in the killing of Alicia Sanchez, I should have been over the moon. Instead, I was worried. Greg didn't think she killed anyone. And if he thought someone was innocent, he would work even harder to find the person that actually had done the deed. If he didn't find anyone before Sherry was arrested, it would haunt him.

As I suspected, Greg was already out of the house when I woke the next morning to my alarm. I went through my morning routine, promising Emma a run when I got home, and then started up the street to the coffee shop and my early morning shift.

I guess if I didn't own the shop, working this shift might get boring or tedious. But I loved my commuters as well as the quiet time the early morning gave me. Of course, as the days warmed toward summer, my quiet time got shorter and shorter. Visitors who were staying at the bed-and-breakfasts in the area liked to stop at the store and get coffee and a bit of reading material before heading to the beach or to a day of sightseeing. And once they tried one of Pies on the Fly's treats, they usually came back.

Today, I didn't have reading time since I was busy building snack bags for Saturday's readathon. The back room was stuffed with boxes of books we needed to get out on the shelves as well as the makings for crafts and the snack bags. It was a good thing I didn't have to do any bookkeeping or marketing this week. I doubted I could find my desk, let alone use it until next week when all of this stuff was gone.

Pat Williams came into the shop just after one of my regular commuters left. From the look on her face, she'd been talking to Sherry. I waved her over to the counter where I had bags set up to fill. "Can I get you some coffee?"

"That would be nice." She pulled out her wallet, but I shook my head.

"Coffee's on me this morning." I poured large cups for both of us and walked around to sit next to Pat. I was pretty sure I knew what she wanted to talk about. "There's sugar and creamer on the counter over there."

"I take mine plain." She took a sip. "It's better this way. Especially when the coffee's this good. I've been known to doctor up bad coffee, but that's not something I have to worry about here."

I realized we were making small talk, but if that helped Pat settle, I'd accept it. "I'm glad you came in. I needed a break from the snack bag prep. We're expecting over two hundred kids this weekend for the festival. I think my idea for a readathon was a little ambitious. Maybe I should have capped it."

"I'm sure you'll be fine. Your shop is so open and friendly." She smiled as she sipped her coffee. "We're having a 'bring in summer' sale on anything without sleeves or above the knee. Business has been picking up. Sherry always worries during the winter, but that's why I keep telling her we need a website. People don't want to just go for a drive when it's chilly outside."

"That sounds like a great idea. I know our sales have picked up since we set up a website. One of my staff, Deek, set it up. If you want, I could send him over. Maybe you could hire him freelance to set up your system. I'm sure it will be worth it." I grabbed a piece of paper, but Pat stilled my hand.

"Maybe this fall. Or once this thing with Sherry gets fixed. You know she couldn't kill anyone, right?" Pat's grip on my hand where she'd stopped me from writing down Deek's number was tightening. Tears were forming in her eyes. "She's not the nicest person, but she's not a killer. You have to know that. You need to tell Greg."

I knew this was coming. "Pat, Greg does know Sherry. And he feels awful about this, but her actions are what's putting her into trouble here. If she hadn't verbally attacked Harper here at the council meeting and then went over to her store too… What on earth was she thinking?"

Pat picked up a napkin and started picking at it. "I know. She feels awful about it but she was reacting. She thinks having a designer in town is going to hurt our sales. But in fact, it's been helping. Women want choices they can afford. Especially in today's economy."

"I think you're right. Surely Sherry has an alibi for the time of Alicia's death." I saw the answers on Pat's face before she even spoke.

"She was shopping in Los Angeles, then came home alone. She's been drinking more, and I'm pretty sure she was drunk that day too. Sherry's been upset about Greg's and your engagement. She doesn't want the guy for years, until he's happy with someone else, then she's all heartbroken. Sometimes, I just don't get her." Pat dropped the napkin she'd shredded into strips onto the counter. Then she drank more coffee.

"Pat, why *are* you friends with her? You seem normal. Reasonable. I'm not saying Sherry isn't, but you two just don't seem like a natural friendship." I saw the jolt run through her. "I'm sorry if that's too personal."

She held up a shaky hand. "I've been telling myself that I'm the only one questioning our friendship. I guess I didn't know that others were as well."

"I should just stop talking," I joked, but Pat didn't smile.

Instead, she looked sadder than she had when she walked in the door. "Sherry didn't use to be this way. We've been friends since high school. She was the cheerleader, and I was the hanger-on. I couldn't believe how lucky I was to be her friend. Sure, she asked for help with homework, a lot, but not everyone had my brain. I was the first female National Scholarship winner in my high school. I had my choice of colleges, but I followed Sherry to a state school. We shared a dorm room. We were on an adventure together."

"It's good to have strong friends like that." I'd been a loner in high school and college. Not wanting to let anyone get close.

"It was, until she got rushed to the sorority. Then I was left in the dorm and she went to live with the sisterhood. Friends aren't half as cool as sisters." Pat shrugged and ran a finger over the lip of her coffee cup. "When I left school that year to go to one of my first choice schools, I didn't think I'd ever see Sherry again. But as soon as I graduated, she was at my parents' house, welcoming me home. I guess she'd flunked out first year and had been working at the mall since then."

"And your friendship struck up again." I guessed the rest of the story.

Pat nodded. "Sherry's so proud of her sorority sisters, but no one has any time for her. They all graduated and went on to good careers or married well. I think that's why she wanted Greg. He was cute, successful, and, in Sherry's mind, on a fast track to someone important. She didn't want to be stuck in a small town and married to the dullest man in town. Sorry, I know Greg isn't dull, but Sherry didn't know what she was throwing away. As fast as they were married, she wanted something or someone else. Her next step."

My heart ached for Greg. From the look on Pat's face, she'd worried about him as well.

"He was a stepping-stone to something or somewhere cooler. Once she married him, she wanted him to take her to the top, or she'd find the next stone. Don't look at me that way. I know what Sherry did was bad. I told her to think about what she had. But just because she was a horrible wife doesn't mean she's a killer."

After Pat left, I thought about our conversation while continuing to stuff snack bags. When Deek came in, I let the conversation go and put the bags into the office. "Hey, you didn't get back to me."

He grinned as he tucked his bag into a cubby and then went to wash up and put on the CBM apron. "Thanks for your help, but I think I found a publisher."

"The one Amy told me about?"

He nodded, but then went to work on setting up the coffee station the way he liked it. "Yeah. It's a good deal."

"Are you sure? Are you giving him money?"

Now his shoulders did tense. "Not much."

"Deek. You know that the one rule for writers is that the money flows toward you, not toward the publisher."

He turned to me. "You don't understand. Brandon has had books on the *New York Times* list. He's a professional. All he's asking for is help getting the book cover and some edits."

"You need to talk to a few of those authors I mentioned. Will you do that before you sign anything?"

He ran a hand over his blond dreadlocks. "Yes. I already had this fight with my mom. She's saying the same thing. I promise, I'll call three different authors and tell them about my deal. I just need to hurry before Brandon goes on to the next book he was interested in. He only has so much time."

"Your book is so amazing. If I were a publisher, I'd be waiting months for your decision. And paying you an advance."

He sighed. "It really doesn't work that way anymore. With so many houses combining, it's hard to get a book even looked at."

"Which is why I gave you those names. People who owe me a favor and are knowledgeable about the book business. I just don't want you to make a quick decision and regret it. I'm not trying to be parental here. If you choose the wrong publisher, it can cost you tons and set your career off on the wrong foot. And your story is terrific. I don't think I've seen the hero's journey done that way."

He smiled then, and I knew I had his attention again. "Thanks. I appreciated your notes. I hadn't thought about combining a few characters to do the same thing."

"I love a good mentor character." I waved at a customer who'd just come into the shop. "Please contact some other people and see what they say. Then you make up your own mind."

He nodded and went to join the customer who had just picked up one of the new releases. I heard him start his bookseller spiel. "I've read that, and if you're looking for a fast-paced thriller, you can't go wrong."

The guy knew his books. Now we just had to get him up to speed on the publishing business so he wouldn't hurt his own chances of being on that shelf someday. I started my shift-closing chores and made notes on where I was on the prep work for the readathon.

I had just grabbed my tote and had said goodbye to Deek when Greg came into the store. I stepped toward him. "Hey. Do you have time for lunch?"

"What did you say to Pat?" Greg took me by the arms and pulled me to a small alcove where the horror books were shelved.

"To Pat? Not much. She mostly did the talking. A lot about her relationship with Sherry. And why she's still friends with her even though she's not a very good friend back." I studied his face. "Why? What did she say? And better question, how did you know she came to talk to me?"

"She said she did. She said talking to you made her realize she couldn't let Sherry take the blame for something she'd done." He ran his hand through his short hair. "Jill, Pat just confessed to killing Alicia."

Chapter 13

"That's crazy." Amy repeated the exact words I'd said to Greg less than an hour ago. I'd stopped at Amy's office to see if she could come to lunch after Greg had turned me down. He'd walked me to city hall, then gave me a quick kiss and told me he wasn't going to be home for dinner. "There's no way Pat could kill a mouse, let alone a person."

"I know. She's saying she was protecting the business. That she was concerned Harper's design studio would kill Vintage Duds. Yet when she came to the shop and talked to me, she said she knew it was going to help the business, not hurt it. She's just trying to protect Sherry. Honestly, I think she believes Sherry actually killed this woman." I searched through my salad for another piece of the crispy chicken, which was the real reason I ordered the item. I didn't find one, but I did find an orange slice. Which was almost just as good. "Greg's keeping her for a few hours, but if he keeps her too long, he's going to have to release Sherry. I think he's trying to blow holes in her statement so he can just send Pat home. This is getting crazy. I'm not even sure if he's started looking into the husband at all. Or even Harper's history. Maybe she has a skeleton or two in her closet that wanted her dead."

"Harper's sister did look like her." Amy looked up at me when I didn't say anything. "I know, I'm not supposed to, but the file was on Greg's desk and Marvin had sent me over to see if he was available for a meeting. He wasn't in his office, so I was looking for his calendar when I found Doc Ames's report. The picture must have been from her wedding."

"No wonder Greg can't keep anything under wraps. He leaves too many folders on his desk." I sipped my iced tea and pushed my half-eaten salad away. I was here more for the conversation than the food today. Emma

and I were going running as soon as I got home. I had too much energy
floating around to settle down to read. "You're lucky it wasn't a picture
from the autopsy."

"Ewwhh. I didn't even think about that. I should be more careful opening
folders on Greg's desk." Amy pushed her basket of fries toward me. "I
never have to worry about that when I snoop on your desk. Or Marvin's.
Although I did find one of those bedroom glamour photo shots of Tina
one day when I was straightening things up."

"Okay, so now I've lost my appetite." I grabbed some fries. "Just kidding.
Anyway, I swear this investigation is getting crazier by the minute. First you
have Harper, who doesn't recognize her sister lying dead on her dressing
room floor. Then her boyfriend just happens to be a lawyer and won't let
her talk. Then the victim is reported weeks ago on social media as missing
by her overprotective husband who kind of gives me the creeps. But the
police don't take his report until just before she was found dead. And now
we have Sherry and Pat getting involved in the carnival."

"Next you're going to tell me that they were all part of some fashion
slave workhouse scandal." Amy leaned closer. "I saw a police bust on one of
those cable stations. They had people and sewing machines shoved into this
huge room like they were sardines. Made me glad I never learned to sew."

"Because you'd be afraid that someone would kidnap you and put you
behind a sewing machine?" I dipped a fry into my leftover ranch dressing.
"Not sure it works like that."

Amy shrugged. "Or worse, Justin would expect me to sew his loose
buttons on his dress shirts. Can you believe he even asked if I owned a
needle and thread? He was hoping to save some money at the dry cleaners.
I told him I don't sew."

"Greg handles his own uniforms. He even does most of his laundry. Of
course, after I blue-dyed a couple of T-shirts when I threw them in with
a new pair of jeans, I don't think he trusts me."

We finished lunch and parted ways in front of Lille's. Amy was going
back into town to work, and I was heading home. But instead of going
home, I hurried across the road and went to Harper's dress shop.

The sign in the window said that the shop was closed due to a death
in the family. That was ironic. Had Harper just not looked closely at her
sister on her floor, or was there another reason she didn't want to identify
her? I checked the doorknob just in case, but it was locked. I knocked a
few times, hoping Harper would answer the door and I could "thank" her
for the dress. Again. And if she happened to tell me something about her
sister? Well, Greg couldn't fault me for that.

Austin called out from his sun chair in the front of his bike rental shop. "She's not there."

I tried not to jump at the sound of his voice. I hadn't seen anyone watching me. And Austin and I didn't have the best relationship anyway. Not since he'd broken Sadie's heart and I tried to get him arrested for his ex-wife's murder. Or at least that's how he saw it. "Hey, Austin, I didn't see you there. Do you know where she is?"

"She left with that dude that's been hanging out here for the last week. If you ask me, he's the one your guy should be asking questions about. He seems a little too clean cut." Austin's gray hair was long and pulled back into a braid. He wore cargo shorts and a Hawaiian shirt, his typical look. Austin thought anyone who wore a suit was suspicious.

"I think he's a lawyer." I tried to explain the reason he might be wearing business attire.

"Figures. I assumed either a cop or a lawyer. No one else would wear that monkey suit on a normal day." He leaned back to enjoy the sun. "The man is always out to get you."

Since his eyes were covered by sunglasses, I couldn't tell if he'd closed them or not, but I figured it was his way of telling me that our conversation was over.

I crossed back over the street and hoped I wouldn't be stopped before I got home. I hadn't learned anything new about Alicia's death today, but I didn't want anything to interfere with my run with Emma today. And if someone said something important, I'd have to let Greg know, and he might change his mind about it being safe for me to run.

Austin's words hung with me, and the more I thought about it as Emma and I ran on the beach, the more I thought he might be right. I needed to talk to Harper. Maybe she'd tell me what was going on with her sister if I came about it from the protection angle. This husband seemed like the type to not take kindly to a wife just up and leaving. Or maybe I was just reading too many mysteries lately.

I was surprised to see Greg's truck in the driveway when I got back from the beach. He leaned over from his place by the stove and gave me a kiss. "I was about to turn this off and come and find you. But I knew you had Emma so nothing could happen."

I watched as he leaned down and hugged my—I mean, our—dog as well. "I had lunch with Amy after work."

"She told me. Amy also said she saw you going over to Harper's shop."

Busted. I took a spoon out of the drawer and tasted the spaghetti sauce he was stirring. "Harper wasn't there. Austin said she and the dude took off earlier. He doesn't like Harper's boyfriend."

Greg snorted. "Austin doesn't like anyone with a real job."

"Hey now, I run a business just like he does, and it's a real job." I dropped the spoon into the sink. "The sauce is amazing."

"I know. Secret family recipe." He grinned as he checked the oven. "Garlic bread will be done soon, and we can eat before I get called back to the station. And Austin doesn't like you, which proves my point."

"Wait, I'm confused. What was your point?" I grabbed plates out of the cabinet and set up the table while we talked.

"You have a real job. You know if Austin didn't have his staff, he'd never rent a bike if it meant he'd have to get up from his sun chair." He drained the pasta and ran hot water over the noodles.

"Oh, that's your point." I pulled out a bag of salad and dumped it into a large bowl. Then I chose two dressings, Greg's ranch and an Italian blend for me. "Why do you think you'll be called back into the office? Is the case breaking?"

"No, but the DA's going to be ticked that I let both Sherry and Pat go. He thinks Sherry is a killer and I'm just the dumb ex-husband who can't see her flaws." He put the spaghetti and sauce into a bowl and set that on the table, then took the sheet of garlic bread out of the oven.

"Do you see her flaws?" I took two sodas out of the fridge and set them on the table.

Greg took his soda and put it back away. He poured a glass of milk. "I need something without caffeine if I'm going to get any sleep tonight."

"Sorry, I should have asked."

We sat down at the table, and after we'd filled our plates, he broke the silence. "If anything, I see Sherry's flaws better than anyone else. But that doesn't mean she's a killer. We both know that. And Pat's confession, well, I blew that out of the water when I asked her what she'd done with the gun she shot Alicia with."

"No. She didn't."

He smiled, but a bit sadly. "She told me she threw it into the ocean. She didn't know what kind it was, as she bought it off a homeless guy in the city. It was kind of genius."

"Except Alicia was killed with a set of pruning shears." I rolled my spaghetti on my fork.

He nodded. "Yeah, there was that."

"I know you don't want to talk about the case, but have you looked into Harper's background? And the dude's?"

He nodded. "Starting some work there. And with Alicia's husband. There has to be something going on with him. Why would she leave her happy marriage? I don't buy that she was kidnapped then found dead two states away from her home. It's more likely she ran and he came looking for her."

"So why isn't the DA looking at him with the same intensity as Sherry?" I took a bite of the warm, fragrant bread. I loved it when Greg was working out things in his head, because that was when he loved cooking.

He caught my gaze. "Because he dated Sherry last year, and she broke it off. Badly."

"Oh, hurt feelings." I returned my attention to my dinner. "So he thinks the two of you should be on the same page with Sherry."

He just looked at me.

The call came as we had just finished cleaning up the kitchen and putting away the spaghetti for another day. Greg held up the phone. "Looks like I'm going in. I'll take this in the office."

"The office is filled with gifts. You probably can't fit," I warned as he moved toward the living room.

"Okay, the back porch it is." He punched the button and answered the call. "This is Greg King."

I wasn't quite sure who had the raised voice that I'd been able to hear through the wall before turning the volume up on the television show I'd found. It was a cooking show and, bonus, one I hadn't seen. I took out the book I'd brought home from the office and curled up on the couch.

Greg kissed me on the back of the neck, and I jumped. "I didn't hear you come inside."

"I'm quiet. How do you think I catch the bad guys?" He glanced at the television. "I saw this episode. They're in Cleveland, right?"

"I think so. I got caught up with the story." I held the book up for him to see. "You're going in?"

"I have to drive to Bakerstown and make an appearance to explain why I let a perfectly good suspect go. I guess the fact she was innocent isn't enough." He leaned down and kissed me. "Don't wait up."

"Okay." I didn't want to sound sad, but I'd been quietly rooting for a night at home.

He pointed to the office. "When are you doing those?"

"I'm not."

When he looked at me with a question in his eyes, I laughed.

"I'm not because *we* are. Maybe Monday when I'm off? I've got a busy weekend ahead." I opened the book again. "Maybe you should come work the readathon with me."

"Not a chance. I'd rather hang out with Mr. Fun here." He waved his phone in my face. "I'll see you later."

I read for a while, then I got restless and went to grab a notebook. I wrote down everything I could think of about the murder and about Harper and her sister. The clue was there with the two of them. I knew it. For the rest of the evening before I wore out, I looked up all the players online and wrote down everything I could find. Including silly things like what kind of dogs they had, if any. You could tell a lot about a person by the type of posts they made about their pets.

Bleary eyed, I studied the pages. Nothing that screamed killer like missing small animals from the neighborhood or lack of parental figures in their childhood homes. Although "dude" had been an only child. And he'd lived in Boise, too, before moving to California for college.

Had he followed Harper here? I hadn't felt the couple vibe when he'd shown up at the shop. Mostly just the lawyer vibe. She said boyfriend, but it didn't feel like they were even friends.

As I turned off the lights and checked that the front door was locked, my attention turned to the flowers. The florist hadn't called me back. Maybe Greg had sent them and he was waiting for me to say something. He couldn't blame me for not, as he hadn't been home a lot since they'd arrived, but I didn't think he'd go this long without saying something. I'd call them tomorrow.

* * * *

With the readathon in just three days, my shift was filled with parents and kids picking out their books for the weekend. When they asked me to choose between two books, I had to tell them that I hadn't read either one. Deek would have known the best choice, but I wasn't Deek. And my usual clientele for the shift were tourists or commuters. Adults.

When Deek came in early that day, I almost hugged him. "So happy to see you. That little girl has been staring at those two books for over an hour. Her mom's over there reading the book she bought for herself."

"April always takes her purchases seriously. Her mom's used to it, but I'll see if I can help her." Deek stuffed his bag under the counter and put on his apron.

"When she asked me, I didn't know what to say since I haven't read either." I dished up a slice of cheesecake for the waiting mom. "I feel like I don't know books at all."

"Kids' books aren't your specialty. You know all the mystery stuff. I'm just not into dead bodies. I'd rather read young adult. April always loves a good fantasy. But she wants to branch out too. Don't worry about it, I'll help." He took off and greeted the little girl.

I gave the cheesecake to her mother. "Sorry I couldn't help her decide."

"No worries. I like April to make up her own mind about things. Deek will steer her to the right book. He's so good with all the kids. I was talking to my PTA group, and everyone loves Deek. You need to hold on to him because I'm sure someone would snatch him up in a heartbeat." The woman took a bite of the cheesecake. "Besides, her indecision gives me time to enjoy a treat while she's pondering."

I hurried back to the counter where the line was beginning to form again. This readathon was going to make this the highest sales month of the year so far. And after a slow January, we could use a good month.

By the time noon rolled around, Evie had come down to start her shift. I was beat. My feet hurt, and I had a bit of a headache. The crowd had slowed a little, but not much. I finished my closing-shift items and groaned. I hadn't done any of the snack bags.

"What's wrong?" Evie came next to me and rang up a coffee for a parent.

"I didn't do any snack bags." I glanced at the office door.

Evie shrugged. "Don't worry about it. I'll stay late and finish them up today. No problem."

"Are you sure?" I felt so grateful, I could hug her too. Now I knew I was tired. I never thought about hugging anyone outside my pooch and sometimes Greg.

"I need the extra hours this month. Homer has a vet appointment and a grooming next week. He's killing me. I think I could raise a kid for less money than I spend on him in a year." Evie smiled, and I knew she was joking. Kind of.

"I know. Emma's annual is next month, and I won't even tell you how much I spend on treats for the dog. But they are our kids, right?" I took off my apron and put it into the laundry basket. "I'm heading home to nap for a bit."

"Enjoy." Evie watched Deek as he went to another young reader by the bookshelves. "He can do all the kids today. I've got the craft table Friday and Saturday, if anyone wants to stop reading for a while. I'm hoping they'll all be too engrossed in their stories."

I grabbed my stuff and left through the back door. I wasn't kidding when I said I was planning on a nap when I got home. And I had three more days to get through before the event was over and I could go back to my quiet morning shifts.

I made my way through the narrow opening between my building and the next that held Antiques by Thomas and almost ran into a man who was coming into the passageway. I held up my hand to stop me from running into his chest. "Whoa. Nothing back there except an alleyway. All the shop entrances are on Main Street."

"Oh, sorry, I was just looking for Exquisite Gowns for You. Do you know where the shop is?" He glanced up and down the street. "I got myself turned around."

"Harper's shop is that way. However, I'm not sure if she's open. I think she does most of her work by appointment only." I pointed him down the road as I wondered why a man would be looking for a dress shop. "Maybe you should call ahead."

"I wanted to surprise her. I'm Scott Draper, her brother-in-law." The man smiled, and I finally recognized him from the pictures that Evie had printed off.

"Oh, I'm sorry for your loss." This was Alicia's husband.

Scott nodded. "Bad news travels fast, I guess."

"It's a small town. When someone's killed here, the news gets around. And there's the fact that I'm engaged to South Cove's police detective." I pointed again toward Harper's shop. "I'm heading that way. I can show you."

"That would be kind of you." He smiled. "I'm always getting myself lost. I guess living in a small town like Meridian all my life has made me a bit out of place when I leave. I can probably tell you how to get to every farm and business in between Nampa and Meridian, but here, I can't find anything."

I thought he was overstating the complexity of South Cove. "It's pretty easy. One main street where the businesses are. One road into town from the highway. At that stop sign, you go left to get to Southern California, right to get to the northern part of the state. You're staying over at the Castle, right?"

He looked shocked. "How did you... Oh, yeah, small town."

"Actually, mostly the fiancé part there." I pointed to the road. "When you leave here, turn right. It's the next road. And you have to turn right at that road. Left will get you a quick splash into the ocean."

"I'm on the edge of the world here." He shook his head as he looked around. "Last night when I walked outside, I thought it was going to be lighter. It wasn't even nine, and it was pitch black."

"There's no light on the other side of the road. Once the sun goes down, it gets dark. You must have some places like that where you're from."

"The mountains or the desert. Even with that, it's becoming harder and harder to find land that's not being built on." He glanced around at the buildings. "It must be the same here."

"Not as bad as in the city, but sometimes." I paused outside the dress shop. "Here you are."

He looked up at the building and blanched. Not the typical reaction of a killer, at least not in my head. "Thank you."

"No problem. And I am very sorry for your loss." I left him standing there and crossed the street. I looked back once, but he was still standing in front of the building. Mourning his wife's passing? Or taking in the place of his last kill? From what I'd read, killers liked to do that. Visit the scene of the crime. And I'd walked him right to it. I shook the thought away.

As I moved past Diamond Lille's, I heard my name being called. Busted again, except walking Scott to his sister-in-law's shop was not my fault.

Chapter 14

"Jill? It is you. It's been a while since you came to visit." Doc Ames hurried toward me from Diamond Lille's front door. "How have you been?"

"I'm good. How are you?" I gave him a quick hug. He looked good. Like he'd been out in the sun more.

"I am so sorry that Carrie and I couldn't attend your party. My workload is crazy right now." He paused for dramatic effect. "People are dying to get into my funeral home."

"Ha, ha. But yes, I understand. Having a party in the middle of a murder investigation seemed a little dicey to me, but Greg didn't want to put it off. This week we have the readathon on Friday and Saturday, so I'm swamped at work. I'm sure Carrie told you about the spring festival."

"That's why I'm here. I came to have lunch with my girl since she's going to have to work the weekend. I sure hope Lille gets someone hired soon." He glanced back at the restaurant like he could see Carrie working. "Anyway, I'm preaching to the choir. You probably work as much as your future husband does."

"Maybe not quite as much." Here was my opening. "Hey, did anything weird come out of the autopsy for Alicia? I swear this is the strangest case."

He nodded toward Scott Draper, who was now knocking on the shop door across the street. "Besides the poor woman's family? The sister doesn't recognize her or at least doesn't identify her. And then the husband comes in and is cool as a cucumber. Wants to know what the police think about the killer. You know me, I'm a vault when it comes to information about a case."

Yeah, except for chatting with me right here on the street. Total vault. But that's not what I said. "He's odd. I was just talking to him."

"He's a cop, or was a cop. I couldn't get the story straight. You'd think a cop would know not to even try to talk to me about these things. It's up to the police what they release to family or hold back because of the case." He rubbed his face. "But maybe they do things differently in Montana."

"Idaho." When Doc looked at me oddly, I added, "He said he was from Idaho."

Doc's gaze went to Scott, who was now walking into the shop. "That's odd. I could have sworn he said Montana."

As I walked home after turning down coffee with Doc, I texted Greg letting him know that Scott and Harper were in the shop together, talking.

When I didn't get a reply, I called his cell.

He answered with, "Yes, I got your text."

"The one I just sent?"

"Yep." He paused. "Anything else?"

"Don't you think that's weird?"

"Family members often get together after a death to do things like plan the funeral or comfort each other. Nothing happening here I can arrest him for unless you found out something I don't know." His voice turned to stone. "Now, I've got to get back to investigating, which is my job."

"Yes, sir." I hung up on him before he could tell me he loved me or even that he was sorry for being abrupt. Now I really needed a run. But I hadn't asked about dinner or, crap, the flowers. I was going to call that florist when I got back from my run.

I didn't even look at the mail when I got home. I ran upstairs, changed, and clipped a leash on a surprised Emma. Typically, our setup time took a while, for me to transition from work mode to home mode. But today, I needed that burst of feel-good juice to push off the less than positive chat I'd had with Greg. And all the work I had to do for the readathon.

When we'd finished and I was walking up the hill, I felt amazing. Like the bad mojo had slipped out of me along with the sweat that covered my body. Emma was even doing the happy doggy walk, even though I could tell she was tired.

And all those positive feelings disappeared when I saw my aunt's car parked at my house. She got out of the driver's side when I walked into the driveway.

"Good, you're here. I didn't want to have to drive back when you showed up." She nodded to Emma, who yipped a greeting to my aunt. Emma loved her. Aunt Jackie pretended like she was immune, but I'd seen her petting Emma when she thought no one was looking. "We need to go over this plan one more time."

"The readathon? It will be fine. Everyone knows what they're doing." I moved toward the house and unlocked the door. "Come on in. I've got to shower and change if you really want to talk about this weekend. There's sodas and tea in the fridge."

As she came inside, she headed directly for the kitchen. "Don't be long. I've got to have dinner with Harrold before I go to work."

"Five minutes. Ten tops." I hurried upstairs.

When I came down, I heard my aunt talking to Emma.

"Who's a good girl? Now sit. Lay down." My aunt paused. "Now stay."

I leaned on the kitchen doorway. "You're good with her."

My aunt jerked and twisted her head toward me. Color filled her face, but then she just nodded. "She just needs a firm hand. That's all. Grab some water and come sit down."

I followed her directions and picked up my own notebook to write down any last-minute assignments my aunt might shoot my way.

We were halfway through the staffing times when she turned to me. "Is Deek leaving?"

"Not that I know of. What did you hear?" Replacing Deek would be hard, if not impossible. He single-handedly had taken over the management and assignments for the book clubs. And the website and newsletters. I didn't know how he got so much done during a shift, but he did. And I knew he wrote during shifts when the traffic was slow. Which happened to all of us.

"Someone asked me to congratulate him on his book deal. I didn't know he had one."

My stress level went down a tad. "He's been talking to a publisher, but I'm hoping he's going to try to get an agent and publish the book traditionally. For a first book, it's really good."

"Oh. I didn't know you'd read it."

"He asked me to read it a few days ago. He just wanted some feedback."

"Oh, well then, are we sure we don't need a temp or two that day?" My aunt pushed past the conversation.

"We have two. Or I think we have two. I haven't heard back yet, but Sadie and Pastor Bill are coming to help chaperone the night session. So we'll have plenty of adults around. You and Harrold should go home to sleep for a few hours. Napping in those chairs is going to be impossible." I wrote down a note to call Sadie and confirm later today.

"I'll see how I'm feeling. Now, let's talk about the readathon rules. Entrants can go home and read, but they have to check out with a bookstore employee who notes on their reading card the page and book they're on. Then when they check back in, they can only have finished no more than that book and one more outside the staff area." She read off the line we'd settled on earlier. "And a staff member has to validate that the amount of reading done outside the bookstore is obtainable."

"I don't think we're going to have many issues with that. But I know some of the kids who are going home to sleep will be reading long past their bedtime." I smiled as I thought of my own bedtime sessions under the covers with a flashlight. "Are we sure we want to limit it to two books?"

"The cards are already at the printer. We can change the rules next year if it's an issue." My aunt read off the rest of the rules, then went through the list of prizes starting with the participation prize of a book coupon and the bag of snacks.

The grand prize was a combo from a lot of the local stores and a weekend for a family of four at the amusement park down the highway, including the room and tickets for the parks. I was adding five hundred to cover food and incidents but Mary Sullivan, Aunt Jackie's best friend, had donated most of the grand prize. "Mary went all out on this one."

"She did, and we should make sure the winning family sends her a thank-you note." My aunt pointed to my list. "Write up something that says thank-you notes for the grand prize can be sent to Mary's address. Maybe that will remind them to be grateful."

I wasn't quite sure that a "please send a thank-you note" reminder was the same thing as being grateful and doing it on their own, but I wasn't going to argue with my aunt. Besides, I still had my own pile of thank-you notes to write, which I'd rather not remind her about. "So what else?"

"Actually, I think we're ready. You prepared better than I'd expected. Especially with this murder investigation going on. I would have thought you'd be too busy playing Nancy Drew to attend to your business duties."

Ouch. That stung. "I don't neglect the store. Sometimes I have different priorities and timelines than you do."

My aunt closed her notebook and tucked her pen into the slot on the side. "You're right. I shouldn't have assumed you weren't on top of things. I guess I'm just trying to convince myself that you still need me at the store."

"What are you talking about? Of course Coffee, Books, and More needs you. I need you. Maybe not to work a shift, especially a night one now that you have a life with Harrold to be concerned about. But you're a vital part of the business. Especially the planning and administration. I'd be lost without you." I pointed to the list. "The reason I'm on top of things is because you already planned out everything and gave me a list. Remember, you were the one who called me to remind me to go shopping.

I'd planned a day in Bakerstown, and it hadn't even occurred to me to do the store shopping too."

"I was looking at the books, and I think we could hire a part-time person to close several nights a week. It would have to be someone we trusted with the bank drop." She tapped her fingers on the notebook. "Unless Evie wants to make some changes to her shifts. That might be better. Then we could hire a day person who could help Deek with covering Toby when conflicts occur."

"Let's bring it up at this month's staff meeting. That way, you could start working days like Harrold, and both of you would be off at the same time. You could work at the office or even just at your apartment." I was liking this conversation more and more. I'd been trying to figure out a way to transition Aunt Jackie into less shift work and more management work. This was the perfect opportunity. "And if we do it soon, we could start applying for a food truck space at the local festivals. I don't think we do that enough."

"That means more staff hours." My aunt glanced at her watch. "Sorry, we'll have to continue this later. My roast is probably done by now."

I walked her to the door, and she paused at the flowers. "These are beautiful. Did Greg send them?"

"They didn't come with a card. They came before the party, so I thought maybe someone sent them as an engagement gift. I need to follow up with the florist again. They were going to call me back."

"Bakerstown Florist is so busy, being the only florist around, you're lucky to get them to pick up the phone." She started her car with the key fob and rubbed Emma's head. "Thank you for letting me go through this again."

"I'm just glad I only have two items added to my to-do list. Let me know if you think of anything else. We still have a couple of days." I watched as she carefully made her way to her car. My aunt looked smaller somehow. I was glad she was taking a step back from working in the shop, but having her as full-time manager was going to increase my headaches as we worked through her transition. But it was all worth it. She and Harrold deserved some couple time where one of them wasn't working. "Come on, Emma. Let's see what we can stir up for dinner. I don't think Greg's going to be here."

I didn't think he'd be in a good mood with me anyway, so having him out of the house for a night probably wasn't a bad idea.

My mind went to Alicia's husband. How had their relationship been? Did Scott have a bad temper as Evie had guessed? Or was he just bad at expressing his grief at the loss of his wife? Looking inside a relationship was hard. A lot of times, the truth was hidden, and even their best friends didn't know what was really going on behind closed doors.

Honestly, I was stuck in this investigation. The people who were the best suspects were all turning out to be poor choices. Sherry, well, she didn't kill the woman. If she'd done anything against Exquisite Gowns for You, it would have been to ruin Harper's reputation or try to stop a fabric shipment. Or worse, try to steal her customers. Pat had only confessed because she was afraid Sherry had gone off the deep end. And now, Scott, the best suspect in Evie's mind, seemed to be what he was, a grieving widower. Maybe I should try to see what I could find out about Harper and her relationships.

I'd done all the online research I could do. I wondered if I knew anyone who knew anyone in the fashion design business. I grabbed my address book I used to send Christmas cards every year and flipped through the names. A lot of them were from years ago when I'd been a lawyer in a large firm in the city. I'd been stuck in family law because of my gender as well as the fact that I didn't like to argue. Yeah, being an attorney was probably not the best choice in careers, but I'd been young and ambitious.

I was almost at the end when I found a name from the past. A designer who had used our firm to help her with a divorce and a property settlement that protected her business. The good news was her ex-husband-to-be was dismissive of her work and didn't realize the gold mine she was sitting on. I just didn't disclose my opinion that I thought this woman was one of the up-and-coming designers of the area. The divorce was final for over a year when she got a call from a large department store who wanted to feature her new spring line with a hefty payment attached. The ex-husband found out and tried to reopen the case, asking for alimony, but with the testimony he'd provided in the first case, the judge refused to reopen it. And I'd gotten flowers along with the payment for my fees. I dialed the phone number I had listed.

"Mahogany Designs, this is Lara Gunn. How can I help you?"

"Hi, Lara, this is Jill Gardner. I was your divorce attorney?" I spun the pen on my notebook, hoping she'd remember me.

"Jill. You weren't just my divorce attorney. You were my guardian angel during that horrible time. Boy, this is a blast from the past. I get your Christmas card every year and tell myself I really have to visit your cute little shop. I have been having my assistant buy all my corporate gifts from you. I hope you're doing okay. I know how hard running a small business can be."

I heard office sounds behind her and realized she was still working. "We're doing well, thanks for asking. And your fashion line! I love everything you put out."

"It's been a fun ride. What can I do for you?"

Okay, so the reminiscing was done. "Hey, just a quick question. Do you know a designer named Harper Sanchez?"

"Harper? Wow, this is old home week. Yes, I went to school with her. She was—is incredibly talented. I heard she opened a shop up your way. Is that in the same town as your bookstore?"

"Yes. This is going to sound weird, but do you know anyone who didn't like her? I mean, any fights or bad blood in the fashion community?"

The line was quiet for a minute. "Jill, hold on a second. Carol, I'm taking this call in my office."

When she came back on the line, the background noise was quieter. "That's better. I don't like to bad-mouth anyone, especially when others can overhear. I take it she's gotten herself in trouble again."

"Kind of. Her sister was killed in Harper's shop." I tried to leave all my preconceived notions out of the information I gave her. I didn't want to be accused of leading a witness. Just in case.

"Oh no, Alicia? She was so nice. I met her during one of our family day fashion shows. The teachers just wanted to fill the seats so it felt like a real fashion show to the models and the designers. Alicia volunteered to be one of my models. She was amazing. I told her she could make a living with it, but she just laughed. She was getting married that summer. Harper didn't like the fiancé, not at all. It became an issue between the two of them." A knock sounded in the distance. "And they found me. Sorry, I'm working on a big project. Anything else you need to know?"

"No, that helps. Thanks Lara, and don't be a stranger. I'd love to see you soon."

A laugh tinkled on the other end of the line. "I'm hoping you do. I hear you got engaged. Anyway, I can be your wedding designer? I've always seen you in a certain design."

"Maybe. We don't have a date yet. I'll let you know. How long of a lead time do I need to get a dress from Mahogany Designs?" My aunt would be happy if I got one thing off my to-do list.

"Six months minimum. I'm pretty busy, but I'd work you in as long as it isn't next week. Then I'd just take you shopping at one of the off-the-rack places. You're going to be beautiful, no matter what."

"No way will it be next week. I'll give you a call in a month or so and let you know what we're doing. I appreciate it."

"Like I said, I owe you one. Or many ones. Gotta go."

I started to say goodbye, but she'd hung up. No one said goodbye anymore. Including my aunt. As I started writing down the information I'd learned about Alicia, something Lara had said popped into my mind. "Is she in trouble again?"

I couldn't call her back—Lara was busy, I knew that—but I texted her a quick note: *When you have a minute later, call me, please. One follow-up question.*

I finished my dinner, then cuddled on the couch with Emma. Greg found me there much later than I'd planned on staying up. I looked up from the movie that was just finishing as he opened the front door. "I know, I should be in bed, but I found this movie when I was surfing, and I couldn't pass it up."

"You're a romantic. That's all there is to it. Did you eat?" He sank to the couch and leaned his head on my shoulder.

"Hours ago. Do you need me to warm something up?" I rubbed the top of his hand.

"No, we ordered pizza from Lille's." He yawned. "I can't believe after all that time I didn't find one reason for our victim to be killed. Her husband is the most likely suspect, but he was working a shift at the station house in Idaho at time of death. Either Doc is totally off, or Scott has an alibi."

"That's too bad. He was my preferred suspect too. Even though he didn't seem like the killer type when I talked to him."

"I'm too tired to fight about why that was such a bad idea on your part." He squeezed my hand. "Can I hope that you did the thank-you notes this afternoon when you were bored?"

"Bored? Never. I have movies." I turned off the television and tossed the remote onto the coffee table. "Anyway, I really didn't have much time. Aunt Jackie came over after my run with Emma, and we went over the plans for this weekend. I'm assuming Toby will be on your service most of the weekend?"

"Sorry, yeah. I'm not getting much support from Bakerstown for this festival. They have their own going on, so there wasn't a lot of extra hours to give me." He yawned again. "I wish Darla would check with me before scheduling these events."

"You could ask her."

He stood and shook his head. "Not now. Maybe after the investigation is over. She'd just see it as open season to ask me about the murder."

Emma whined.

"I'll let her out. Then I've got to get some sleep." He stood and kissed me on the head. "I'll be gone before you get up. Another fun trip to Bakerstown in the morning."

"Hey, before you go. Did you send the flowers? I was going to call the florist, but I got sidelined today."

He shook his head. I could see the confusion fighting with the fatigue in his eyes. "Was I supposed to send flowers? Did I miss something? Can't be first date."

"No." I pointed to the flowers by the door. "Those flowers. They came last week with no card. I thought maybe you just hadn't found the time to ask me how I liked them."

"They're pretty, but I thought they came from someone who couldn't attend the party." He moved toward the kitchen. "I'll send you flowers just as soon as this investigation is over."

"Not my point," I called after him. Then I went back to the slowly dying arrangement and pulled out a couple of stems where the flower had died. I studied the flowers that were left. "Who sent you?"

When the flowers didn't answer and I heard Greg heading upstairs behind me, I checked the door lock and turned off the living room lights. I moved through the downstairs, starting the dishwasher after locking the back door. Then I turned off the last light and went upstairs and to bed.

Chapter 15

Wednesday morning was usually a strong morning for commuters, and today was no different, so I didn't even have time to finish my opening chores until Evie showed up at eleven. "Good to see you. I need to ask you something."

Evie paused as she was putting on her apron. She looked cute with her hair all pulled back into a bun and an African-print scarf wrapped around it. "Did I do something wrong last shift?"

"What? No. Not that I know about anyway." I sat on one of the stools. We were alone in the shop but not for long. The lunch crowd would be here in just a few minutes. "I wanted to ask you if you were interested in the closing shift? Maybe not totally if you didn't want all of them, but Jackie is stepping away from direct customer work, and we need someone to move into that slot. Deek's already said he would rather not work nights, so if it's not you, we'll need to hire someone."

"You want me to close? Already? Isn't that a pretty important shift?" Evie turned away and poured herself a cup of coffee. "Are you sure I'm ready?"

"You're kidding, right? You've been amazing since you started. Of course, you can close. We haven't asked you before because my aunt loves closing. She's a bit of a control freak, so you can expect some close scrutiny the first couple of weeks, but she'll calm down, eventually." I grabbed my to-do list for the shift. "And you'll have to do the nightly deposit, but the bank's just down the street. If you don't feel comfortable walking there, we can have one of the boys on shift escort you. Neither Toby nor Tim would mind. They're usually pretty bored on nights."

Evie came around and sat next to me. She sipped on her coffee, then set it down. Before I could react, she reached out and hugged me. "Thank you."

Laughing, I dropped the clipboard and the pen. "You're welcome. But I'm not sure why. You earned your spot here. You've been amazing."

She wiped her eyes and then laughed. "You have to understand my history. I came from a place where I was told no one would ever trust me or even hire me. I was lucky he was taking care of me. Of course, I knew that was wrong, but when you're told that, over and over, you start to believe it. Even a little. Thank you for having trust in me."

"You're a hard worker. You're a nice person. And you're Sasha's cousin. That's three strikes in your favor. You earned this. Although I'm not sure it's a promotion, it does come with a shift differential since you're working later, and sometimes there are more bookstore sales than coffee shop buyers. I'll warn you that the tips are lower." I was trying to let her know that the shift wasn't all that amazing, but Evie was having none of it.

"I'd be delighted. And it works out with my plans. I was going to tell you when I got accepted, but I'm going back to school in the fall. This way, I'll be able to work full-time and still go to school during the day. It's perfect."

"It's a done deal then." I grabbed the clipboard. I'd text Aunt Jackie and let her know that Evie needed to take over her shift. That would make her feel better about giving it up. Next up was to hire another day person. We'd bring it up at the staff meeting. "Now I have to get my work done before you get swamped with customers."

By the time I got out of the shop, it was almost one. Too late to talk to Amy about lunch, so I headed home. I had sandwich stuff at the house anyway. When I went past Exquisite Gowns, Harper was sitting on the bench in front of her shop. She appeared to be crying. After the tiff with Greg, I should just ignore it and keep walking. Instead, I crossed the street and sat next to her. I pulled out a packet of tissues from my tote bag and handed it to her. "Are you okay?"

She considered the tissues in my hand, then sighed and took them from me. "I'm fine. I guess I'm just reacting to losing my sister."

"Okay. Not that I'm questioning your grief process, but why the tears now? Did it have anything to do with Scott stopping by your shop yesterday?" I was probably pushing and definitely being less than thoughtful. So I leaned forward, my forearms on my thighs, trying to be supportive.

"How did you know?" She shook her head. "Never mind. He said someone showed him where the shop was. He's good at using people."

"I was walking this way, so I showed him where it was. Anything wrong with that?"

She didn't say anything for a while. "You probably don't know this, but I wasn't happy when Alicia married him. I thought she could do better, and I was worried about how he'd treat her. I was right on both counts. You probably did hear about his story on how she was missing. Well, she wasn't missing. She ran away from him. And I was so hopeful that she'd be okay now."

"And then she was found dead."

When Harper didn't answer. I pushed. "Harper, do you think Scott killed Alicia?"

She shook her head. "He couldn't have. He was working. He told me yesterday. His alibi is solid. And your boyfriend has already checked it. So he didn't kill her." She shivered again. "Look, I've got an appointment coming in at two. I need to get some stuff done. Thank you for the tissues."

I watched as she hurried back inside her studio. And, I was certain, she'd locked the door after her. Which was curious since she had a client coming in. It made me feel like maybe I was the one she was locking out of the shop. But why?

Harper was a brilliant designer, but she had some demons in her life. I wasn't sure I wanted to know why she did anything she did. I typically really liked everyone who moved into South Cove to start their life over, but there was something about Harper I wasn't sure I liked. And I definitely didn't trust her.

When I got home, it was run time. The flowers taunted me, but I didn't want to make Emma wait to run. I'd call as soon as I got back. Which took longer than I thought since I was stopped by Esmeralda just to chat. Then when I came back up to the house after my run, Toby had just pulled in the driveway. "What's up?"

"I'm crashing for a couple of hours since I have the night shift tonight. Greg says hi and he should be home for dinner." Toby yawned as he locked his truck. "How's CBM? Anything I should know? I always feel so checked out when Greg has me doing these doubles."

"Nothing big. Aunt Jackie's going to step down, and Evie's taking her evenings slot." Something in Toby's face made me pause. "Crap, don't tell me you wanted it. I didn't even think. I'll tell Evie you get first crack at it."

"Jill, I don't want to work evenings. I'm just surprised Evie wants to. She must be feeling a lot more comfortable here than she was." He must have sensed my follow-up question because he shook his head. "No, I'm not telling you anything more. I'm just surprised that Evie wanted the shift. Look, I've got to crash. If my truck's still here at five, knock on my door and wake me up please. I'm setting my alarm, but when I'm this tired, all bets are off."

"Sure, I'll be glad to." I paused before diving in again. "Are you sure Evie's all right?"

"Talk to her, not me. I'll see you after this crazy time is over. Sorry I bailed on you for the readathon." He moved toward his apartment.

"No worries. I don't usually count on you during festivals anymore since Greg seems to book all your time up before I can. Hey, I told Evie she could call the station for an assist if she felt uncomfortable walking to the bank at night with the deposit. You think that's going to be a problem?"

He turned and rubbed a hand through his hair. Yawning, he answered me. "Probably not. There might be some nights we'll be too busy to help, but she can just lock the deposit up downstairs, and you can take it in the morning."

"Go get some sleep. We'll work out the details at the next staff meeting." I took Emma inside the house and locked the door. The flowers were almost all dead, and I still didn't know who had sent them. I grabbed my phone and looked up the florist. No answer, and then I got voicemail. I left a message without much hope I'd get a call back. With that off my to-do list, I glanced at the only item left. The thank-you notes. I moved the item to my Sunday list and then closed my planner. I was free the rest of the day. Technically.

I made lunch, then sat outside on my back deck with a book. Emma took the time to explore the yard and check for any intruders like rabbits, or worse, turtles. She hated turtles with a passion.

Greg was home before I even had time to finish the book. It was like musical trucks in the driveway. Toby took off about four thirty, probably going to Lille's for a meal before reporting to the station. Greg came home about five. He saw me when he drove up, and instead of going in through the front door, he came through the yard and greeted Emma, who had been waiting for him to get out of the truck.

"Hey, what are you doing out here? I thought you'd be busy writing thank-you notes." He came up on the deck and gave me a kiss.

"Keep dreaming. I pushed it off until Sunday. Hopefully you'll be done with this investigation and you can help. You have better handwriting than I do. Not to mention better tact. What if your mom sent us a really ugly piece of sculpture I don't like? I might offend her before even getting the role of daughter-in-law."

He laughed as he sat next to me. "Won't happen."

"You are overestimating my tact meter." I wrapped my fingers around his.

He shook his head. "Nope. I just know Mom sent us a check and not an actual gift. I'm thinking we should put any monetary gifts into a vacation account. Then when we find time, we have the money set aside. Rather than have time but no money. I've played that game. It really isn't much fun."

"You're the practical one. I feel like a jerk now all the times I asked to go on a trip and just put it on my credit card."

"We're entering a different stage of our lives. Now we make decisions as individuals. What's good for you or me in case it's just you or me in the future. After we get married, we'll be an us. Then we can talk about what we want to do with our lives and our money." He held up a finger. "Unless you don't want to have joint finances."

"Wow, so much to think about. I thought getting a dress was going to be the big issue." My stomach was hurting a little.

"We can keep doing what we're doing. Or we can combine our finances into joint accounts. We just need to talk about it sometime." He patted my leg. "And by the look on your face, you need to talk about it some other time. You're looking a little freaked out."

"Guilty as charged." I didn't want to offend him, but I'd been on my own mostly since I graduated high school. Even when I was married before, we didn't have any shared assets. Which made it easy to do the divorce papers later. A little too easy. I wanted this marriage and this relationship to be permanent, but I guess I'd never thought about money issues. "Should we make dinner before this becomes awkward?"

"That ship has passed, but yes, let's make dinner." He kissed me. "You can go back to trying to trick me into saying something about the investigation, and I'll dodge all your questions. Then we can forget we even started this discussion."

"Sounds good. I got pork chops out. Grill or fry?"

He leaned his head back. "It's too nice to go in and fry them. What are we going to do for sides?"

And with that, the financial talk awkwardness was gone. Now we were talking about food and our days. I would have to weigh the pros and cons and talk to Amy and maybe my aunt to see what they were doing. I figured my aunt was going traditional and combining everything. Maybe Amy and Justin were taking a different tactic. It didn't hurt to learn from others' successes and mistakes. I'd find some time to talk to Aunt Jackie and Amy over the weekend. I didn't want to have the deer-in-the-headlights look again. Greg put up with a lot from me, and I wanted to be able to discuss this topic fairly the next time it came up.

I wondered how other couples got around these land mines in their relationship. And what other ones Greg and I hadn't even started to explore. Maybe we were just too different.

My heart told my brain to shut up.

After dinner, Greg opened the door to the office and took out ten packages and the thank-you cards. "Go get a notepad and write this all down while I do the thank-you cards. If we do ten gifts a day, we might be done with this before the wedding next summer."

"Good plan." I hurried into the kitchen and came back with a brand-new notebook. One that didn't have my notes written about the current murder and who had said what and when.

We'd gone through the ten gifts, and Greg and I'd agreed not to return any of them. They were all surprisingly useful. I needed to replace several items in the kitchen anyway, and the gifts we'd opened were like we'd gone shopping for them ourselves. Including a new set of kitchen towels and hot pads. "Tomorrow I'll get a box set up in the kitchen, and we can put the stuff we replace into that for the community center charity yard sale."

"Just don't get our new stuff tucked in there. Someone might think we didn't like the gift." His phone rang. "And now it starts back up again. Thanks for getting me out of my head for a few minutes."

I kissed him quickly. "Thanks for getting a start on the pile in the office. I thought we'd never get these done."

"You forget who you're living with. I can't leave a project undone." He hit a button on his phone. "King here, how can I help you?"

I went upstairs to get the hamper and wash at least one load of clothes tonight. Especially since my weekend was going to be shorter than normal. By the time I got the washer going, Greg was standing in the kitchen with his keys, waiting for me. "Wait, let me guess. You're out of here."

He chuckled. "For a few hours. I'm interviewing someone over Skype from Scott's station to confirm his alibi. There's just something about the guy I don't trust."

"I know, I feel the same way." I glanced around the kitchen and shrugged. "I guess it's an evening of reading for me. The laundry's started. The kitchen is fairly clean. And I don't have anyone to talk to if I wanted to chat."

"You could talk to Emma. She's a very good listener." He pulled me into a hug. "Did you talk to the florist?"

"About the delivery?" I shook my head. "No. I called and left a message. Again. The flowers are going to be gone before I know who to thank for them."

He frowned at the offending bouquet. "Maybe I should call. Or stop by."

"It's just flowers. If they were poisoned, we'd be dead by now." I rolled my shoulder. "Someone just isn't going to get a thank-you note if we don't find out."

"Maybe we'll find out before we finish the notes?" He grabbed his hat and headed to the door. "Lock up after me."

"Yes, Dad." I followed him and watched him pause on the deck until I threw the deadbolt. Of course, I could just throw it open again after he was gone, but he had a point about me being here alone. Esmeralda was my closest neighbor, but I don't think she'd even hear if I started screaming.

I looked at Emma. "What do you think? Reading or ice cream?"

When she woofed, I nodded at her. "You're right. Why limit ourselves? Let's do both."

Chapter 16

Harper came into the shop early on Thursday morning. She ordered coffee, then went strolling through the bookshelves. I still had commuters in the shop, but when the last one left, she came back to the counter with two self-help books about getting your life together after divorce.

"Is this all? Or do you want a treat to go with your reading material?"

Harper shook her head. "The books are for a friend. And I'll pass on the treats. I need to slow down on the sweets. I've been mainlining sugar for the last month."

"Stress will do that." I rang up the purchases and told her the total. "Is the shop doing well? Anyone who saw that dress you made me would have you make them a dress even if you were working out of a barn in the countryside."

"I might be there sooner or later. Buying the building was a great idea, but now he's saying I'm partners with him. And he's not the easiest guy to get along with. I've got Colton looking at my partnership agreement with Alicia to see if he has any inheritance rights." She shook her head. "Sorry, you don't want to hear my sad story."

"I'm a barista. You should hear the stories I get." I poured myself a coffee and came around the counter, perching on a stool. "I'm sorry about your sister. I hope this doesn't sour you on South Cove."

"Oh, no. I mean, it's fine." She avoided meeting my gaze as she sipped her coffee. "Alicia would want me to go on with my life."

Go on with her life? It had been less than a week. Man, this woman had no attachment at all. "That's nice. Hey, we have a friend in common. Lara Gunn was one of my clients when I was a lawyer."

Harper looked up sharply from her coffee. "You know Lara?"

"I helped her with her divorce." I set my cup down. "I used to do family law. I have to admit, I like running a bookstore more."

Harper's hand rested on the books I'd put into one of our CBM bags. "Working with divorced people must be hard. It's hard to put your life back together, right?"

"Sometimes. Sometimes both parties are ready. And in the extreme cases, one needs to be out of the relationship for their own sanity. So like I said, it depends." I nodded to the books. "Are you going through a divorce? Not to get personal or anything. I just thought with the choice of reading material, you might be."

"No, I've never been married. Like I said, the books are for a friend." She pretended to glance at her watch. "Look at the time, I need to open the shop."

"Come back anytime. I'd love to get to know you better," I called after her, but when she turned, the look on her face was pure panic, not friendly.

"Sure, that would be awesome." And then she hurried out of the shop.

Greg came in the shop a few minutes later. "Hey, you look bored. I thought you had a big event starting tomorrow?"

"I do, but I guess everyone bought what they wanted. Besides, Deek and Evie will do the stocking on their shift. I don't want them to be bored. I can read or something without feeling guilty since I'm the boss." I leaned into him and gave him a quick kiss. "Why are you here?"

"I just saw Harper leaving the store. What did you say to her? She ran down the street." He climbed on a stool and pointed to a chocolate chip cookie. "Can I snag one of those? My brain is fried from trying to figure out who would want to kill this woman. Did you know she taught Sunday school? And sang in the choir? From what everyone tells me, she's pretty close to being declared a saint. Mostly for staying with her husband. Not a lot of people outside the cops he worked with liked the guy."

"One cookie coming up." I held up a cup. "Coffee?"

"Water. If I drink another cup of coffee, my hands are going to shake." He took the glass of water from me and then bit into the cookie. He set it down. "Okay, spill. Why don't you want me eating a cookie?"

"What are you talking about?" I stared at him, confused.

He took my hand. "You have that look. Like something's bothering you. I figured it was the cookie. Is it me?"

"No you don't. You don't get off that easy. You've promised to marry me, and I'm holding you to it." I shook my head. "It was what you said about Alicia. If she was the kind of woman that everyone loved, why isn't her sister at least a little upset about her death?"

Greg scratched his head. "Now, that's a good question."

I watched as he finished his water and picked up his cookie.

"I'm going back to see if I can find someone to answer this. Maybe they weren't as close as we're guessing."

As he walked out, my aunt walked in. "Good, I caught you at a quiet time. I wanted to see how much of the stocking for this weekend was done."

Busted. I smiled and greeted my aunt. "Actually, I've been swamped all morning. A lot of lookers. I guess they're getting ready for the readathon. I was just about to pull out the boxes and see what I could get done before Deek and Evie come on shift."

"So you haven't done anything. Seriously, Jill, you can't always leave things to the last minute. What are you going to do when I'm not around anymore?" My aunt went to the back to store her purse, then came out and put on an apron. "You go grab boxes. I'll do the inventory and watch the front while you're stocking. What time is Sadie delivering tomorrow?"

"She's coming today with our normal order, then she'll bring more tomorrow morning. Hopefully she'll grab some sleep before showing up tomorrow night to be a chaperone." I nodded to the window. "And there she is. Do you want to handle her delivery, and I'll start bringing out boxes?"

"Sounds like a plan as long as no customers come in." She sighed. "I wish she'd come earlier in the day. Your shift isn't as busy as the midday one."

"It's still my shift now." I smiled at Sadie, who was bringing a tray of goodies inside. "Hi, Sadie. Aunt Jackie's going to check the order in while I move boxes."

"I think she got the better end of that deal." Sadie laughed and set the first tray on a table. "Jackie, here's the checklist. You mark off what you accept, and I'll go get another tray. I have three today."

I left them to figure out the details and went into the office to find the first box of books we'd ordered for the readathon.

By the time Deek arrived, I had more than half of the boxes shelved, and my aunt had put away all the treats from Sadie's delivery. He joined me in the office and grabbed another box. "I thought you were leaving this for Evie and me?"

"Jackie had other plans." I stretched my arms above my head. "Man, hauling all these boxes is crazy hard on my back and shoulders."

"You aren't working out." Deek paused with two boxes in his arms.

"I run almost every day," I protested as I followed him with one box.

"That's not working out. You need to work with weights. You'll build muscle, and this stuff won't bother you." He nodded at my aunt, who was now talking to a customer about a new release in the women's fiction section. "Jackie and Harrold have joined my gym in Bakerstown. I see them there every morning. At least during the week."

"You're kidding, right?" I dropped the box and cut it open with a cutter, being careful to not damage the books inside.

"I swear. You can ask her." He opened his boxes. "A lot of South Cove residents go there since they stopped having classes at the rec center. In fact, I thought the new dress designer had joined, but when I talked to the woman, it was someone who just looked like her. She said a lot of people had been confusing her with Ms. Sanchez lately, but she didn't even know how to sew."

"We're kind of pushy that way if we see one of our own out in the world." I was just as bad. Anytime I saw someone in Bakerstown that lived or worked in South Cove, I always waved or stopped to talk.

He shook his head. "Not pushy. Friendly. I like how close knit the town is. If I could find an apartment to rent here, I'd move in a second, but even if one would open up, it would be too spendy."

"Talk to Kyle and see when he's getting married. His apartment might be available if you don't mind living so close to work." I emptied my box and started on Deek's box. Even though they were children and young adult books, the covers drew me in, and I wanted to sit down and read one or two of them.

"Living close to work wouldn't be a problem. Having Josh Thomas as a landlord, that might be an issue. Although I hear Josh might be moving out when he gets married this fall." Deek shelved faster than I did, but then again, he didn't study each book as it came out of the box.

"Wait, Josh is getting married? I need to go talk to him."

Deek picked up the boxes. "Don't yet. I think he's still getting up the nerve to ask. But it could be an empty apartment."

"Not to change the subject, but did you talk to any of the names I gave you?" We walked back to the office with the empty boxes.

"Yes, and I've sent out the book to three agents. I'm not sure why I'm waiting, but everyone was so nice and offered to have their agent look at it, I didn't want to move until I hear back. So I did what every real author does when they're waiting."

"Drink?" I grabbed another box and held the door open for him.

"You're funny. No, I started a new story. This writing thing is pretty fun. And if I never sell a book, I can see how people get attached to it. I keep getting calls from Brandon. He's not happy that I sent the book off to an agent. I didn't think I'd hear from him again, he was so mad, but he called the next week and asked if I'd come to my senses yet."

"Unless he hands you a check, that doesn't bounce, for a sizable amount, you need to wait to hear from the agents." I might have delayed Deek's publishing career, but I wanted him to have all the information. Not jump at the first offer. "Thanks for listening."

"No trouble. Between you and my mom, who had a real bad feeling about this guy, I decided it was better to wait. He's coming to the readathon to support us. You can meet him Friday."

I thought I might just have a little bit to say to the man. And if I got a business card, I could do some of my patented "internet" research on him and see if he was on the up-and-up or not. "After this box, I'm heading out. Don't let Aunt Jackie work too long."

"I'm not telling her to go home, but I can tell her everything is set for tomorrow. From what I saw, we only have two more boxes. And the bags are done. All we need now are the readers and the timer to start." Deek had bought a big digital timer that would sit on the treat table and let the readers know how long they had left to read. "This is going to be a blast. We'll want to do it every year."

"If you say so." I put the last book on the shelf from my box and stretched. "And I'm done. See you tomorrow."

"Sounds good." He was studying a book that he'd pulled out of the box. Even my booksellers got caught by a book every now and then.

I went to the back to get my tote. On a hunch, I picked up my aunt's bag as well. I opened the door and looked over to where she stood, watching the nearly empty shop. "Are you ready to head home? We can walk together."

She turned and looked at me. Something was on her mind, I could see the wheels turning, but instead of telling me, she nodded. Then she called out to Deek. "We're leaving. Make sure you break all those boxes down, but don't get rid of them. We may have to store some things for next year."

She took her purse from me, and we made our way out to the street. She didn't look at me as we walked toward her new home, the Train Station. Or to be precise, the apartment above the Train Station. "How are you and Greg?"

"Good. He's busy with this investigation, but we're good. We got to eat dinner together last night and got a start on the thank-you notes." I knew what she wanted to hear, so that was what I told her.

"I hear he's been visiting Sherry. Are you sure everything's okay?"

Her bluntness never seemed to surprise me, but this time, it caught me off guard. "Aunt Jackie, Greg and I are fine. Nothing to worry about. He's been visiting Sherry because she was a suspect in the latest murder, that's all."

She made a noise, and I turned toward her. The look on her face was priceless. "I'm just looking out for your best interest."

"And I appreciate it. But we're good."

We walked a little farther before she spoke again. "I could see Sherry being the type to kill. She has issues."

"Aunt Jackie! I can't believe you said that." I started laughing, and she chuckled.

"Well, it's the truth. That boy is lucky he found you and lucky he survived his first marriage." She glanced over toward the police station. "But he is a hard worker. I'll give him that. Harrold says the men's group is always talking about the things Greg is doing for the town. Have you two set a date yet?"

"Not yet. We've been a little busy with everything going on." I didn't want to talk about this. I knew it was something my aunt wanted me to move on, but I wanted to get past this emotional roller coaster and then set a date. "Do you and Harrold have joint finances?"

"That's quite a change of subject, but the answer is complicated. If you really want to talk about joining financial lives after marriage, we can have lunch together. I'll just call Harrold and tell him I'll be a little late."

I debated telling her I was too busy, then I realized that I wasn't too busy. I didn't know how many opportunities I'd have left to spend time with her. It was time to seize the moment, so to speak. "That would be nice. Greg said something, and I need to work out my response to it."

"Does he want to take over the Miss Emily fund?" My aunt got right to the heart of the matter.

"Not specifically, but we were talking about joint finances. What does that actually mean? What's normal for couples? What's one step over the line?" I took her arm as we crossed the street to Lille's. "It's so confusing."

"It doesn't have to be. Some couples go old fashioned with 'what's mine is yours' and go all in. Your Uncle Ted and I were that way. Mostly because neither one of us had anything when we got married. So we built our lives together." She nodded to Lille, who grabbed menus and took us to a booth near the back. Aunt Jackie smiled at her as she sat down. "Thanks, dear."

Lille grunted, probably for my benefit. She was nice to my aunt since Jackie married Harrold. Lille had been good friends with Harrold's first wife, so when he and Aunt Jackie had started dating, Lille had been a little protective of him. But she liked Jackie. It was me that she didn't really care for. "Carrie will be right over."

After Lille left, I pretended to study the menu. My aunt took it as a sign to keep talking.

"When Harrold and I started talking about marriage, we decided that we would have a joint account that we paid the everyday expenses out of. He has his business account and several other things going on. We've both made provisions for each other for when one of us leaves. But we don't worry about keeping all our money in one big pot." She set the menu aside. "It's different when you're older. I don't need anyone to take care of me or leave me set up. I've rebounded from that whole stock issue nicely. So if Harrold leaves first, I won't be penniless."

"When I was married before, we didn't combine anything. I moved into his apartment and paid half the rent and utilities. We split the costs and kept all our money separate. Of course, that relationship didn't work out anyway."

Carrie came up with two iced teas. "I hope I guessed right today. I'm trying to save some steps. I'm so beat by the time I get home, it's pitiful. What can I get for the two of you?"

My aunt ordered a soup and salad combo, and I followed her lead and ordered a taco salad. "No beans though."

"Not a problem. I'll just tell Tiny it's for you." She grinned as she took the menus and left, picking up plates as she moved through the dining room.

"So what does Greg want to do?" my aunt asked.

I shrugged. "I'm not sure. I got so freaked out when he said joint finances, I didn't hear the rest. I'm a control freak, right?"

"No, you're not a control freak. You're going through some changes in your life. Change is hard, and you need to do what you want to do. I would keep the Miss Emily fund separate. And don't put him on your house. You can leave it to him in the will, but Miss Emily left that to you. I'd hate to see you lose it if something happens between you and Greg."

As I was walking home, I thought about my aunt's advice. Could I be half in on this relationship regarding my money and still be all in with my heart? Would it hurt Greg's feelings if I said I was keeping it separate just in case? So many land mines. I decided it was time to go for a run.

That was my answer to any stress in my life. Run with my dog. It didn't fix everything, but it did make things look more positive when I got home.

When we were finished, I decided to put the topic of Greg and me on the back burner. Instead, I opened the notebook and read through what I'd found out about Alicia's murder. She'd been identified by her sister a day after she was found in the dress shop. Okay, that was weird but not unexplainable. Harper could have been in shock. And if she hadn't seen her in a while, maybe she didn't realize it was her sister?

The husband had come into town and confirmed Harper's identification after a short pause, according to Doc Ames.

What was it about this victim that made the two closest people in the world to her not see her for who she was when she was dead? I grabbed my keys to the Jeep and loaded up Emma for a short road trip. I needed to talk to someone.

Chapter 17

This time when I pulled into the mortuary's parking lot, my Jeep was the only vehicle there. Well, not counting the minivan that had been turned into a hearse after Doc bought it last year. I rolled down the windows far enough that Emma could get air, but not low enough to risk her getting outside and running after a random rabbit.

The front door was unlocked, and I stepped into the cool, air-conditioned lobby. It always freaked me out when I visited, due to the richness of the room's decor. Dark wood and velvet, it looked like what I suspected a gentlemen's smoking den would have years in the past. I turned toward Doc's office and saw a notice that Alicia Sanchez's funeral would be held on Sunday at two.

I picked up one of the flyers that they gave out at these things and studied the content. The funeral would be here. Alicia's body would be cremated afterward, and a second service held in Meridian, Idaho, at another funeral home next week. It made sense in one way, her sister did live in South Cove now. Maybe Harper had insisted on the two services? Another question. I scanned through the songs and Bible verses and saw that neither Harper nor Scott were delivering a eulogy at the service. A man with the last name of Sanchez was speaking, but I didn't know how the man was related to Alicia and Harper.

"What are you doing here? It's such a nice day, you should be out with that dog of yours, running. Or reading on the beach. I'm sure Greg's too busy to hang out with you, at least this week, but that doesn't mean you need to be shut up in the dark." Doc Ames was dressed in an old pair of jeans and a worn dress shirt. He looked like someone's grandfather, not the county coroner.

"I just popped in to see you. I had a question that's been bothering me." I gave him a quick hug. "Emma's in the Jeep, so I can't stay long."

"Well, let's go outside then and talk by the picnic area. You can let her out if you have a leash. I hate to see her get too close to the road."

"Sounds good." I followed him outside and then hurried to the Jeep. I always carried one of Emma's leashes in the car, just in case. Along with a dish and a bottle of water, which I pulled out. She could have a drink while we talked.

Doc was already sitting when I got to the picnic area near the back of the building. I filled Emma's water dish, then set it on the ground near the table. Sitting across from Doc, I took in the small, park-like area. "This is nice. I didn't know this was here."

"I don't have much of a backyard, so this takes its place. It's a good area to come and sit during the evenings when I need a minute to think." He studied my face. "What's bothering you?"

"I've been thinking about what we talked about last time we met. How neither Harper nor her brother-in-law had recognized Alicia when they were first asked to identify the body. Does that happen a lot?" I didn't have anything to write on, but I thought I could remember this conversation at least until I got back in my Jeep and found a notebook in my tote.

"More than you'd think. I think the issue is the lack of a soul. Pain, worry, and even happiness has an effect on how you look. So when your soul leaves, that drain shows on your face. When loved ones see the body, they don't see their loved ones. Their personality is gone, so it's hard for someone to navigate the thought that this body in front of me is the person I loved." He studied me. "Why are you asking?"

"I just thought maybe it was someone else. Did you do DNA testing or fingerprinting?"

"The tests are all still out. If Greg hadn't still been looking for a killer, I would have fired him and canceled the tests. The county isn't made of money, you know." He watched me as Emma came around the back of the table and sat in front of him. She loved visiting Doc. He spoke her language. "Who's my girl? Sit pretty."

Emma followed his commands. Like I said, she could be a perfect dog when she wanted to be. Especially when she was showing off for others. "So the body could be someone besides Alicia Sanchez."

"You've been reading too many of those mystery novels you like to shelve. Exactly why would both her sister and her husband identify the woman if it wasn't Alicia?" He smiled as another car pulled into the parking lot. This one parked in the back close to the hearse. "Carrie's home."

"She's living here?" I blurted out before remembering Greg had told me about the new living arrangements.

He blushed as he stood to greet her. "She moved in last week. We're keeping it quiet for a while."

Carrie hurried over and gave Doc a kiss. Then she greeted Emma and me in that order. "I can't believe I'm seeing you outside the diner. Do you want some iced tea? I made some this morning before I went into work."

I shook my head. "I'm fine. Emma and I need to get home and make some dinner soon."

"Well, it was nice to see you. Are you coming to the funeral on Sunday? That poor girl doesn't have much family here. I'm sure Harper would love to see you." Carrie sat next to Doc.

Her comment surprised me. I hadn't thought that Harper had made friends with any people in South Cove in the short time she'd been here, but I'd been wrong. "How well do you know Harper?"

Carrie put her arm around Doc. "She ate most of her meals at Lille's for the last few months since she opened her shop. Career girls, they never think they're going to need to cook. I guess she thought she'd live in the city for the rest of her life."

"Did she ever talk about her family? About Alicia, at least before she was killed?" This was getting interesting.

"Of course. She hated the husband. She said Alicia was no more than a prisoner in that marriage. I guess Harper had tried to talk her out of it, so they didn't talk for a few years, but when she came to visit a few months ago, she basically admitted to Harper that she'd been right. I guess she was trying to find a place near here to move to." Carrie rubbed Emma's ears.

"Why do you say that?" I needed to keep Carrie talking. She was a gold mine.

She rolled her shoulders. "I found some of those house flyers on the table when Harper left one day. The houses were all nearby, just more inward. They can be a little cheaper if they don't have an ocean view."

"Carrie's daughter has been looking at houses nearby," Doc added as if that explained Carrie's interest.

"Oh, well, thanks for chatting with me. I should let you two get started on your evening." I figured the first thing Carrie would do was take off her shoes and maybe soak in a hot bath. Then, I didn't really want to know what they had planned. "See you soon."

"Thanks for stopping by, Jill." Doc waved as I walked back around the building and to my Jeep.

Doc and Carrie were an official item. Which was totally cute. And might explain Greg's information leaks. Could Carrie be spreading information she didn't realize was confidential?

I called Greg's cell as I drove back to South Cove. "Whatcha doing?"

"Looking at cell phone transcripts. Did you know Alicia was making plans to move down here months before she disappeared?" Greg asked.

"I just heard that she was looking at houses. Or at least Harper was looking at houses for her." I had the windows down, and Emma had her head out, catching the breeze with her tongue hanging out.

The other end of the call was silent.

I thought I'd lost reception around a curve. "Greg, are you there?"

"I'm at the station. Where are you?"

"Driving back from Bakerstown. I went to ask Doc something." I grimaced. I hadn't wanted to tell him I was grilling Doc for information. He might think I was the leak. "Carrie's already moved in."

"Good to know. But how did you know Alicia was looking at houses here?"

Me and my big mouth. I told him about the real estate flyers. "Carrie talked to Harper at the diner when she came in for meals. I guess she talked about her sister a lot."

"The sister she didn't recognize for twenty-four hours." He groaned. "I'm coming home for dinner. I keep going around and around, and nothing is making sense. I think we should work on the thank-you notes after dinner."

That was a change of subject. "Okay, but don't you have a game to watch?"

"Probably, but this is more important. It's our first action as an engaged couple. Besides, your aunt called and asked when we were planning on finishing. I guess she asked Mary if she'd received our card yet."

I laughed. "Leave it to Aunt Jackie. We had lunch today. I guess she thought my answer wasn't good enough. I'm sorry she bothered you at work."

"It's fine. Like I said, I need some time away from this, so maybe I could see the missing puzzle piece."

"Okay, I'll take some meat out when I get home. Chicken, fish, or something else?"

"Let's do fish. And that lime rice you make. I'll see you soon."

I ended the call and turned to see Emma grinning at me. "Yep, your boy is coming home tonight. Maybe you can talk him into a few rounds of fetch before we cook dinner."

Emma barked, and I thought she was saying "no maybe about it." Or she was upset at a seagull that got too close to the car.

Greg's truck pulled into the driveway right after I did. So much for me getting out something for dinner. We'd have to defrost it in the microwave unless he was serious about taking the entire evening off. I waited at the door for him. Emma jumped on his legs as he walked toward us.

"I told her that you were coming home." I unlocked the door and turned on the lights. Home. "Are you really taking the entire night off?"

"Unless someone walks into the station and confesses to killing Alicia Sanchez, yes." He paused. "Let me rephrase that. Unless someone besides Pat walks into the station and confesses."

"She knows she can't take the blame if Sherry had really done the deed, right? You're too good of a detective, you saw right through her fake confession." I moved toward the kitchen and let Emma out in the backyard.

"Pat would do anything for Sherry. They're just that close." He opened the fridge and got out a soda. "I wish she just would have trusted me a little more. There was no way Sherry was going to be charged with something she didn't do. Not on my watch."

"You're a good man, Detective King." I got out the tuna I'd stuck in the freezer after my last trip to Bakerstown to shop. "I can do a watermelon and feta salad to go along with the rice."

"Sounds perfect. But are you being sarcastic about the good man thing?" He put his arms around me and pulled me close to him. "You know there's nothing between Sherry and me anymore. History is just that. History."

"I know. And yes, I meant it. But I was thinking of how you didn't just shirk off all the thank-you notes because I'm the girl." I felt safe in his embrace. Something I'd never get tired of feeling.

"You have horrible handwriting. You should have been a doctor." He let me go, then went to the back door. Emma stood there, looking in at us through the screen door. Her tennis ball was in her mouth. "I'm being called into the game. Are you coming outside?"

"As soon as I put this fish in the microwave." I watched as he went outside and threw the ball for Emma. We all had our happy moments, and for Emma, she had a top two. When she ran with me and when Greg threw the ball. She knew she was loved. And really, that's all that matters sometimes.

* * * *

Friday morning, I had changed my alarm to an hour later. My commuters were going to be upset, but if we were staying open through the night for the readathon, I needed at least a little sleep. And I'd warned them. But typical me, I was up at my regular time anyway. I used the time to pack an overnight bag with some people-appropriate pj's as well as a few things to make me look at least a little less drained the next morning.

Greg was still downstairs when I came down with my overnight bag.

"You look like a preteen packing for a sleepover rather than someone going to work." He leaned over to kiss me. "Now you be good with the other kids and don't give the parents a hard time."

"Sadly, I am the parent in this situation. Did I tell you that Sadie and Pastor Bill agreed to come help with the sleepover part? They have experience with lock-ins at the church." I filled my travel mug with coffee and sat at the table. Reaching down, I gave Emma a hug. "I'd bring you with me, but who knows what kid is going to be afraid of dogs or allergic to dog hair."

"I'll bring her over for a short visit after I get home tonight." He snapped his fingers, and she moved over to his side of the table. "I'm going to grab takeout from Lille's, then come home and watch a game."

"No thank-you notes?" We had made a big dent in the pile, but we had one more session to finish everything.

He shook his head. "Not going to happen. This is a you-and-me event. It can wait until Sunday morning. Are you still on with Amy for brunch?"

I shook my head. "We canceled this weekend. She's spending time with Justin on Sunday to talk about his bringing work home all the time."

"Fun times." Greg finished his coffee. "Speaking of work, I need to head into town and make some calls. Something triggered a new lead last night, and I need to see if it goes anywhere."

"Sounds promising. Hey, Carrie asked if we were going to Alicia's funeral on Sunday. I think she's trying to get a good showing from South Cove to help support Harper." I eyed the muffins on the table but knew I'd be eating junk all day long with this readathon. Instead, I grabbed a banana and peeled it.

"Not a bad idea." He put his coffee cup in the sink and grabbed the last muffin I'd been eyeing. "It might just provide some clarity."

"The funeral might provide clarity?" I studied him and could see the wheels turning in his head. "Exactly what is this new lead you're looking at?"

He paused in the doorway. "It's just been bugging me all night. Why would a perfectly happy wife, in a good marriage, according to her husband and his work friends, be looking at moving two states away?"

Chapter 18

The shop was a madhouse by ten. There were kids everywhere, a book in one hand and typically a piece of candy or a soda in the other. We had free water and plain coffee available for the participants and the parents, but most had brought a cooler of sodas as well as healthy snacks. But I didn't see a lot of cheese sticks being finished.

Deek stood next to me, surveying the room. "This is bigger than my wildest estimates. The television station called just now and is sending down a crew for the late news. As long as we don't get bumped by a ten-car pileup or a mass murderer running around loose, you and Coffee, Books, and More are going to be on the news."

"Is it bad I'm hoping for the pileup?" I rang up a large mocha and a romance novel for one of the mothers. "Thirty-seven fifty."

"Just swipe the card. Or open me a tab. I saw you have the second and third book on the shelf too. This is amazing. Just think, I get to spend the time reading *and* be a good mother. That doesn't happen a lot." The woman giggled and took her drink and book over to the corner where her daughter was deep into a young adult fantasy.

"We're filling an unmet need." I leaned back on the counter behind the cash register. "Just don't ask me to do this again for at least a year. Maybe two."

"You'll probably change your mind when you see the sales reports. I've sold more books in the last hour than I did all last week. Even with the book club last Saturday." Deek pointed to a family of four huddled around a table near the front. "I've seen the mom in here with the kids, but this is the first time the dad's come in. And he bought three books on California history. He's a pirate nut. So I'm ordering in a few more he might like. We're making reading cool."

I laughed and saw Aunt Jackie waving me over to the bookshelves. "I'm being paged. Although if it's about a book, maybe I should send you."

"Jackie knows who she wants to talk to. Sending me would just delay your arrival." He reached out to take a book from a woman who'd came up to the cash register. "Can I get you anything else? The brownies are pretty amazing. I've had two this morning already."

"You had me at brownie." She grinned. "Thank you for doing this. My Caroline doesn't like reading, but she's been talking about this event all month. Her friends are all here."

Lucky us, I thought as I smiled and walked away. My aunt stood next to a man in his fifties. He had the typical rich tourist outfit of polo shirt and well-maintained linen shorts and a tan that made his whitened teeth gleam. "Hey, what can I help you with?"

"Max Winter. So nice to meet you. I'm a developer for upscale communities, and I'm looking for a building site near South Cove. Your aunt says you own the property near the highway? Are you interested in selling?" He handed me a card.

I didn't reach for it. "Actually, no. My home isn't for sale."

"We are always looking at future development too. Maybe you'd be interested in an option? We'd pay you a set amount just to have first dibs on the property in case you changed your mind or circumstances change. It happens sometimes." He kept holding out the card.

I didn't like him. I didn't like his rebound any better. But as several people had told me lately, the future wasn't just mine to plan anymore. What if Greg got offered a new job in a bigger city? Would I keep both the house and the business? Doubt must have shown on my face, as he continued.

"You don't have to make a decision today. I just came in to purchase a few books for my vacation. Take my card. You can call me later and tell me no over the phone. It's easier to be direct when you're not looking at someone in the face." He jiggled the card.

This time I took it. "My answer won't change, but I need to chat with my fiancé first before confirming. I have no current plans of moving or selling."

He laughed, and it didn't sound fake at all. "That's the thing. Most people don't until they do."

After he walked to the register with four hardbound purchases, I turned to my aunt. "Why did you tell him I owned Miss Emily's house?"

She shook her head, watching him pull out cash for his purchase. "That's the thing. I didn't. All I did was confirm that you were the sole owner.

He already knew me and you. I'd been watching him for several minutes before he approached me. He came in, grabbed the books off the shelf, and then pretended to read the back of one while he watched the room."

"What do you think he's up to?" I waved as he left the shop. Books in hand.

My aunt watched too. "If I were to guess, I think he thought you'd be alone this morning. I have a feeling he's a smooth talker. When he walked in and the event was going, he had to change his strategy."

"I'm not selling. I don't know how many times I have to say that." I picked up a candy wrapper and dropped it in a nearby trash can.

"Probably a lot. That property is worth a lot of money. And will just continue to appreciate in value."

My aunt's words continued to haunt me as I worked the rest of the day. Around noon, I had a delivery of Tiny's sub sandwiches come in from Lille's for the staff. I started sending people off the floor to the office to eat. My aunt took hers and one for Harrold and left the shop. She'd go to the Train Station to eat and relax for a bit before coming back.

Greg showed up about one. He looked around the crowded but quiet store. People were eating lunch or reading or just relaxing. The coffee and water stations were filled, and the kids had all fallen into a book or were on their second one. I'd already checked in several cards that had more than one book finished. I wished I was reading along.

"You alone here?" He sat on a stool near the register.

I shrugged toward the office door. "They're on break. I get mine in about fifteen minutes. Do you want some coffee?"

"Actually, I came to see if I could steal you for lunch." He pointed to the Diamond Lille's bag on the counter. "But it looks like you already ordered."

"We can have sandwiches in the back if you want to hang out for a few minutes until Deek or Evie get back."

"Sounds perfect. I'm waiting for some callbacks anyway. I told Esmeralda to patch it through to my cell if anyone responds." He looked around the shop. "Looks like the readathon is a success."

"I think so. It's a lot of work, and we need more people on staff when we do this again, but it's been fun and everyone has been great to work with." I handed him the card. "And I got an offer on the house today."

"I didn't know it was for sale." He studied the card. "Coastal Investment Properties?"

"I think it's a retirement community. He came in to talk to me, but he was surprised by the readathon. I don't want to sell Miss Emily's house, but I thought I should talk to you."

He shook his head and tried to hand the card back. I hesitated. "Why would you talk to me about the house?"

"We're engaged. Maybe you see your future in a bigger city running your own department." I held out the ring. "This means where you go, I go."

He took my hand and kissed it. "That means we talk about our future goals and plans together. Not that you follow me. As of today, I have no plans of leaving South Cove. If I went to a bigger department, I'd have more people questioning my decisions. And then Mayor Baylor would probably hire one of his friends to take over, and Tim and Toby would quit, then South Cove would turn into a drug den for thieves and malcontents."

"Wow, that's dark." I was kind of impressed at the detail he'd thought about our lives. "Thorough, but dark."

He grinned. "Sometimes I have a lot of time to think. So don't worry about where the future is taking us. My home is here." He pointed to my heart. "Where you go, I'll follow."

"And back at you." I leaned my head on his shoulder.

"Excuse me, I need to check in this book and buy the next one." A girl of about twelve stood in front of us. "And a cookie, please."

"Let me know when you're ready to take a break. I'm going to look for the next book in that action series Deek suggested last month." Greg nodded to the little girl as he left the cash register. "She's all yours."

It took a little over twenty minutes for me to get free for lunch, but Greg didn't seem to mind. For someone who had a murder investigation on his plate, he didn't seem distracted. Instead, he stopped and chatted with several families while I checked off books read and sold more cookies. When Evie arrived to work after taking Homer for a walk, I lifted a hand to get his attention.

We headed to the back and packed up sandwiches, chips, and a couple of sodas, then took the haul out to the back parking lot. Greg had set up a picnic table over on the other side of the road where a creek ran behind the buildings. Several of the locals used it for a quick break away from their shops.

"You seemed at home with the madhouse in there." I unwrapped my sandwich and took a bite. "I think you were even enjoying your discussion with the Randell boy. What were you talking about?"

Greg set his sandwich down after taking a bite. "Star Wars. The kid knows it backward and forward. Even stuff I didn't know, because he's read the companion books. It's crazy how much trivia he has about the movies."

"Everyone has a passion. Maybe he's going to go into space when he grows up." I opened my chips. "I assume you read crime novels when you were a kid."

He shook his head. "I was more interested in music."

"Seriously? I didn't know that." I studied him. I couldn't see him as a band kid. "What instrument?"

"I sang choir for six years. I even got a scholarship to college because of it. Then I took a criminal justice class, and I was hooked. I wanted to serve and protect. I knew that was my calling. The music, it was just the means to get me into college. My mom was pretty disappointed. She sang backup for years before she settled down and married my father. I think she thought I was going to earn the star status she never obtained."

"This explains so much about your mom." I pulled a slice of ham from my sandwich and ate it. "Why didn't you mention this before?"

"It didn't come up before now. What was your reading passion as a kid?"

I thought about it as I ate another bite of my sandwich. "Everything. I loved reading and learning. I found some old textbooks about animal husbandry—basically raising cows? I read those along with *Gone with the Wind* and the book about the guy who went to Africa. If I ran out of 'good' books I'd picked up from the library, I read what was around. Including my mom's copy of *Flowers in the Attic*. I had to sneak that out of her room. But then later I realized she didn't really notice anyway."

"You don't talk about your mom much." Greg didn't meet my gaze; he focused on the sandwich. "For all I know, you came down from space when you were a teenager and started your life with your aunt."

"I know. Someday we'll have that conversation, but today I've got to get back to the readathon." I saw a couple walking up the alley, talking. "And I think we're about to have company at the table."

He finished his sandwich and tucked the wrappings into a bag. Then he opened his chips before turning to look down the alley. His hand froze on the way to his mouth with the first chip. "That's Harper and Colton, the lawyer. This should be interesting, if they don't run the other way when they see me sitting here."

As they came closer, I saw it on Harper's face when she realized who was sitting at the table they were aiming for. Colton held a bag from Diamond Lille's. She stopped walking, and he turned back to ask her what was wrong.

"Come and sit down," I called as I waved them over to the table. "We're almost done and out of here. We can share for a few minutes. It's too pretty of a day to eat inside."

Harper looked like she wanted to be anywhere but there at that exact minute. Colton whispered something, and she nodded. Then she pasted a smile on her face and marched to the table. "That's so kind of you."

"Not a problem. We're just taking a break from the readathon inside. Did you hear about it? I don't know if the spring festival idea works for your shop. You probably don't get a lot of walk-in traffic, do you?" I chatted about the business rather than the elephant in the alley, her dead sister.

"Not much, but I have had several people stop by today to look at my designs, and I had one consignment. So I guess the marketing plan worked for me too. A readathon was a great idea." She glanced at the bookstore. "I'm not much for a lot of kids around though. I never was. My sister, she was the party girl. She loved being around people, even when we were kids. I was her shadow."

"I'm sorry for your loss." I should have known that we wouldn't stay away from the subject for long.

She looked surprised for a minute, but before she could speak, Colton answered, "Harper appreciates your condolences."

"Yes, yes, you are so kind." She smiled as Colton set a takeout container in front of her. "Sometimes I forget that she's even gone."

"I can't imagine." I tried to change the subject again. "Oh, I hear you joined the Bakerstown gym. My aunt and her husband along with one of my baristas work out there. I guess it's the place to be."

"Unless you have a home gym." Greg reminded me of his ultimate plan.

"Yeah, but I hear it has a pool. How are you liking it?"

She met Colton's gaze, and a long moment passed between them. Then she nodded and turned to me. "I'm just getting settled in. I'll have to let you know. Are you thinking about joining?"

We talked for a little while longer about South Cove and the issues of living in a tourist town, like having to go somewhere else for groceries, then I stood and gathered my leftovers. "Sorry to have to leave. I've got kids waiting to check in books."

"And I need to get back to the station. I'm sure there's been some sort of emergency since I've been gone." Greg took my arm and nodded to Colton and Harper. "Enjoy your lunch."

When we got back into the shop, I threw away the trash and boxed up the leftover sandwiches for another snack or meal. "Is it me, or did Harper not know what I was talking about with the gym?"

"Or her sister being dead. I wonder if they have her on some meds that are dulling her responses?"

"Maybe." I started to say something else, but then Evie popped her head into the office.

"Good, you're here. We have an issue."

"I'll be right out." I kissed Greg and brushed crumbs off his uniform shirt. "Back to work. I'll see you tonight."

"I'll be here." He followed me out to the front, where two children were yelling at each other over a book. He managed to swallow a chuckle as I moved in to negotiate with a couple of five-year-olds whose parents seemed to be MIA. He called out as he escaped out the front door, "Have a great day."

"Whatever." I took the book they were struggling over and held it out of their reach. "What's going on?"

By the time Greg came back to the shop, the kids and parents had been fed and settled down for the sleepover part of the adventure. Some were curled up in our bookstore seating area for an evening of storytelling with Deek. Others had their sleeping bags in corners where they'd piled a bunch of pillows to lean against walls to keep reading. I'd already checked in hundreds of books. One teen had almost ten books on her list, but she'd been smart and chosen the ones with fewer pages to start. Now she was in a series that Deek had suggested, and she looked like she'd finish the first three books before morning. If she stayed awake.

He glanced around as he brought in Emma. "Rodney isn't here, is he?"

"The health inspector from Bakerstown? No. I haven't seen him since our annual. Why? Do you think he'd have a problem with Emma?" I leaned down to give her a hug. "I'm sorry I missed our run, girl. Maybe tomorrow if I wake up in time."

"We walked up from the house, so don't let her guilt you. She's getting some exercise." He noticed a bunch of kids in sleeping bags over near the kids' section, where there was usually a reading table and tiny chairs. "I think you might want to keep the fire marshal out of here too. You have to have close to three hundred, counting parents."

"The count ebbs and flows. We'll lose a lot of these after story time ends. They're just letting their kids pretend like they're out for the evening." I pointed over to where Sadie and Pastor Bill were playing Chutes and Ladders with a group. "Those parents just left to grab dinner at Lille's. I'm thinking we're babysitting a lot of kids right now for a bit of quiet time for their parents. But it's all good. Most of them are still reading, and we've had an amazing day of sales. Now to just get through the night."

"Are you hungry, or have you eaten too many cookies?" He held up a bag from Diamond Lille's.

"I've had my share of cookies, but I'd love some dinner and a break. Let me get Evie up to the counter. Aunt Jackie and Harrold just left for the evening." I nodded to the office. "Meet you out back at the table? Or do you want to eat inside?"

"The table will work fine. Who knows, maybe Alicia's killer will come sit down and confess while we're there." He kissed me on the cheek and moved around the counter and out through the office door.

Chapter 19

A little girl stood, watching him go. She grinned as I walked over to her. "Your puppy is pretty. Mommy says I can have a dog as soon as I get into fourth grade. I'll be responsible then."

"That's Emma. She's a golden retriever."

The girl nodded. "I know. I have a book of dog breeds, but Mommy says we'll probably get a mutt from the pound. I want a Maltese. They're pretty, but they're expensive."

"I've never seen a Maltese." I was impressed. This girl knew her dog breeds.

"They're little and always white. At least I've only seen white ones." She frowned and glanced at the books. "Maybe you have another book on dogs, and I can show you. I bought my book here last summer."

"That would be great, but I need to grab some dinner. My boyfriend and Emma are waiting for me." I motioned for Evie to join us. "Evie's taking over for me at the counter while I go eat. Maybe she can help you find the book."

"I wanted to show you." The girl sighed deeply. "But I can find the book and show you when you get back."

"Perfect."

Evie stepped in and took the little girl's hand. "Let's go see if we can find the book. Jill, I'll watch the register while you're out."

"Thanks." I hurried away and out the back door before anyone else could sideline me. I really appreciated my slow morning shifts right now. I saw Greg sitting at the table with another man. As I came closer, I realized it was Doc Ames. "I don't see you forever, and now I've seen you twice in the same week. Don't tell me you're discussing work. I'm starving and just can't go back into the shop with those kids. At least not until I've eaten something."

"Oh, no, I don't mean to impose on your dinner. I'm just waiting for Carrie to get off. I like to pick her up on Friday nights; then we can go sit by the beach and watch the sunset. If she gets off in time." He checked his watch. "Which, since she hasn't texted me, I don't think is happening today."

"Festival weekends everyone's super busy. I'm afraid Lille's probably keeping her late." I sat next to Greg, who was unpacking the bag. "Do you want to share our dinner?"

"No, I'll wait and dine with Carrie. I've got a pot roast in the crockpot waiting for us to get home." He nodded. "Go ahead and eat. I'm sure you'll need to get back to the bookstore soon. I walked by a few minutes ago, and it looked like you had everyone in South Cove who had a kid or was a kid in there."

"The readathon has been a big success." I opened my takeout box and grinned. Greg had brought me fish and chips and even grabbed the malt vinegar packets and salt. He totally knew me. "But honestly, I'll be glad for tomorrow when it's over. This level of participation is a little overwhelming for me."

"Maybe next year you should have it at the rec center. That way you don't have to squeeze everyone into your store." Greg opened his takeout. He had Tiny's pot roast, which was one of his favorites. "Hey, Doc, I've been meaning to ask you about this, and don't take it the wrong way, but do you lock your office door?"

Doc chuckled. "I've been meaning to apologize to you as well. I slipped up and left the autopsy report for Alicia on my counter in the kitchen. I know, I'm just not used to having people over. Well, Tiny was helping Carrie move in one day, and he saw it and peeked inside. Carrie didn't know until she heard him say something to Lille, and well, she came to me about it. I'm your leak."

"I wasn't blaming you, but at least now I know where Lille got the information she told Harrold. And I know she was just trying to be supportive of him. She really cares for Harrold. I'm sure when she heard that the killing might be random, it bothered her." He glanced at me. "I know keeping things from the people we love is sometimes hard to do."

Doc Ames chuckled. "Especially when they're bright and curious like the women we choose to share our lives with."

"Hey, now how did this become about me?" I set down the fish I'd been eating with my fingers. "Carrie and Tiny were the leakers, not me."

"True." Greg didn't look up. "This time."

Doc's phone buzzed, and he checked the message. "And I'm saved by the bell. I hope I didn't start a fight here, but Carrie's ready to go, so I'm out of here. Still got time for a bit of the sunset."

"You're a romantic," Greg called after him.

He paused and looked back at us. "It helps at my age. And I think it's something else that I have in common with the two of you. Have a good night."

I watched as he made his way through the buildings and back out onto Main Street. "I love seeing him happy. And the fact it's with Carrie is just icing on the cake."

"They're good together. I thought maybe my leak was coming from Doc's place, but I didn't want to accuse Carrie and start a fight. The fact he already knew about what I was going to say helped." He held up a fork filled with mashed potatoes. "I swear, Tiny makes the best mashed potatoes in California. Maybe in the US."

That's what I loved about being with Greg. He had his priorities straight.

After dinner, Sadie and I sat at the counter and talked. The kids that were staying had mostly settled in for a round of ghost stories and microwave smores and hot chocolate. Pastor Bill and Deek were leading the charge there. Evie had gone upstairs to spend some time with Homer. And the families with small kids had packed it in with a promise to be here bright and early for coffee.

"So, you and Pastor Bill. How's that going?"

Sadie blushed and glanced over at her boyfriend and the local minister. "We're taking it slow, but he told his deacons about us last month. And last Sunday, he told the congregation. Of course, most of them already knew. I guess we weren't so sneaky."

"How does Nick feel about it?" Sadie's only son, Nick, had been my summer help for years until he'd graduated college and went off to intern at a high-end financial company. I wasn't even sure of what he did, but he would be graduating with his MBA next year and working full-time in London. He was a good kid and a better young man. Any mother would be proud of him.

"He likes Bill. He said it was my life and I needed to be happy, no matter what he thought. But he likes Bill. He's coming home for a week before he goes off to London for the summer. I'm sure he'll stop in and see you." Sadie beamed when she talked about Nick. "Anyway, you're the one whose life is about to change. Have you set a date yet?"

"A date?" I knew I should know what she was talking about, but my brain felt dead.

She tapped my ring finger. "For the wedding?"

"Oh, yeah. Not yet. We're going away for a few days if he ever finds time, and we'll set it then." I rubbed my neck. "But it can't be soon, because I need to sleep for a week after this."

"You can go in the back and lay down if you want? Or go home for a few hours. We've got this." Sadie looked concerned.

I shook my head. "No fifteen-year-old is going to stay up longer than I do. I'm in it for the long haul. So what else should we talk about?"

Sadie pressed her fingers on her lips. I think she was trying not to laugh in my face. Then her eyes widened. "I saw Harper in Bakerstown the other day. She was coming out of that gym that has all the body builders. I was sitting outside the coffee shop waiting for Bill, and she just walked by me. I tried to say hello and catch her gaze, but she looked right through me. Maybe I need to be coming to more of your meetings. Especially when I'm not recognized by someone who I'd just met at the last meeting."

"She can be a little hard to get to know." I'd mentioned the gym to Harper too, but got a wishy-washy answer. I wanted to give Harper the benefit of the doubt, but she'd been off with me as well. Maybe she just wasn't fitting in well in South Cove. We were a special breed.

"I talked to her about doing my dress." She blushed and looked over at Pastor Bill. "I mean, if Bill asks me to marry him. I don't want the big white thing, but I want something special, you know? She seemed to get it when we talked at your party. Then she just walked by me like she'd never met me before. Although, she does have a lot on her mind."

I thought about Deek saying he'd seen Harper in the gym, and she hadn't said anything to him either. But no, he'd said the woman had told him she'd been confused with Harper a lot lately. Maybe that was who Sadie had seen. I wondered if I should stop by and talk to Harper about how small South Cove was. It wouldn't do to have Harper seen as antisocial.

"I see that look in your eye. Don't be thinking you need to talk to her on my account. I don't get my feelings hurt. I just think she needs to understand we're a small, tight group here. She needed to at least smile and wave, even if she was late for whatever." Sadie stood and poured herself another coffee. "I swear, if I hear that you browbeat her for not talking to me, I'm going to be upset."

Sadie's upset was anyone else's slightly bad mood. She just didn't have it in her to be over the top with her negative emotions. Which was why she'd make an amazing wife for Pastor Bill. "Sometimes, you're too nice."

"I just want everyone to get along. I'm not sure that's being too nice." She nodded to someone over my shoulder. "Can you excuse me? Bill needs a refill on his coffee."

I watched as she got a coffee and delivered it to the man sitting next to Deek. They made quite a pair. The minister and the surfer dude telling ghost stories to a group of kids like they were sitting around a campfire. It was cute.

Something outside moved across the window, and I turned back to see a man staring in the window. When he saw that I saw him, he took off. Weird. I went over and checked the lock. We had closed the shop and locked the door after the last family left. Maybe it was just someone who had seen our lights and had wondered if we were still open.

I opened the door and stepped outside. No one was on the street. Wherever he'd gone to, he wasn't in view now. Or maybe I'd imagined him? I rubbed my eyes and felt a hand on my shoulder. Turning around, my hands were up in a boxing move, protecting my face.

"Whoa, slugger." Deek held up his hands in a defensive stance. "What's going on? Why are you out here?"

I dropped my hands and turned back to the street. "I thought I saw someone out here."

"A parent?" He frowned and studied the empty street. "I didn't think anyone was coming back tonight. Maybe one of the kids got homesick."

"Maybe." I shook my head and moved back toward the door. "Or maybe I'm just seeing things."

"Have you been listening to our ghost stories?" Deek held open the door and waited for me to go inside. Then he locked the door again. "Just kidding. Anyway, no one's out there now. Maybe you should go take a nap. The kids are starting to settle in. Several of them are already asleep."

"This was a great idea. You have a real knack for events." I studied the room. He was right. Most of the kids who were left were either sleeping or tucked in a chair with a book. If I was going to get a nap in, this was as good a time as any. "I'll go crash on the couch in the office. If you need me, just shake my shoulder. I'm a light sleeper."

"Okay, but if you hit me when I'm trying to wake you up, I'm filing workman's comp." He stopped by a chair where a girl had her head on the table. "Genny, let's go find your sleeping bag. You're done for the night."

I made my way to the office. Deek was right. I felt beat. I laid my head down and wondered what Greg and Emma were doing. Before I could reach for my phone, I fell asleep. I dreamed of books and maple syrup.

I blinked at the sunshine in my eyes. I must have slept through the night. I rolled off the couch and headed into the café to grab coffee. Sadie stood next to the pot.

"Can I get a cup?"

She looked at me. "Girl, you can get a pot. Maybe you should go wash up in the bathroom and comb your hair?"

I reached up and pulled it into a pony, using the band I had kept on my wrist. "Better? Why does it smell like maple syrup in here?"

Sadie handed me a cup and pointed to a table where Pastor Bill was making pancakes. "We've got bacon going too. Go get cleaned up, and I'll bring you a plate. Parents are starting to arrive, and you need to look like you didn't sleep on the couch all night."

"But I did." I sipped the coffee. "I'll be out in a few minutes. I'll get a plate then."

It was actually more like fifteen minutes, after I found my bag with a change of clothes and popped into the shower. Aunt Jackie had thought it was a mistake to leave the three-quarters bath down in the office, but this wasn't the first time I'd used the shower. And it made a great place to store mops and other things for the cleaning crew.

When I came out, my hair was still wet, but my mood was lighter. I got food from Pastor Bill and then found an empty table. Evie joined me. I noticed she was either still in the same clothes or had several pairs of tan capris. My aunt had wanted to design a uniform, but I'd talked her out of it. I don't think she wanted to wear polo shirts any more than the rest of us. "Did you get some sleep?"

She nodded. "I'll take a nap after we close down today, but I'm good. Deek was a machine. That guy can do an all-nighter and still be up and fun with the kids in the morning. I'm in awe."

"He's a natural at all this event stuff. I'd be lost without him." I picked up a slice of bacon. "And thank goodness for Sadie and Bill. They love this stuff."

"They're good with the kids. It's not really my jam. Don't tell Sasha. I mean, I love Olivia, but after spending a day with that girl, I'm ready to get home to my Homer. He's all the kid I need. Someone to care for and to talk to, but he doesn't talk back or ask why." She finished her pancakes. "Did your man find out anything more about the husband? I'd lay money on him being involved in this. He's just too perfect. Even his reactions when someone talks to him. I swear, he takes a beat before he answers, just to make sure he says things the exact right way."

"He has an alibi, at least he did the last time I talked to Greg." I stood and grabbed my cup and held my hand out for hers. "More coffee?"

"Please."

The conversation went on pause as I went to get coffee. Evie took the plates to the trash can and came back to the table.

I set her cup in front of her and rejoined her at the table. "I have to admit, he's a likely suspect. And I know he's hiding something. I just can't figure out what it is."

"The entire family is that way. I saw Harper yesterday walking outside and popped out to tell her how sorry I was for her loss. She looked at me like I was speaking another language. But then she caught what I was saying and thanked me for my concern. Then she asked me when the kids were going to be gone. That she'd like to come in and browse, but she wasn't comfortable around kids." Evie sipped her coffee. "I told her to come in before noon because we were closing for the weekend after we announced the readathon winners. She said she'd come in on Tuesday and miss the crowd."

"I can relate." I wasn't sure what Evie was getting at except she clearly didn't like either Harper or Alicia's husband. I agreed with her assessment mostly. It was hard to not like a fellow business owner. They'd put their hopes for a future into the business in our town, and that was pretty cool.

"Well, I guess we'll see if she does come in or if she orders online." Evie stood and finished her coffee in a couple of gulps. "If you don't mind, I'm running upstairs to take Homer for a quick walk. Then I'll be down to finish this readathon up. I'm sure the kids that went home will be showing up soon."

As I finished my breakfast, my mind wandered back to the new people in town. Was it weird that Scott was still in town? Had it been him outside the window last night? Or, more likely, had it been a parent of one of the kids sleeping over just checking to see if we were locked up tight? Either way, the thought made me shiver.

Chapter 20

The last kid walked out of the shop with a pile of books he'd just bought. He'd won the readathon, so he had a gift certificate, which he'd spent and then some. His mom handed over her credit card without a problem. She dropped her voice as he headed to the door, one of the books already open as he walked. "Reading wasn't his thing until he started coming to your book club. It's made all the difference."

With the readathon over, the group of staff and volunteers huddled around a table in front of the cash register. My aunt wanted to debrief to see what had worked and what hadn't before we disbanded and closed for the rest of the weekend. I was beat and my hand was cramping from writing down the books on the kids' cards. "We need to make their check-in cards bigger."

My aunt frowned. "Why?"

Deek held up his writing hand twisted into a fake grip. "Because I won't be able to write for weeks. Who's going to type out all my good ideas for books if I can't use my hand?"

"Baby." Evie slapped his hand, and he groaned in fake pain. "I think we should actually do it over three days. And the last night could be a lock-in. We'd let a certain number in to sleep over, and then we'd start the party the next morning."

"If you had more help, you could do the lock-in either at the church or the rec hall," Pastor Bill offered. "You can't fit more kids in here, but the rec hall you could have twice the number. Maybe even more."

I groaned.

My aunt started to say something and then bit her lip. Instead, she nodded. "I think Jill's right. We need to table this until next week's staff meeting. Sadie, Bill, thank you so much for your help. We couldn't have done it without you."

"True that." Deek held up his hand for a high five from Pastor Bill. "And wicked ghost stories. You had me freaking out along with the kids. Tell me they weren't true."

Bill stood and held his hand out to Sadie to help her up. "There is no light without darkness, Deek. Have a great weekend, you all. And maybe I'll see some of you on Sunday?"

He didn't wait for an answer, just put his arm around Sadie and grabbed their bag. They left through the front door.

"What? Is that dude kidding?" Deek turned to me.

"I didn't hear the stories. But we do have some good ghost stories here at South Cove. I'll have to tell you one." I held up a hand when I saw the light flash in his eyes. "But not today. I'm beat and heading home."

"Sounds like a plan." My aunt glanced at her watch.

"Did you drive up here?" I cleaned a few cups off the table next to us. "Or can I walk with you?"

"I'll let you walk with me." She glanced around the shop. "We probably should do some cleanup."

"Not today. I'll do some on Tuesday when I open. We're all off the clock."

Deek and Evie had paused by the office door when they heard Jackie mention cleanup.

I waved them off. "Go on and get out of here. We'll see everyone Monday afternoon at three for a staff meeting. We can clean then."

After they left, I grabbed Aunt Jackie's purse and my tote from the back room, locked that door, then came out front, turning off lights and machines as I went. I looked inside the almost empty dessert case. "Do you want cookies to take home? I have three sugar and a brownie."

"I'll take one of the cookies for Harrold, but you can have the rest." My aunt pulled out a mirror and lipstick from her purse and freshened her makeup. Newlyweds. Harrold loved her for who she was, not how she looked. "I think our sales from the event are going to make up for closing early today."

"I know they are." I pointed to the bookshelves. "Deek's going to have to do some ordering to get those refilled. Especially with summer coming in fast. We don't want to be low on books."

"Deek's a real asset to the bookstore. Have you thought about a possible promotion for him?" My aunt put her makeup away and slipped the cookie into her purse.

"What are you thinking of?" I knew we wouldn't be able to keep him as just a bookseller for long, but on the other hand, my aunt ran the bookstore's financial budget. "I don't think I can take him off the floor. He loves working with people."

"Let me think about this, and I'll give you numbers and a proposal next week. I'd like him to be able to step in for me when I decide to retire and travel."

I hid the smile that came from her words. My aunt had retired once and had to come back to work for me after losing a lot of her retirement savings. Now, with Harrold, she was feeling strong enough again to start thinking about traveling and not working. It was a good sign. "Sounds like a plan. We'll have to see what Deek's plans are. You know his ultimate goal is to be a professional student."

"Yes, but I think his mother has other plans for her basement." My aunt stood and adjusted her blazer. "Are we done, then? Harrold is probably ready to eat lunch."

"After you." I finished shutting off the lights and locked the door. We started walking, and she took my arm.

"I've been thinking about that developer who was interested in your house. Do you have a break-even point where if you're offered above that, you'll take it?"

"No." I turned and looked at her. "Where would I go? Where would I take Emma? Greg and I are making a family there. It would have to be a lot of money and come with a new place for me to live before I'd even think about it. And I don't move for chump change. Not anymore."

"How does Greg feel about the two of you moving?"

I looked straight ahead. "He agrees with me, and we're not moving. I wish the rumor mill worked in my favor, not just against me."

"I didn't mean to make you upset." My aunt paused, then she patted my arm. She nodded to the dress shop. "Now that's a woman who needs some positive rumors, and soon. Everyone is saying horrible things about her, like she killed her sister so she wouldn't have to be partners anymore. Lille said that brother-in-law is telling everyone how Alicia hated her sister."

"Funny, I'm hearing the opposite. That Alicia and her husband weren't seeing eye to eye. I guess you never know what's going on in someone's personal life." I started walking again. I was going to regret asking, but she was my aunt. "Greg and I are going to Alicia's funeral tomorrow. Do you and Harrold want to go? We can ride together in the truck."

"That's a lovely thought, dear. I'm glad you are going. I'll ask Harrold if he has plans." She paused at the door to the Train Station. She hugged me quickly. "Thanks for everything."

"Have a great weekend," I said, blinking back tears. I didn't know why this conversation was making me so emotional, but right this minute, it seemed like I might never see my aunt again.

"You're a sweet girl, Jill." She patted my face and then opened the door to go inside the model train shop.

I stood outside for a second, watching her through the window as she greeted Harrold and gave him the cookie. They were truly in love. I could see it through the glass. I turned and left before they caught me watching and thought something was wrong.

Love, sisters, murder. The words were all running through my head. Something had happened before Alicia wound up dead on Harper's floor. And we knew she'd left her home and husband weeks ago. So where had she gone? The easy answer was to Harper's. But were they speaking to each other then? Lara had made it seem like they had a falling-out a few years ago. How long had that lasted? Surely not through her applying for the business license here, since she'd put her sister on as a partner in the building. At least in the eyes of the South Cove business community. I needed to make a timeline.

Greg was gone when I arrived home, which made it easier for me to execute my timeline. I pulled out some butcher paper from the office and laid it on the table. I took out my notebook and tried to see dates. I didn't have to go back to when they were kids, but maybe back to when Harper had come out to California? I checked her website and found what I'd been looking for. Her graduating date from the design school. That would be the start date. Then I put today at the other end. I added Alicia's death date and then started adding in other days as I knew them. Probably stupid, but it gave me something to do since I didn't have the energy to run with Emma.

As I added things, I kept coming back to what Sadie had said about seeing Harper in town. What if she hadn't seen Harper? What if it was Alicia? Was that stupid? Maybe Alicia had run here to hide from Scott, and he'd found her.

I shook my head. That didn't work. He had an alibi for the day and time of death. One that was miles away.

I grabbed a quart of ice cream and went into the living room to watch a cooking show. I was still there when Greg showed up later. "Hey."

"Hey, yourself." He picked up the now dead flowers and carried them to the kitchen. "Did you ever hear from the florist about these?"

"Nope. And I forgot to call today. I'll call on Monday." I picked up the empty ice cream carton and my spoon and followed him.

He threw the flowers away in the trash can and then picked up my timeline. "What's this?"

"My mind was rambling on me, so I thought I'd put everything down." I sank into a chair. "I know, I'm not supposed to be thinking about this stuff."

"No, I've said you can't investigate this stuff. You know, like go talk to people and get yourself in trouble." He tapped the paper. "This is good stuff. Why are Sadie and Deek on here?"

"They both saw Harper in Bakerstown and thought she was ignoring them. Deek said the woman said she was getting confused with Harper a lot. I thought maybe they'd seen Alicia instead. But the timeline doesn't work for that either since Sadie's encounter was after Alicia died." I studied the freezer. Maybe there were two more cartons of ice cream and that could be dinner. If there was only one, I'd probably have to share. "What do you want for dinner?"

"Hummm?" Greg was still looking at my timeline.

I leaned forward. "What, did I miss something?"

Ignoring my question, he pointed to Lara's name. "What's this note?"

"Who is that note, you mean." I rolled my shoulders. "Lara was one of my old divorce clients. She was a fashion designer, so I took a shot that she might know Harper. She actually knew both Harper and Alicia. But it was a dead end, except she told me that Harper didn't want Alicia to marry Scott. Apparently, there was bad blood at the beginning, so the sisters didn't talk for a while. One good thing, she wants to design my wedding dress."

"Harper?" Greg wasn't looking at me.

"No, Lara Gunn. The designer I called. Why is this important information?"

He turned to me. "Because neither Harper nor Scott said anything about the sisters not talking for years. And Scott said he and Harper were close. Which we know from Lara is a lie. I just wonder what else he's lying about?"

I stared at the timeline. "There's something I'm missing, and I just can't figure it out."

"If a piece of information isn't true, it will throw off the whole idea." Greg moved over to the fridge. "I'll grill the steaks if you'll make a pasta salad."

"Okay." I glanced back at the timeline. What piece of information on here wasn't true? "Are you going back to work tonight?"

He shook his head. "Nope. Tonight we're finishing the thank-you cards and deciding what to do with the gifts. I've got a feeling I'm going to be busy tomorrow."

I poured two glasses of tea from the pitcher in the fridge. "Are we still going to the funeral tomorrow? I told Aunt Jackie that she and Harrold could ride with us."

"Maybe they should take their car. You might need a ride home." He grabbed the tennis ball and showed it to Emma. "Ready for some fetch?"

He and Emma went out to the backyard, and I put some water on the stove to boil. He'd seen something in my timeline and wasn't telling me. Now I just needed to find out what I didn't know.

I salted the water and watched Emma and Greg play outside. I loved my life. And the fact Greg hadn't fussed at the timeline was another reason we were good together. His phone buzzed on the counter where he'd left it before going outside. I glanced down, hoping it wasn't the station or Esmeralda. It wasn't. Sherry's name showed on the display.

I wanted to ignore it. To let him find her call later, when it was too late to ruin our perfect evening. Besides, he was the one who had promised we were doing the rest of the thank-you notes tonight. But the angel on my other shoulder kicked the devil off, and I picked up the phone. "Hey, Sherry, hold on, I'll go get him."

"Oh, well, thank you," Sherry responded.

I could hear the subtext, like *Why are you answering his calls?* But I just took the phone out to the porch and held it out toward him. "You've got a call."

He groaned and threw the ball one last time. Emma took off to the edge of the yard. He jogged toward me. "Don't tell me it's the station. Toby's on tonight. He wouldn't call unless there was something bad happening."

"It's not the station. It's Sherry." I handed him the phone and almost laughed when he rolled his eyes, but I smiled and went back into the kitchen to work on dinner.

He followed me inside. "Hey, Sherry, what's up?"

He listened for a while, finally settling down at the table. She must have taken a breath, because he jumped into the conversation. "Look, I can't help it that your customer traffic is down. I'm sure it doesn't have anything to do with the fact you were questioned regarding the murder. Have you talked to Pat about this? Maybe you should just step away from direct customer work for a bit and let Pat work her magic. She always was better with people."

I heard Sherry's response, and as she went on her tirade, Greg grabbed one of the cookies I'd brought home. He must have found another opening because he set the cookie down. "Sorry you feel that way, Sherry, but Jill and I are just getting ready to sit down to dinner. I need to go. We're writing thank-you notes for the engagement gifts we got last week. Have a great night."

And he ended the call. He returned to the cookie and finished it. "Sherry feels that I should put out an all-points bulletin to all the people in South Cove stating she isn't a murderer. She says her traffic today was slow."

"She shouldn't attack people in the business-to-business meetings if she wants to be seen as a good person. A lot of people think she's mean, and that doesn't bring people to your shop, especially at the prices they charge for used clothes. I know they're designer but give me a break. This is a beach town. Maybe she should sell swimsuits and beachwear." I dumped the pasta into a drainer and ran cold water over it to stop the cooking process. I was pretty happy about the engagement poke he'd given her when he ended the call with Sherry.

"Maybe you should add beachwear to your 'more' section. That way you can get into the clothing business too." He laughed and went to pour more iced tea. "Never mind, then my Sherry calls would increase."

"Not to mention my interactions with her. I'd rather stay off her side of the business road and out of her awareness." I poured the dressing into the bowl where I'd been putting chopped peppers, onions, and tomatoes.

He came up behind me and wrapped his arms around me. "I'm afraid it's too late for that. Sherry sees you as competition now that I put that ring on your finger. I'm afraid the attention is just going to get worse. But I'm fifty percent certain that she's not a killer."

"That makes me feel so much better." I shrugged him off with a laugh. "Start grilling the steaks while I finish this salad. I'll need my strength to fight off the challengers you're setting against me."

"I don't control Sherry. Crazy is as crazy does." He kissed my neck. "But you might want to watch your back for a while."

Chapter 21

First thing Sunday morning, my aunt called to let us know that she and Harrold would be driving themselves to the funeral, as they were taking a couple of days and heading into wine country. As she ended the call, she said, "Make sure you wear something appropriate."

I set the phone on the table and rolled my eyes at Greg. "I guess wearing the banana costume to the funeral is probably not what my aunt would call appropriate, right?"

He spit a bit of coffee out as he started to laugh. "Seriously, you need to warn me before you say things like that."

I threw a napkin at him. "I just wish she realized I'm an adult and I know what funeral-appropriate is."

"I'd give you a buck if you did wear the banana costume." He stood and refilled his cup.

We'd finished the thank-you notes last night, and all I had to do was take the lot to the post office tomorrow. The box of sealed and stamped cards was sitting on the table where the unknown flowers had been before Greg threw them away. In addition, there were several bags of gifts I needed to take back to stores and get a different item. If I found one on sale, I thought I might just have enough for a new food processor.

"Not going to happen. You haven't seen Aunt Jackie really mad yet. I don't think I have the strength to deal with it. I could do the returns today, and if I stop at the grocery store too, I won't have to go to Bakerstown tomorrow." I had my planner open for meal planning for the next week. Monday looked busy. If I combined all these Bakerstown trips to today, I'd have reading time. "What's your plans for today?"

"I'm not sure yet. Either I'll be busy, or I can help with the grocery shopping. I'll let you know after we leave the funeral." He glanced at the clock. "I'll put the returns in the back of your car before I leave. I need to get ready and get out of here. I'm meeting someone before the funeral."

"Who?"

He ignored my question and headed upstairs to change.

"It's not nice to keep secrets," I called after him. Emma woofed in agreement. But I also let her outside, just in case she was announcing something else. I had at least thirty minutes before I had to get ready, so I took my coffee and a book out to the back porch.

Greg came out to the porch before he left and said goodbye. Emma didn't even move from her spot near the stairs.

"You're risking getting Emma hair on that suit." I studied him. It didn't matter what Greg wore, he looked good. His sandy-blond hair was cut short. And the suit was one I'd bought him last year. He'd needed a new one, and I knew he wouldn't pay what I paid for it, so I gave it to him for his birthday. "You look good, Greg King."

"She seems to know not to approach when I'm wearing this. Did you tell her how much it cost?" He kissed me. "Don't get lost in your book and be late."

"I won't." Okay, so I had before, but I had a timer set on my phone to remind me to get ready. I ignored the jab on the cost of the suit. Greg didn't worry about fashion, but even he knew the difference in the suit. "See you soon."

"I put a change of clothes in the car, just in case I go shopping with you. So don't leave them there, okay?"

Always thinking a step ahead, that was Greg. "I'll bring a sundress for me too."

"Maybe we can do lunch at one of restaurants with the deck over the ocean we've been meaning to visit."

"Now you're just teasing me. Let me know what your plans are when you know them." I went back to reading.

"You'll be one of the first to know." He went back inside and left through the front door. I saw him get into his truck and wave as he backed out of the driveway. I guess he knew I'd be watching.

I tried to go back to reading, but Greg's clandestine meeting had me wondering what was going on. I went back to the kitchen and rolled out the timeline again. Nothing stood out to me, so the missing item must be something Greg knew, and when he added it into the timeline, it stood out. And he thought the mystery might be solved at the funeral. This whole thing was turning out to be more like one of the novels I liked reading and less like real life.

I sat down and tried to work it out. Sherry had been a suspect because she'd fought with Harper. The dead woman looked like Harper, so maybe Sherry had killed the wrong sister. Then Pat had confessed and Greg made short work of both of their guilt. Meaning, neither one had killed Alicia. So who had?

Greg had stopped thinking it was random when he let me start running alone again. I marked that day on my timeline. So no masked random serial killer was running around South Cove, or Greg would have kept me inside.

Evie had thought it must be the estranged husband, because, well, it's always the husband. And she'd found some weird stuff with his Facebook story when he was keeping everyone updated on the search for his missing wife. But Greg had verified he'd been at work two states away when Alicia was killed.

Which left Harper. Had she run out of the shop after a fight with Alicia? Then gone to Diamond Lille's for lunch? She'd known I was stopping in to pick up the dresses. Maybe she'd planned for me to find the body. That was cold. Especially when it was her sister. And where had she been going with her lawyer buddy, Colton? And the big question that never got answered: Why didn't she identify her sister as the victim when Greg took her inside the shop?

Maybe I'd have some time to gently ask some questions today at the funeral. Especially if I got there early. If I knew what her relationship with Colton was and when Alicia actually arrived, that might answer a few of the questions. Or it might just give me more.

I rolled up the timeline again and tucked it on the kitchen desk. Time to get ready for a funeral.

* * * *

Greg's truck wasn't at Bakerstown Funeral Home when I arrived. There were several cars in the front parking lot, and I worried I'd gotten there too late to talk to Harper alone. I checked my lipstick in the mirror and applied more before going inside. Makeup wasn't an everyday thing, and I didn't want to look off. Especially after my aunt's admonishment that I dress appropriately. Having clown makeup would probably not meet my aunt's standards.

I stepped into the cool lobby of the funeral home and saw a lone person sitting on one of the velvet couches. Harper. I moved toward her and sat next to her. "Harper, I'm so sorry for your loss."

Harper looked up at me, confusion in her eyes. Then she blinked and it went away. "Jill, so nice of you to come. I know you didn't know Alicia, but you would have loved her."

"I heard good things about her from Lara Gunn. Remember I told you that I worked with her a few years ago on a legal issue."

The confused look came back. "I don't understand. You ordered books for her?"

I smiled at that. Sometimes I forgot that not everyone knew my history. I must not have clarified in our last conversation. "No, sorry, before I owned the bookstore, I was an attorney in the city. I did divorces, family law, really."

"Oh, yes, you mentioned that. Her husband was less than supportive of her career." Harper tightened her grip on the small clutch she carried. "It happens a lot. People get married to the wrong person, and then they find out who they really are after a few years. Alicia's marriage was that way. I know you've met Scott. He's very controlling."

"Is that why you're having two funerals? One for you and your friends here, and one for his friends in Idaho?"

She nodded. "It was a good compromise. Although I would have been fine going to Idaho for one combined event, he thought this would be better. I think he'll get more attention if I'm not there. Who could love Alicia more than he did? Who had the bigger loss?"

Harper was still acting strange, but at least she was talking. "You were against the marriage." When she looked up sharply at me, I continued. "Lara mentioned it. That you hadn't talked to your sister for several years because of the fight over the marriage?" I was pushing, but I didn't have much more time before people would show up. Like Colton.

"We argued. I'll admit that. But that was years ago. She made a bad choice. It didn't mean she needed to pay for it the rest of her life."

"No, that would be horrible. Did she come down here when she vanished from Idaho?" I was guessing, but from the surprised look on Harper's face, I'd hit the nail on the head.

"She did. She was filing divorce papers and needed a place to stay." She looked up past me and nodded.

Colton Canyon hurried over to her, his black suit even more expensive than the one I'd bought Greg. The man was making money as an attorney. I tried to remember what I'd found out about him. Everything about him seemed to fade into the background. Except for one fact: he was from the same town as Harper and Alicia.

"The service will have a closed casket." He squeezed Harper's shoulder, then focused on me. "Good morning, thank you for coming today. Harper appreciates the support from South Cove, but I'm sure you all had better things to do."

I let a small smile curve my lips. He didn't want me or anyone from South Cove here. That was obvious. And we'd just ruined his day. "We're a tight-knit community. I think you'll find we support our own, in good times and bad. Being here for Harper, it's our pleasure."

Colton took Harper's arm and helped her up from the couch. "Sorry, we've got some final preparations for the service to attend to."

"Thank you again for coming." Harper smiled and then turned to follow Colton back to Doc Ames's office.

A voice came over my shoulder. "I don't think he liked you talking to Harper one bit."

I turned and saw Greg watching the retreating pair. He must have come in from the back door. "I didn't see your truck here."

"I parked in the back. I've been chatting with Doc Ames. Apparently, this Colton insisted on a closed casket even though Doc assured him that the body was more than presentable." He nodded to the chapel where the service was being held. "Do you want to take a walk with me?"

I wouldn't say I jumped to my feet, but clearly Greg was letting me play investigator for some reason, so I moved quickly. "Of course. Where are we going?"

"I just want to check out the chapel for a minute. I'm curious about the setup." He took my arm, and we stepped to the chapel doorway. Opening the door, I noticed the overpowering smell of roses. Cold roses. The altar was filled with arrangements. On one side was the casket, and on the other, a stand with an oversized picture of Alicia. It was an old picture. She was in her wedding dress, standing at another altar and smiling for the camera. But her smile seemed sad. "I didn't realize how much she looks like Harper."

"Yeah, even though they chose a picture where she was a lot younger. I wonder why?" He studied the photo. "The photo they used for her missing person's picture was just a year or so old and showed her face better. Why would they use this one?"

"Maybe Scott insisted?" I touched the coffin. "I'm always sad when I hear about a woman who lost so much time in a bad marriage."

"Especially when they don't have that much longer to live." Greg put his arm around me. "Let's go sit out in the lobby and wait for your aunt."

"What are you talking about?" I moved with him, looking up to watch his face.

"According to Doc, Alicia had advanced cancer that had metastasized. She probably only had a few months to live anyway." He held the door open.

I paused and looked back at the casket. "Then why was Harper looking for houses for Alicia to buy? If she'd come here to die, why would she buy a house? That doesn't make any sense."

He followed my gaze and nodded. "Good question. There's a lot of things that don't make sense. I've got some tests running at the crime lab now. I think once we find the truth, it will lead us to finding whoever killed this woman."

"Jill, Greg, I didn't think you two would beat us here." Harrold waved at us from the lobby area. They'd just come inside, and my aunt was checking her hair and makeup, holding up her small compact she took everywhere with her.

"We wanted to miss the traffic." Greg walked over and shook Harrold's hand. "It's nice of you to give up your day off to attend this."

"From what Lille tells me, this Harper girl needs some support from the South Cove crowd." He looked around the empty lobby. "I hope my final appearance is a little more well attended."

"Don't talk like that." I gave him a hug. "You need to be around a long time so you can run buffer between Jackie and me."

He laughed and squeezed me. "That's my pleasure."

"Airing our dirty laundry in public isn't funny, dear." My aunt sniffed as she put away the compact. "Do we have time before the service starts to sit down? My feet are killing me after yesterday's event."

"I heard it was a knockout." Greg took her hand and led her to a couch, where she sat. And, I noticed, he sat in a wingback chair that gave him clear access to see the entry door.

I waited for Harrold to sit, then sat next to him. The couch was huge. A few more people wandered inside, several I recognized from the South Cove business-to-business meeting. Then Lara Gunn came in, and I stood to greet her. "Excuse me, I'll be right back."

She watched me approach and held out her hands. "Jill, it's so good to see you. When you told me about Alicia's death, I had my assistant send flowers. She used the same florist that sent you the bouquet for your engagement, I hope they were satisfactory. You didn't say, and I was so thrown by your call, I didn't think to ask. And as I'm standing here, I realize I never called you back. Sorry, it's been crazy."

"You sent the flowers?" The mystery arrangement was finally solved. "Actually, sorry, I didn't mean to ignore you, but there wasn't a card."

"Oh no! I bet you thought they were from your secret admirer. Is that your fiancé over there?" She pointed to Greg, who waved.

"Guilty as charged. He's a police detective in South Cove. Loves animals. Very active in community events." I was listing off his attributes like he was on a dating site or something. "Do you want to meet him? My aunt's over there with her new husband too."

A side door opened, and Doc Ames came out of a hallway. "Everyone, if you'd make your way into chapel one, there's an usher at the door to give you an order of service."

"I guess we'll have to do introductions some other time. I'm heading to the airport after this to jet off to New York City. I've got some buyer meetings to attend." She kissed me on the cheek. "Wish me luck, okay?"

I went back to the couch where Greg was still standing.

"Your aunt is going to hold a seat for us." He nodded to Lara, who waved as she disappeared into the chapel. "Is that your designer friend?"

"Yes. And she sent us the flowers. One mystery solved." I stood next to him. "What are you watching for?"

"I'll know it when I see it." He put his arm around my waist. After everyone was inside, he nodded toward the door. "Ready?"

I nodded, but then I saw a woman come inside. She had on a black hat that covered her face, but for a second, I thought it was Harper. She followed us into the chapel but paused at the doorway. Walking up the aisle, I saw that Colton and Harper were already seated in the first row. Doc Ames must have brought them in through a side door before announcing the start of the service. I glanced backward and saw that the woman had backed out of the chapel. When we were almost to the row of seats next to Aunt Jackie, I stopped and whispered to Greg. "Sorry, I need to use the restroom, and I don't want to get up during the service. I'll be right back."

Greg started to say something, but I hurried away before he could stop me. He might have seen the woman too. If he even thought I was going to talk to her, he'd be tying me to one of the pews. And he'd be talking to the mystery woman instead of me. Besides, she was probably just a friend of Harper's.

I scanned the lobby without seeing anyone. Then I went left thinking the restroom was that way, but that was the men's room. I'd walked inside before realizing I was in the wrong room. Luckily, it was as empty as the lobby. Or at least as far as I checked.

Turning back, I saw a figure in black move through a door. That had to be where the women's restroom was. I hurried over, opened the door, and stopped. The room had a hallway that led to a small sitting area and wash station. I'd used the room once and remembered the stalls were farther back. Someone could sit and refresh their makeup without being right in with the other section of the bathroom. It reminded me of the bathroom at the theater where we'd gone to see a play last year. And the acoustics were just as good.

"What in the heck are you doing here? Are you crazy?" Harper asked the woman in black.

"I wanted to see my funeral. It's not often you get to witness how others deal with the loss of you in their lives. I'm kind of disappointed at the turnout."

Alicia? The woman I'd seen was Alicia? Then who was in the casket? Who had I found on the floor of Harper's studio, dead? And why the elaborate lie to hide the truth? All I knew was I needed to get back to Greg and get him out here before Alicia left and I looked like a crazy person.

"You should have stayed in the chapel," a man's voice whispered in my ear. And I felt the hard barrel of a gun shoved in my back. "Let's go make some introductions. I have a package to pick up."

Chapter 22

I stepped into the restroom, and Harper moved in front of Alicia. "Jill, I'm so happy you're here. We better get back in the chapel. Doc Ames is getting anxious to start. I keep getting emotional and having to step back."

"Good try, Harper, but she's not alone." The man stepped around the wall and waved his gun. "Jill, why don't you go join the woman over near the mirror. Maybe you can swap makeup tips while I figure out how to get my wife out of here and back home where she belongs."

"I'm not going with you." Alicia took the hat and veil off her head. "I left you for a reason, and you can't make me go back."

"Now, see, you're wrong. I can. And your sister gave me the perfect out. If you go to the cops now, she'll be charged with obstruction of justice. Since she identified that poor girl in the other room as you." Scott shook his head as he looked at me. "Too bad your boyfriend can't just let a cut-and-dry case be solved. I gave him all he needed to arrest that bubblehead ex-wife of his. I was actually doing him a favor. I know how troubling wives can be. But now I have mine all to myself, like it's supposed to be."

"How are you going to explain to the neighbors that I'm not dead?" Alicia moved so she was standing in front of her sister and trying to block me at the same time.

"Oh, we won't be going back to Idaho. I have a new job and a new house already set up for us in Utah. You won't need to leave the house. I'll have everything brought in for us." He smiled and used his other hand to wave her closer. "You'll be taken care of, just like I promised. Until death do us part. Of course, you kind of already died, so now you belong to me."

"You're crazy. And I'm not going with you." Alicia folded her arms. "I told you in my note that we were done. I want a divorce and for you to be out of my life."

"Dear, it's too late to play that game. You're dead. And you have a choice. You can be really dead and your sister up for charges for killing you, her, and that woman in the casket." He pointed his gun at me. "Or you can come home with me and these women can stay alive."

"Don't go with him. He's not going to leave me alive. I'm a loose end." I grabbed Alicia's arm as she started to move. "He's lying. I'm pretty sure he'll kill your sister too. He doesn't care."

Alicia froze, and Scott swore under his breath.

"Jill, I've heard things since I've been in town. You're too nosy for your own good. So this might just be the investigation where there really was a serial killer in town. Someone who doesn't like people living this perfect small-town life. And one night, I might just break into your aunt's house and get rid of them too. A serial killer explains a lot of death. Especially in a tourist town. You all just angered the wrong person." He glanced at his watch. "This service is probably close to being over. What's it going to be, Alicia? Are you coming home and letting these people live? Or are you dying with them?"

Alicia met my gaze. "I'm so sorry about this. I should never have come here after I ran away."

Harper grabbed her hand. "No, it's not your fault. He's the one to blame. He's the one who couldn't take no for an answer. Don't go back to him. You've suffered enough."

"I can't let him kill you and her because of me." She turned toward Scott. "I'll go with you, but you can't hurt Harper or this woman. That's my offer."

"No more running away?" His eyes locked on hers.

She shook her head and stepped toward him. "I promise. I'll never try to leave you again."

I saw the move before Harper made it. With Alicia distracting Scott, Harper was outside of his view. The chairs were made of iron with a thick cushion on the seat. She reached over, never breaking eye contact, picked up the chair, and knocked him out cold.

"Hands up," Greg called as he rushed into the bathroom. A Bakerstown cop followed him inside. He looked around at us and the prone man on the floor. He holstered his gun into his shoulder harness and bent down with a bag he pulled out of his suit pocket. He picked up the gun and handed it to the other officer. "Cuff him."

The officer nodded, and Greg turned back to us. "Does someone want to tell me what's going on? And Harper, I think you need to introduce me to your sister. The one who's supposed to be in the coffin in the chapel, right?"

I leaned against the counter. "Can we do this in a conference room or somewhere else besides this bathroom?"

Greg nodded but didn't address me. I figured I was going to get a lecture when we were alone, but for now, all I wanted was a chair and a cup of coffee. And maybe a cookie.

We moved into a conference room by Doc Ames's office. Doc had waited to let the service out until Greg had given him the all clear. Scott was in a police car on his way to Bakerstown jail. Colton joined us in the conference room. He'd come out of the chapel looking for Harper just after Greg allowed us to move into the other room. Colton kept trying to talk, but Greg kept shutting him down.

Finally, when we were all sitting around the table. Greg sat down and picked up a notepad and a pen. "Who's talking first?"

"Harper, don't say anything. I'm her attorney, and I'll speak for her. You need to let us talk before we do this." Colton puffed out his chest as he pounded his finger on the table.

"Wrong answer." Greg held up a hand, and Colton stopped talking. "Jill? What were you thinking?"

"I *was* going to the bathroom," I said, not meeting his gaze. Finally, when he didn't say anything, I sighed and sat up. "Okay, fine. I saw Alicia come into the funeral home. But I didn't know it was her, I just kind of thought it was."

"How on earth did you figure that out?" Harper stared at me. "We've been so careful."

I leaned forward. "Deek said he saw you at the gym the other day, but you didn't talk to him. He's a pretty popular person, so I thought maybe you just didn't see him. But then Sadie said you snubbed her in Bakerstown at the store. Which is by the gym."

"And by your apartment, Alicia. You said you were being careful." Harper leaned back in her chair and stared at her sister. "You knew Scott was in town. What if he'd found you?"

"Which he did," Greg reminded the sisters. "Just now. I don't get why you would risk coming to your own funeral?"

Alicia rubbed her arms, trying to push off the cold. "I was bored. Harper said that Scott was going home a few days ago, so I decided to see what a funeral would look like. You don't get the chance to actually attend your own funeral, well, that you know about."

"Alicia, Harper, you both need to shut up. I'm your attorney of record, and you don't understand what you're saying." Colton folded his hands. "So how long are you going to hold us here? What are the charges?"

"There's plenty of charges to go around." Greg glanced at me, then back at Colton. "What I don't understand is who killed Marsha Kilenger. Who wants to explain that?"

I saw the look the women gave Greg and then each other.

Harper asked the question we were all wondering. "Who's Marsha Kilenger?"

"She was a single mom who was dying of breast cancer. Her daughter and her ex-husband just got an anonymous gift of five hundred thousand dollars two weeks ago, just before we found the body at Harper's studio. I can't believe you thought this mix-up would work." Greg was staring at Colton now. "Especially when she tried to give the money back because she got into a new drug trial."

"We don't know anyone by that name." Colton stood. "And I think we're done now. Harper, Alicia, let's go."

Harper didn't move. "Colton? What's going on? You said she died of a drug overdose."

"There were no drugs in her system. Except for her normal cancer pills." Greg pointed to the chair. "You might want to sit, because if you leave, I'm charging all of you."

"You have no proof. Of anything." He grabbed Harper's arm, but she shrugged him away. "We need to leave now."

"We were just trying to save Alicia. Scott had put her in the hospital last year, and she was afraid." Harper took her sister's hand. "This is my fault."

"No, it's mine. I should have been brave and just divorced him. I could have gotten a restraining order." Alicia started to cry and grabbed some tissues out of the box on the table.

"Shut up, everyone." Colton stood and moved to the door. "I didn't have anything to do with any of this, no matter what they say."

He stepped out of the door and slammed it.

I looked at Greg. "Aren't you going after him?"

He moved the tissue box closer to Alicia, who was being comforted by her sister. "The Bakerstown deputy outside the door is taking care of him. You can go home. I need to talk to Alicia and Harper some more."

I stood and patted Harper's shoulder. "If you need anything."

"We'll be fine." She smiled at me sadly. "It's time to be truthful."

* * * *

My phone rang on the way back to South Cove. The display said Aunt Jackie and that I had missed seven calls. "Hello?"

"My word, girl, don't you ever pick up? I was beginning to worry. There were cop cars all around the funeral home, and I couldn't find you anywhere." My aunt's voice was tight, frightened.

"Sorry about that. I was talking with Greg." I didn't know how much to say, so I left it at that.

"Now don't you be coy with me. I know this has something to do with that dead girl." Aunt Jackie sighed. "But as long as you're all right, that's all I need to know for now. Harrold and I are heading up to Napa for the night. I'll be back on Tuesday to work."

"Sounds fun." I turned onto Highway 1 and snuck glances at the ocean to my right. It was a beautiful sight. "I'm glad you're getting out and enjoying yourselves. It was a busy weekend."

"It was, and I want to talk to you about next year's event."

In the background, I heard Harrold say, "Jackie."

One word, a warning about working on vacation. And it even worked.

My aunt sighed. "I've got to go. I'm just glad to hear you're all right. I was worried."

"I know. I'm sorry you were worried. But go have fun. We'll talk when you get back." I hung up first this time. I bet that surprised her. The thought made me smile, and I rolled down all the windows to let the air run through the Jeep. Maybe I'd take the roof off later when Greg got home. I felt the need to let the sunlight inside all parts of my life.

Chapter 23

Greg and I didn't talk until Monday morning before he left for the station. He came in late Sunday night, and I'd already been in bed. Now, we sat across from each other and drank our coffee. In silence.

"Look, I know you're mad at me, but I didn't think I was putting myself in danger." I wrapped my hands around my coffee cup and stared at the engagement ring. From his demeanor, I might not be able to keep the ring much longer, so I should enjoy it while I had it on.

"You have a knack for being at exactly the wrong place at the wrong time." He refilled our cups. "You're lucky you weren't killed."

"He might have killed Harper and got away with Alicia if you hadn't come looking for me." I pointed out a factor that could be in my favor. I had saved a life and foiled a kidnapping.

"We already had police on site. If he'd tried to leave with Alicia, he would have been arrested."

"Or it could have turned into a shooting gallery. This way, he went down easy. He was trained with firearms. You don't think he would have thought twice about shooting?" I leaned forward to emphasize my point. "I saved lives yesterday."

"You did, but you put your life in danger. And if you keep doing that, I'm not going to be able to keep forgiving you. Jill, I want you to be safe. To be with me. Putting yourself in the line of fire isn't smart."

"I don't mean to get into trouble." And that was true. All I'd wanted to know was if Alicia was really still alive. The thought of why she'd run in the first place and what Scott would do to get her back had been secondary. "Does Marsha's family know what happened?"

"I talked to her ex-husband last night. He cried. He said he didn't realize how much stress she'd been under due to the cancer treatments." Greg shook his head. "I understood his frustration about someone you love doing something stupid."

"Okay, I get it. But all I was going to do was see if the mystery woman was in the bathroom. I would have waited for her to get out of the stall, said some polite small talk, then come back to you and told you that the woman who was supposed to be dead was in the bathroom." I reached for a cookie from a bowl on the table. "I had a plan."

"Yes, you did. And since I already knew the body in the casket wasn't Alicia, I had a plan too." He laughed when he saw my confusion. "You see, as a law enforcement officer, I get tests from the labs, and when I review them, they tell me things. Like the woman's name. She'd done a DNA swab for a bone marrow transplant list, and when Doc found the cancer pills, we asked for additional help."

"You knew Saturday night that Alicia wasn't dead." I broke the cookie in half and offered part to him. He shook his head. "Did you think it was Colton?"

"Actually, I thought all of them were in on it. But Harper explained that yes, they'd been looking for a body to trick Scott into thinking Alicia was dead. But she never thought Colton would kill someone to get it. He convinced her to go along with the plan and told her that Sherry had probably killed the woman thinking it was her. He was her only hope to stay alive here. Like we're some sort of den of vipers."

"Well, we do have our share of murders in town." I ate his half of the cookie first so he couldn't change his mind.

"So let's get out of town. Let's plan a trip up to that fake Dutch town and just relax for a week. Can you get away from work?" He rubbed the top of my hand with his thumb.

"Not this week. Or at least not today. We have a staff meeting, and I hate to leave the staff without a buffer for Aunt Jackie. What if we go next Saturday after I get off and stay the week?" I was getting excited about some time away. "Maybe Toby could watch Emma?"

"He should be able to. If things go south here, we'll have to come back, but we always run that risk." He stood and came over to pull me to a standing position. "I know what you're thinking. One fight and we're done. But relationships don't work that way. We have to just try to work things out. We're committed. And it's important."

I had a full day planned, and he was telling me that he'd never leave. "This is why I love you, Greg King. You're always watching out for the little guy."

"White knight syndrome, I'm afraid. Do you want to break up? Is this too much?" He rubbed the middle of my back.

"We're good. I'll let you know if you hurt me and I have to leave." I found myself in a full bear hug as he pulled me closer. "Until then, remind me why we're so good for each other?"

"It's a million little things." He kissed me, warm and soft.

Emma barked and put her nose in between our legs.

"We have company." I giggled as he brushed his lips over my cheeks.

"She can wait. She's telling me it's time for me to go to work so you two can run. She's so selfish." He gave me one last kiss. "But she's not wrong. See you tonight."

Alone again. I had a list of things to get in Bakerstown as well as a recipe I wanted to try. And a book to read, if not more than one. My life was perfect. We were alive, in love, and with a roof over our heads. And I had a vacation planned. Life was good.

About the Author

New York Times and *USA Today* bestselling author Lynn Cahoon is an Idaho expat. She grew up living the small-town life she now loves to write about. Currently, she's living with her husband and two fur babies in a small historic town on the banks of the Mississippi River where her imagination tends to wander. Visit her at www.lynncahoon.com.

Recipe—Lemon Drop Pie

I didn't use to like lemon desserts. I guess the bite from the lemon cut the sugar hit for me when I was younger. Now, I love them. And for the same reason I didn't like them before. A bit of a citrus bite makes the richness of the sugar and dairy all the more lovely.

Lemon Drop Pie

I use a premade graham cracker pie crust. So easy and just as good as homemade.

Preheat your oven to 350F.

In a medium bowl, whisk the following together

1 14 oz can sweetened condensed milk

5 egg yolks

½ cup lemon juice

Pour the mix into the crust and bake for 25 minutes. Let the pie chill for at least 2 hours before serving. Serve with whipped cream.

Keep reading for a sneak peek at
the first in a brand-new series from
Lynn Cahoon
The Tuesday Night Survivors' Club
Coming soon from
Lyrical Books

And don't miss her other series
The Kitchen Witch Mysteries
The Farm-to-Fork Mysteries
and
The Cat Latimer Mysteries
Available wherever books are sold!

Chapter 1

Rarity Cole was living and loving her second shot at life. If she'd been a cat, she would have five more. Right now, she was just grateful to have this second chance after living through the breast cancer that had been almost too advanced to win against. Now, in the bookstore she'd cashed in her corporate stocks to buy, she felt at home. She shelved the last book from the box that had arrived this morning into her new healing section. It still looked a little sparce, but she was determined to give others like her options when the c-word was thrown around by a team of doctors who seemed to think they had total control over you and your body.

Which reminded her, she still needed to find an oncologist in the area. The doctors from St. Louis had explained how important it was to keep up with the medical regimen they'd started her on, which meant not only taking a pill every day but getting regular bloodwork and mammograms to make sure she was okay. She'd been here long enough pretending she wasn't still recovering from the cancer treatments. It was time to check into her body again. She took the empty box back to the main counter and wrote the task on tomorrow's to-do list that she kept on the counter.

The air conditioning blowing out of the nearby vent made her shiver, and she rubbed her arms before finding a sweater to put on. If she turned it down, she started to sweat every time someone opened the door to The Next Chapter, her new bookstore in downtown Sedona, Arizona. Her shop was positioned right between a fortune teller's shop and a place that sold crystals. The crystal shop was owned by Rarity's best friend from high school, Sam Aarons. Sam had talked her into moving here and away from St. Louis a few months ago.

Honestly, she didn't mind the new location. It was in keeping with her theme of the new her. When you walk away from ringing the bell at the oncologist's office, you tended to reevaluate your life. Gratitude for what you gained and what you currently had.

Which was, in Rarity's case, a few extra pounds around the middle and the need for a nap at least once a day. Eating right and exercising hadn't stopped the ten-pound weight gain that had circled her waist. And stuck.

Rarity blamed the chocolate. She'd eaten a lot of chocolate, and ice cream and fast food, during her year of treatment. Then the visits had just stopped. She'd seen her doctor once since she was cured and once before she'd left St. Louis. They'd drawn blood to check to see if the cancer had returned. Or worse, if the treatment was now killing her instead of the disease. Doctor visits were always a barrel of fun. The bell over the door sounded, and she saw someone walk toward the counter.

"I'm here for the meeting tonight." A forty-ish woman stood in front of the counter. "I know I'm early, but I was so excited when I read about your new book club in the Sunday paper. I'm Shirley McMann. I finished treatment two years ago. Although, I'm still going to my oncologist every six months. They call it a well-baby checkup. And I'm rambling. George always says I ramble, and since having cancer, I'm worse. I guess I wanted to get out all my words before something else happens because tomorrow's not promised."

Rarity took an instant liking to the woman. Shirley's chattering was refreshing after hanging out in a slow bookstore and then going home to an empty house. "I'm Rarity Cole, owner of The Next Chapter, and I'll be leading the group tonight. I'm almost at a year. Survivor. I always hated that term. But you work with what you're given, right?"

"I feel like I should have done something heroic to be called a survivor. Like survived a month in the desert or walked away from a plane crash. I just went to every appointment and did what they told me. Well, except for losing weight. I started baking again, and George doesn't eat sweets. So there's that." Shirley glanced around at the area by the fireplace. "I see you found Annie's Bakery. She bakes the best cookies in town. Well, besides me."

"Go grab a drink and a few cookies." Rarity looked at the clock. It was almost seven, and Shirley looked like her only participant in the book club. Rarity had needed books when she went through treatment, but maybe having a group called the Survivors' Book Club was off-putting. Like what Shirley said. "We'll get started in a few minutes."

Shirley handed her a piece of paper. "Before I forget, George wanted to know if you could order these books for him. They're all on World War I or maybe II. I forget what he's currently researching. He makes planes and boats and stuff. You should see our basement. It's filled with his models."

"Sounds like a fun hobby." She glanced at the list. "I don't think I have any of these in stock, but I can have them for next week's meeting. I'll just need a credit card to charge them on."

Shirley dug in her tote and pulled out a wallet. She handed over a card. "Set me up a tab because I'm going to be your best customer. George hates driving into Flagstaff to get supplies. And when I was going through treatment, he'd complain for a week after I had chemo about how long the drive was."

"I bet you were glad for the company." Rarity thought about how Josh hadn't come once to her treatments, saying that hospitals made him sick.

"Yeah, as much as he griped, he'd bring games and cards. We had fun." Shirley smiled at the memory. "Which I know sounds totally weird. Anyway, I'll go get settled. You do what you need to do, don't worry about me."

It was already ten after seven, so Rarity ordered George's books, set up a contact file for Shirley and George, and then took the credit card back to where Shirley was sitting. She had pulled out a pile of pink yarn and a crochet hook and had started working on the project in her lap. Rarity held out the card. "Here you go. That's pretty."

"It's for my granddaughter. Karen and her husband are expecting. I've been working on this off and on for a month. I need to get it done, but it's so hot sometimes. Sometimes I wish we still lived in Idaho. Getting through the winters there, I needed a project on my lap." Shirley tucked the card into her wallet. "I'm sorry we didn't get more of a crowd. I'll bring someone next week. I promise. I hope you're not thinking of canceling the club."

"No, there's no need to cancel. It takes time to build a group." Rarity sat next to the pile of books she'd chosen for possible discussions. "Have you read any of these?"

Shirley shook her head. "During treatment I didn't read anything but cozy mysteries. I could lose myself in the plot or the setting. I'm looking forward to expanding my reading choices."

Rarity moved the cozy mysteries she'd pulled into a side pile. "Okay then, I'll take these off the list."

"Maybe someone else will want to read those," Shirley protested.

Rarity glanced around at the empty chairs. "I don't hear anyone complaining. Let's look at the women's fiction. I wanted to start with a book that didn't talk about cancer but instead dealt with a woman struggling with other problems."

They discussed the books until there were only five left on the table. Rarity heard the clock chime for eight thirty. "We did a lot of work tonight."

"We didn't even choose a book." Shirley pointed to the table. "We still have five up for contention."

"We can make the decision next week. I'll put these on the counter with a flyer about how we're going to start choosing one to read next week. Maybe that will draw some more people into the group." Rarity could already see the flyer in her mind. She'd make it first thing in the morning.

"You're really good at this marketing thing." Shirley tucked her blanket into her tote bag. "I'm happy you moved here and opened your shop. I've missed being part of a book club."

"I'm glad I did too." She glanced around at the old building with high ceilings with tin plating on them. She didn't know what the utility costs would be to keep this place cool, but she loved the look of the old brick and the warm wood floors. "It's beginning to feel like home."

* * * *

Wednesday morning, Rarity made the sign and display for the book club and then went about what was becoming her normal routine. She'd worked as a business analyst at a large corporation before leaving St. Louis, and she'd thought her days were busy then. Owning the bookstore meant no day was the same. She needed to start setting up some systems, though, to get a kind of normal routine.

Sam Aarons came into the shop with two cups of coffee in her hand. She looked like a Roma gypsy in her flowy skirts and white peasant blouse. Sam believed in dressing for the part. And her long, curly red hair topped off the look. She came up to the counter and handed a cup to Rarity. "Hey, neighbor. How did your book club go last night?"

"Didn't your crystals already tell you?" Rarity took a long sip of the coffee. "This is just what I needed. Why is coffee from a shop so much better than what you brew at home?"

"Because Annie brews it with love. At least that's what her sign says above the coffee bar. And my crystals don't tell the future. For that, you need to go to Madame Zelda's next door. She'd be glad to tell you what's going to happen in your future. I just give you the gems to protect yourself from bad juju. Like the clear quartz I sent you when you were diagnosed. It's a master healer stone."

Rarity reached up for the necklace she still wore. "I love it. Even if it didn't cure me."

"You of little faith. Anyway, is the fact you have a book display up for the group a good sign? Lots of attendees?"

Rarity shook her head and held up a finger.

"Why do you want me to wait?" Sam frowned. "Why can't you tell me now?"

When Rarity took a drink rather than answering her question, Sam got the message.

"You have got to be kidding me. One person showed up? What a waste of time." Sam nodded to the chairs. "Can we sit for a bit? These boots are new and horribly uncomfortable. My feet will be killing me long before I close the shop today."

"What we do for our image. Sorry, of course we can sit." Rarity crossed over and sat in the same chair she'd occupied last night. "It wasn't a complete waste of time. The woman who came brought in a big order, so at least there's that."

"Are you doing okay with the store financially? Walk-in traffic will start picking up soon. Summers can be a little slow. People don't realize it's not going to be as hot as they think here."

Rarity nodded. The business had been slower than she'd hoped, especially since it had taken longer to remodel the building than she'd planned. She'd only been open a few months. "I'll be fine. Tell me about your date last night. How did it go?"

"Do I have to?" Sam groaned and then sipped her coffee.

Rarity giggled. "That bad?"

"We met at the restaurant in Flagstaff because he couldn't drive all this way on a work night. Then he was almost an hour late. He was all Brooks Brothers suit and tie. And he insisted on splitting the bill. Just so we wouldn't feel obligated for anything après dinner." Sam rolled her shoulders. "I'm never going to find Mr. Right. I should just give up the search."

"You're perfect the way you are, and if there's a Mr. Right in your future, he'll find you." Rarity leaned back. "Or we could ask Madam Zelda."

"You are so bad." Sam leaned her head back and closed her eyes. When she spoke, she let her voice waver, imitating the fortune teller. "You will meet a man where you least expect to meet him. He will be tall, dark, and handsome. Please hand over your credit card for payment."

The bell over the door sounded, and Madam Zelda walked into the store.

Rarity stood, and as she hurried past Sam, she hit her arm to alert her. "Madam Zelda, so nice of you to visit. What can I help you with?"

Madam Zelda narrowed her eyes and stared at Sam, who was now also standing but by the fireplace. "I came in to see if you had a flyer for your survivors' club. I have a client who might be interested in some social interaction around the subject matter. She's very timid, though, and I might not be able to get her to come."

"We're a small group." Rarity added, *of two,* silently. She picked up a flyer from the counter, writing the book list on the front. Then she handed it to the fortune teller. "I'm sure she'd enjoy the discussion. These are the five books that we're considering reading."

"Hey, Rarity, I need to go open. I'll chat with you tonight." Sam circled around the furniture, and Madam Zelda, and almost ran out of the store.

"That girl needs to relax. She's wound up like a clock ready to bust a spring." Madam Zelda watched Sam through the window as she hurried to open her store. "It's not healthy to be that anxious."

"Sam's always been a little high-strung." I nodded to the flyer. "I hope your client decides to visit at least once. Can I have her name?"

"I do not divulge my client's information. Surely you can understand the privacy needed for a job like mine." She tucked the flyer into a pocket on her dress and left the shop.

Rarity waited for her to disappear out of view of the window before responding. "As if people who visit fortune tellers are expecting privacy like it was their doctor. Things just keep getting weirder here. Maybe that's just life in Sedona."

Rarity didn't have time to think about Madam Zelda's privacy policy much that day because she had several customers show up, one after the other. A few took a flyer about the book club, others asked her to order a book for them, and one walked through the bookstore checking out the stock, and just left.

When she went to lock the door at five, she glanced outside at the empty sidewalk. Or almost empty. The man who'd been window-shopping her store sat on a bench on the other side of the street reading. He must have felt her watching him, because he looked up from his book and nodded after meeting her gaze.

Now she felt stupid. He'd just been killing time. Or looking for his online ordering shopping list. Maybe opening a brick-and-mortar store hadn't been the smartest idea with the book world changing in front of her eyes. It didn't matter though. This was her dream, and she wasn't going to waste any time on worrying about opening at the right time. Action is rewarded. Worrying never did anyone any favors.

She went back to the storeroom and grabbed her purse out of the small closet. Then she checked the back door to make sure it was locked. Finally, she turned off the lights and, holding her keys in one hand, went to the front door to leave and then lock up.

The man on the bench was gone when she turned and dropped her keys into her tote. She glanced up and down the street but didn't see him.

"Hey, are you ready? The restaurant's this way." Sam stood outside her shop, waiting for Rarity to join her.

She shook off the vague unease she felt, but before she went to meet her friend, she reached back and checked again that the shop was locked. Then she slowly walked the few steps to meet Sam.

"Everything all right?" Sam's face echoed the fear that Rarity had felt when she'd seen the guy watching her.

Rarity took her arm. "Everything's fine. I'm just hungry, that's all."

Made in the USA
Monee, IL
03 March 2022

92211122R00111